# Henry III

Book 6
in the
Border Knight Series
By
Griff Hosker

i

Published by Sword Books Ltd 2018

SWORD
BOOKS

SWORD
BOOKS
HOME OF EPIC HISTORICAL FICTION

# Prologue

Men often make mistakes. Real men learn to live with them while weaker ones bemoan their fate. I had made many mistakes in my life and endured more misfortune than most men would expect but I had still been a man and faced the adversity stoically. I had recovered from the death of my father at Arsuf. I had reclaimed my lands stolen from me by King John. However, the death of my son, Alfred, at the hands of Sir Jocelyn de Braose and his squire John, aided by the London whore, Morag, almost drove me over the edge of reason. When my aunt, the last of the line of the Warlord's family, died, leaving me as the sole survivor, I was in a pit of despair out of which I thought I would never rise. The death of my son seemed to suck the life force from this great lady. I was with her at the end and I wept as much as I had when my son had died. On her death bed she had told me how her life had been made full through mine and my son's. When we buried her in the small cemetery in my castle it felt as though I was burying part of myself. That was when my life was at its lowest ebb. That was when I felt true despair. My family and people walked around me for they feared my temper. I was a man of action. I had been a sword for hire and yet I was unable to follow my son's killers. That added to the weight I bore. That sent me deeper into the pit that was becoming my life.

The death and funeral of my aunt delayed my hunt for his killers. My wife, Margaret, told me that it was a sign from God that I should let him punish my son's killers. She was wrong. I was God's tool. Sir Jocelyn and his squire would die at my hands and no other. The delay had not cooled my anger. I was like a sword. I was tempered and hardened. I did not listen to her. I could not let this abomination crawl upon the surface of the earth any longer for Alfred had been the knight I had trained to be Earl of Cleveland. He was my future. He left a young wife, a daughter and a son. They had no father and Matilda's tears needed vengeance. I ignored my wife. In the end I knew that my departure would hurt others. It allowed enemies to ravage my land and to hurt the innocent.

There was worse for the hunt for the killers also took me away from the young King Henry. The Earl Marshal had charged me with his training and, in the wars against the Welsh, we had made a good start. When I left for France on the hunt for a trio of killers, I abandoned him. I made the mistake of trusting others. I was not made of the same steel as the Warlord. He had never abandoned his charge and he had kept his oath. My blind search for vengeance cost England dear. Had I stayed at the King's side who knows if things might have turned out differently?

# Chapter 1
# The King's Command

It was months after my son's murder that I finally left Stockton with my fellow hunters. After we had buried my aunt, I had her estate to settle. My aunt was rich and her money, as she had proscribed in her will, was to be equally divided between my three surviving children, my son's widow and myself. The money meant nothing to me but I was honour bound to administer her estate. I then gathered my closest knights, Sir Edward, Sir Fótr, Sir Geoffrey and Sir Peter. I held a feast in my Great Hall for I was saying goodbye. I also invited David of Wales, Henry Youngblood and Ridley the Giant my three captains. They all knew what I intended and the mood was sombre rather than the normal joyous one. My wife's face told them all of our arguments. The closer the day came to our departure the more heated became the words. Her nights were sleepless. She was the supreme hostess, normally, but at the last feast she was largely silent and spoke only to my son's widow, Matilda. My son, William, tried to enliven the meal but he failed.

As the sweet meats were brought in, I stood, "My friends we are gathered here to mourn my son and celebrate his life. He had a short life but a glorious one and now I must leave my land to seek his killer. I go first to London for I must speak with the King. Then I will take ship for France. De Braose's trail will be cold and so the men I take with me will be hunters. Save for my son, William, none of those in this hall will be coming with me." As I had expected my announcement brought uproar to the feasting hall. Everyone had known of my plans and they each thought and expected that they would come with me. My selection of William had been the cause of contention and argument with my wife. She had lost one son and I was taking with me her last. My son,

William, had barely begun his training as a knight. He was raw unmoulded clay and I was taking him into great danger.

Sir Edward had been the son of a hawker and was the most plain spoken of my knights. He could be rough around the edges but, in a battle there was none better to stand behind a knight. He openly criticised me, "My lord, this is foolish beyond words. Do you not see the experience around this table? Have we not served you well? David of Wales and his archers are the finest in England. Ridley and your men at arms are a steel wall through which none can penetrate. And I believe that Sir Fótr and myself have done valiant service too!"

I smiled at him. His words were sincere. "And that, my old and most valued of friends, is why I do not take you. We all know that we live on the edge of a precipice here. The Scots are always ready to slip over the border and cause mayhem. I need my most experienced men here to defend my family, my people and my land. This country of ours is not settled yet. The King clings on to power. He may yet order me to stay but I pray not. I know whom I will take. It will be a small retinue for we go not to fight battles, but to seek a snake. That treacherous knight and his whore will be hiding. Snakes hide in rocks and dark places. To find them we will have to go in disguise. If I take Ridley the Giant then all the world will know that it is the Earl of Cleveland who comes. A column of archers will confirm it too and if I have my knights then the snake will hide deeper. I go in disguise. I do not go as Sir Thomas of Stockton. I will assume another identity. I have had a plain grey surcoat made. I will travel as a sword for hire." I laughed and touched the back of my wife's hand, "It was how I met my wife. This is not a rash move. I was cold when I conjured my plan. I have spoken already with the men I will take." I saw the look of surprise on the face of my three Captains. "They are my men and I made them swear an oath. They know what we do and are all happy. None are married. If we die then… I charge you, Sir Edward, with watching this border. You will be the seneschal of the North. You will command in my absence."

I saw him nod.

"As for the rest of you? Vigilance is all. Sir Hugh of Craven showed us what can happen when we do not watch. You are my watchmen!"

4

Each of them came to speak with me before they took their leave. My wife played the hostess and watched them depart. Left with my family I took my leave of my daughters, Rebekah and Isabelle and my son's wife, Matilda. "I leave you all with heavy heart. My world is here in this room. The three bairns who lie asleep upstairs are more valuable to me than any crown or throne."

Rebekah said, "I have but one brother left. Do not take him from me!"

I saw William stiffen. He had helped me with the planning. He was as anxious as any but he was determined to avenge his brother, "William here knows the dangers."

Matilda said, "My husband is dead. Do not take my father from me! My own father was murdered and my son, when he grows, will need your guidance. Killing his killers will not bring back my husband."

"Your son shall have my guidance for I intend to return but I must do this. I know you find it hard to understand but Alfred would."

That night, as my wife lay in my arms, I thought about the journey, the quest I was about to undertake. She had sobbed herself out. I think she believed that until I told my men then I might not actually leave. Now she knew the truth of it. "It was hard enough to lose my first born but to have my husband and my remaining son leave me is too hard to bear. What if you do not return?"

I squeezed her a little tighter, "Do you remember when we lived in Sweden?" I felt her nod. "There they spoke of sisters who spin their webs. We both thought it nonsense."

"Ridley and his wife believe it still."

"And perhaps there is something to this. If I do not end this now then we will have the threat of a knife in our backs for the rest of our lives. Rebekah and her husband might be threatened. Young Henry Samuel might be in danger. I killed the man of the woman who was with them. She must be destroyed too. They have enjoyed success and our indolence might encourage them to inflict further hurt upon us or others. Sir Jocelyn might forget about us but I doubt it. We robbed him of his father and his inheritance. I have to do this so that we may sleep easier in our

5

beds." I kissed her, "And I will be in no more danger than when I fight for the King. This way I know that the eight men I take with us are the best and that I can trust them."

That seemed to content her and soon I heard her begin to breathe steadily. She was asleep. I lay there for a while running through my plans and the quest I would undertake. The King would not be happy. He had recently fallen out with one of his advisors, Peter des Roches. The Bishop had left England a year ago to go on a crusade. That left the King with just myself and Hubert de Burgh. Hubert de Burgh was a vindictive man. He had alienated many of the Poitevin lords. He had confiscated their English estates. Poitou was now openly opposed to the King. Until the King married and had children then he would always be threatened with insurrection but England, at the moment, appeared quiet. There was never a good time to leave the King but my quest had to be undertaken.

I rose before dawn and left my wife sleeping. I went to the stables. Already William was helping to select the horses we would take. The archers and men at arms we would take were there already. "Morning, my lord!" Their cheerful chorus told me that they were looking forward to what they considered an adventure.

"Morning."

I was taking Richard Red Leg, Padraig the Wanderer, Sam Strongarm, William of Lincoln, Dick One Arrow, Cedric Warbow, Walter of Coxold and Mordaf, son of Tomas. All were single men. Some had had wives and they had died. The plague claimed many folk. Some were older and some younger but what they had in common was that they were the best in the land at what they did. "Richard, make sure the four sumpters we take are hardy. I am not sure we will find more in Gascony and France."

"Do not worry, lord, the horse master has chosen them all."

"Where is he?"

"He was walking Blaze around the walls to make certain he is ready for such a long journey."

Blaze was a palfrey and a good one too. He was almost the size of a courser. He would do. "Good. Remember we keep the grey surcoats hidden until we board the ship to France. I want the Earl of Cleveland to disappear and Sir Thomas of Kastelholm to land

6

in France. And your arrows, Dick One Arrow, how will they be hidden?"

"We will not fit the heads until we need them. That way they will not take up as much space. We will fletch them in France. We have disguised our bow bags as best we can. Do not worry, lord, we can carry off this deception." He laughed, "I think it is Master William who is unhappy that he will have to wear a plain pot helmet!"

William flushed, "I do not mind, Dick One Arrow. It is just that it is not as good a fit as the one my father had made for me."

"And that is why you wear it. Squires of swords for hire take helmets and weapons from the battlefield. They do not have expensively made mail and weapons. It is why I wear an old helmet and have a ventail." I nodded. "This is good. Bring the horses around to the inner ward and I will send John down with my travelling bag. I too, my son, am travelling lighter than I normally do. We are on a quest. A quest for justice."

By the time I reached the hall all were awake. They knew that their lord was leaving and everyone was busy. My servant John was unhappy to be left behind. As I had told him a sword for hire could not afford a servant. I went to the table and poured myself some ale and cut some ham to have on the fresh bread. I was taking plenty of money. I had it secreted beneath my mail in a belt. I had had it specially made by the tanners in the town. My purse would carry just the coppers we needed to get by. The belt of coins was my reserve.

John appeared, "Your bag is ready, lord."

I could hear the criticism in his voice. "Good then give it to Padraig and he will fit it on the sumpter. Make sure the shield cover is on the new shield. It would not do to give away the fact that I had a plainer shield." The grey surcoat had just a sword on the left breast and my shield, painted a dark blue, had a grey sword in the middle. I had seen such designs when in the Baltic. It would add to my disguise.

This was the first time I had left without my aunt waving me off. I knew that she would not approve of my actions. Her brother had gone off to the crusades and never returned. Her husband had perished fighting the Scots. Had she been alive she would have told me to stay! She had left me her cross in her will and I

7

fingered it now almost as an apology to her. When I had finished my meal, I donned my cloak and headed for the church. There I bade farewell to my family who were buried there. Their tombs and bodies lay in the small chapel. It had grown for now Alfred and Aunt Ruth had joined them. I said a prayer and then left. Before I left the church, I touched the tomb of the Warlord and asked him to help me in my quest. I stood in the door and looked at the tombs of the dead. I would keep them in my head while I was away. My men were all mounted and waiting. The four archers each led a sumpter. They were laden. The four men at arms would ride both before and behind them. We would not be using scouts while in England and William and I would ride at the fore. All of us would play the part of a small company seeking a lord to serve. My wife kissed us and wept. My daughters, looking like little more than children, waved from the gate as we headed to the ferry. We were on the long road south. The journey through England took many days. I was still Sir Thomas, Earl of Cleveland, and we either stayed in the halls of those who knew me or had good accommodation in inns. We made the most of England for once we were in France then we would have to rough it.

I did not like London. I mistrusted both the people and the lords who lived there. I think that the second King Henry had turned out as well as he had because the Warlord had kept him as far from London as he could. The present King Henry was a creature of London. He had spent coin to improve both the Tower and his palace of Westminster. We had ridden down Watling Street and entered London close by the Cheap. I was wearing my livery and I was recognised. It meant that people were wary of upsetting me. We were not crowded in the narrow streets. I was not welcomed for I was a supporter of the King. The King taxed them and they did not like that but they knew me to be a warrior and a warrior to be feared. We were afforded more room than most. We passed the inn called *'The Earl Marshal'* and left the city to cross the bridge into the Tower.

King Henry had begun to improve the castle. I saw that the two new towers, the Wakefield and the Lanthorn were progressing well and that there was a water gate next to the Wakefield Tower. I knew from my conversations with the young King that he intended to have his quarters in the Wakefield Tower. We were admitted for I was well known but the sentries viewed us with suspicion.

We entered the inner ward and dismounted. Two sentries stood by the steps which led to the White Tower. I saw that there were now two halls in the inner ward, "Are they the new warrior halls?" The sentry stared at me as though he did not speak my language. I walked up the steps and put my face close to his. "Are you new here that you do not recognise the Earl of Cleveland?"

His eyes flickered to his companion who grinned, "I am sorry, lord. Dick is a little slow and must have misheard you. Aye, they are the warrior halls and they have stables newly built."

I turned and saw that my men were also amused by the man's reaction. "Get the men settled. If we are not to stay here, I will send William with a message." Brushing aside the two sentries I entered. I had seen their type before. They were nothing more than human door stops. If trouble came, they would not last more than a few heartbeats. Both were overweight. That worried me. The King should be surrounding himself with men who could fight and defend him. The King and his household ate well. I doubted that they would practise with their weapons. I hoped that the King had surrounded himself with young knights whom he could trust.

When I entered the hall, I saw that the King was there with Hubert de Burgh and some younger knights. One was Humphrey de Bohun who was heir to the title of Earl of Hereford. I did not know the other six. I came to know their names soon enough. Outnumbering the knights were the clerics, bishops and priests. I shook my head. If trouble came to the King then they would be of little use.

The King saw us and we bowed. In those days he was still fond of me. He smiled and came over, "My condolences, my lord, on your loss. That a knight could resort to murder is beyond the pale. Especially one in whom we placed so much trust."

I nodded. I would not tell the King my plans whilst in this company. I did not trust any of them. "Thank you, King Henry. We have all taken it hard. It is one reason why I have delayed my return."

Hubert de Burgh did not like me and made no attempt to hide his disapproval, "Your Majesty if we could return to matters of state!"

"Of course, and we now have the Earl of Cleveland. These are military matters with which we deal and there is none better than Thomas of Stockton! Sir Thomas, we would welcome your advice on these matters."

"If I can be of any help, Your Majesty, but I would speak with you in private when time allows."

"Of course," he nodded. "Go on, my lord. You were outlining the position."

"Now that King Louis is dead it is his twelve-year-old son, Louis, who rules France. There are many in France who see this as an opportunity for you to reclaim Normandy, Poitou and Gascony. The Duke of Brittany has sided with us. We need to take an army to France and reclaim that which is rightly yours."

I saw the eagerness on the young King's face. "Then let us do it! What is stopping us?"

"Coin, majesty. We can use the forty days' service owed by your barons but it would take more than forty days to recover all the lands which are yours. We would have to raise money from the people or by raising taxes."

I said nothing. People, especially those in the north, were unhappy about being taxed for wars on the continent. The same was true of the people on the Welsh border. We had domestic enemies who were a bigger threat.

"Then raise taxes." The King's words made it sound as though this was a simple thing to do.

I ventured, "What about those barons and lords who have land in Normandy, Poitou and Gascony? Is it not in their interests to have their land returned to them? There you have the heart of an army and they can help to fund it."

The Earl of Kent, Hubert de Burgh, gave me a patronising look, "Earl, finances are a complicated matter."

I shrugged, "Ask them, majesty. Sound out their opinion. If they will not then you can always resort to taxes but I wonder if there is an appetite for war? We have just fought the Welsh and the peace has been barely brokered. If they broke the peace then we would need an army to fight them."

"I am disappointed, Sir Thomas. I would have thought that the hero of Arsuf would be more than happy to fight the French!" The mocking words of the Justiciar of England, Hubert de Burgh, annoyed me. He was not a warrior. King John had selected him to be Prince Arthur's gaoler and, in my opinion, he was not qualified for that position either.

"I am always willing to fight for my King but we are not talking about fighting in England. There is a sea twixt France and here. If we get there and find that there is no support then we could lose the war before we begin. You would not wish that, would you, King Henry?"

I had expressed doubt. I saw that the King was reconsidering. Hubert de Burgh, who was also the Earl of Kent said, "But we have had a delegation of lords from Normandy, majesty! They said that there was much support for you in that duchy."

I saw that the King still listened to me. He went to the map which lay on the table and ran his finger across the English Channel. I had raised doubts and he was thinking about the problems. Hubert de Burgh glared at me. The young knights just looked bemused. Humphrey de Bohun was even younger than the King. I doubted that he had ridden to a tourney let alone a war. A servant brought in a brand to light the torches in the sconces. The afternoon was almost gone and the light was fading.

"I have much to think on and I would speak with the Earl in private. We will resume this on the morrow. Lord Justiciar, I would have you give me an estimate of the cost of the war and how much tax we would have to impose. One night cannot make a difference eh?" Without waiting for an answer, he took me by the elbow and led me towards the door which lead to the fighting platform on the north wall.

"I have missed you, Thomas, and your son, Alfred. I do not know how you can bear the pain of such a loss." We stepped out into the cool air of the north wall. He led me east. "I will show you my new towers. At the end of the week I leave for my palace at Westminster. It is more comfortable than this one. When I have finished the two new towers then it will be my home. I came only to chivvy the builders. Unless I personally supervise the work then they drag their heels. So, what do you wish to speak to me about? Do you want William here dubbing?"

11

William was following a few paces behind along with one of the King's pages, Geoffrey. I laughed, "That will be a good many years off." I turned, "William, Geoffrey, walk further behind, I pray you." We reached the north east corner and I said, "Majesty, I would go to France to find the killer of my son and avenge him."

He stopped and turned, "That would be murder!"

"And it would not be in England. The crime, if crime it was would be in France."

I saw the King considering my words, "You could bring him back and he would stand trial."

"Majesty, Sir Jocelyn was well connected. He has friends. Who knows they may try to use this to threaten your rule. The last thing you need is a martyr in England around whom your enemies can rally."

He nodded and continued walking, "But how will you find him? France is big. He may have fled further afield."

"He may have but he will have left a trail. I will go with a handful of men and we will go in disguise. We will pick up his scent. We served with the man and I know his habits. He is with a whore. She is a beautiful woman. She will have been noticed. If he rids himself of her then it will be harder but I am confident we will pick up their scent."

We had reached the Lanthorn Tower. Men had stopped work. I could see that they had almost reached the top of the wall. The King pointed to it, "This will be a stronghold once more when I have finished. I have too many enemies! They surround me!" He stopped and turned to me, "Sir Thomas, can I trust these Norman lords? Sir Hubert seems positive but I know that he dislikes the Poitevin lords. Can I trust his judgment about these Normans and Bretons? They betrayed my father. They may try to betray me. How can I trust them?"

"You only need trust them if you wish to have your lands in France returned to you."

"And I do."

"Then you must find out whom you can trust."

He continued walking. We picked our way through blocks of building stone which had been left on the fighting platform. We looked west and the sun was setting along the river. "And that is easier said than done. Sir Jocelyn fought well against the Welsh. We both thought we could trust him and he betrayed us."

"He disguised himself, majesty."

The King stopped, "I have it! You are going to France in disguise. Find Sir Jocelyn but also find out what is in the hearts of the Norman barons. Report back to me."

"Be a spy?"

He shrugged, "I do not care what you call it. You would be serving England and me. I trust you and I trust your judgement. You will not be going as the Earl of Cleveland. You will be a mercenary. Men will speak with you." He smiled, "This is perfect. I will tell my Justiciar, the Earl of Kent, that you have displeased me and I have sent you from court. He does not like you and that will please him. You will disappear." He nodded, "I command you, find out whom I can trust!"

I nodded. I had no choice for, it seemed to me, that I had no life outside that allowed by the King. I had been better off when I had been a sword for hire. When I took the manor of Stockton I was tied to the King for good or ill.

The King began his deception that evening as we ate. William and I were sent to the furthest extremity of the feasting hall. It is amazing how much joy our apparent misery caused. There was much laughter from those around the King and fingers were pointed in our direction. I had not had the opportunity to speak with William and he was quite distressed. "What have we done wrong father? We are seated with knights who have no influence."

I shook my head, "Do not be so arrogant. A true knight does not worry about influence or power. Be at peace and I will explain tomorrow when we take the road to Southampton." He seemed mollified. I noticed that several of the lords from the Welsh campaign had joined us: Gilbert de Clare and his son Richard, the Earl of Norfolk and his sons Hugh and Roger. They had not been at the meeting I had interrupted and I wondered if that was a deliberate ploy on the part of Hubert de Burgh. Was he isolating the King from lords who could aid him? What were his motives? I had not liked Peter des Roches but at least the Bishop had balanced out the influence of de Burgh.

When we left, the next morning, we crept out as thieves in the night. My archers and men at arms were also puzzled because they had heard of the treatment we had received. I waited until we had crossed over London Bridge and ridden a good five miles south before I spoke. I told them what we had been asked to do. All of them, William included, appeared relieved.

Padraig said, "It didn't seem right, lord. You having done so much for the young King."

"This makes it harder for us though, father."

Richard Red Leg said, "I do not want to disagree with you, Master William, but you are wrong. If anything, this helps us. We can now pretend that we are looking for a lord to follow while we look for Sir Alfred's killer. We have a reason to be wandering around asking questions."

He was right, of course, and I had been guilty of seeing only the negatives. "We all have to stick to the story. I chose you all as you understand some Swedish. It will give credence to our story."

"We will find an inn to spend the night. Keep your surcoats covered by your cloaks and we will change into our plainer surcoats before we eat."

They chattered like magpies. This was something new and, to them, enjoyable. I was less certain about William. One thing I knew, he would grow up on this journey. After Arsuf I had been alone and had to grow up quickly. William would not be alone. We would have to endure adversity but the eight men I had with us were more than I had had in the Holy Land.

# Chapter 2
# The Road to Paris

We found an inn by the river in Southampton. I went with Padraig to negotiate berths on a ship. With fourteen horses we required a big one and that meant spending coin. I also needed passage to a French port and that, too, restricted the choices. Eventually we found the *'Maid of Rye'*. The captain was happy to take us although the price he demanded made me wince. He was picking up a cargo of pots in Dieppe and was happy to have ballast on the outward voyage. He had been waiting for a commission such as ours. I suspect I could have beaten his price down but I was just pleased to be sailing on an English ship. As we ploughed east towards Dieppe, I sat beneath the piece of sail which the captain had rigged by the forecastle. It kept both the sun and the rain from us. The ship had a small crew and they were all busy. We were able to sit and talk. Although I had agreed to be the King's spy that was not my priority. I would find out that which the King needed to know but it would be while seeking the three fugitives.

I had a wax tablet before me. I drew a crude map of England and France. I put a cross on it. It represented York on the Ouse. "This is where we lost the three of them. What do we know?"

William said, "Five ships left the river at the same time. They could have been on any one of them."

Sam Strongarm said, "I can narrow it down a little, lord. Three of them were heading for London and the other two for France."

Sam was a good warrior but always quiet, "How do you know?"

"Harry was my friend. He was murdered and I knew that the woman had something to do with it. When you were with the

Archbishop I went down to the river and asked questions. The two ships sailing to France were heading for Calais and Nantes."

"Thank you, Sam." We were heading for a port between the two. There would be no evidence of them in Dieppe.

William asked, "Might they not have boarded a ship to London? They could have disappeared within England."

My son had a point but in my heart I did not think so. "Sir Jocelyn was prominent in the campaign against the Welsh. He was at court with the King. He would have to hide and that begs the question where? His family disowned him and he had neither land nor coin in England. I am not certain if he had money from his father. He seems to have inherited his father's men. He will be with the French. They are our natural enemies. He will be safer there. Perhaps he was in their pay all along. Had he escaped by land I believe he would have gone to Scotland but we managed to force his hand."

Padraig was carving a piece of bone. He did it when he was thinking. Padraig and Richard Red Leg were my most experienced men at arms. They had been with me a long time. Like Ridley the Giant and Henry Youngblood they had helped to make my son into a knight. Without children of their own and now unlikely to father any, they were as determined as any to wreak revenge. Padraig's wife had died of the pestilence and he seemed resigned to being a man at arms. "It seems to me, my lord, that we look for the doxy, Morag. I know not how long she was with Sir Jocelyn or how she came into his company but she did for Harry. As I recall your words, Sam, she was a stunner."

I heard Sam grumble, "Aye, the treacherous bitch."

"And she must have helped to arrange the passage too. We found money when we ended the life of One-Eyed Waller but what if she took more? That would explain why Sir Jocelyn needs her. Harry was killed in Wales. I am guessing that, with a name like Morag, she came from Wales originally. It would explain why she remained unnoticed save by Harry. Sam, you saw her. What does she look like?"

Sam stroked his beard as he cast his mind back. "We were drinking in an alehouse. All of us, even Harry, were celebrating our victory. There were no enemies." He turned to Padraig, "You were doing that trick where you stand on your head and drink a horn of ale."

"Aye you are right."

Richard Red Leg said as he recalled the events too, "Aye. we were all watching. Men were placing bets on you."

Sam became excited, "Harry was laughing. He said he had to go outside and make water! You had fallen over and we were collecting and paying off the bets." He closed his eyes. "There was a woman with chestnut hair. It was long and tied at the back. She had eyes that were like deep pools. A man could drown in them. She had red lips painted with cochineal." He shook his head as though she had enchanted him and he wished to clear the memory. "I remember she looked over at us and then she left. I helped you up and then she was gone. I saw Harry, he was just coming back in when she passed him. He turned and ran after her. I shouted to him but he did not answer me. I thought, at the time, he just wanted a woman. I misjudged my friend. He must have remembered her from London. She must have been Morag." He shook his head, "I am a fool. Why could I not have remembered that before we went to York? I might have seen her. I could have looked for her."

Padraig stopped whittling, "You are looking back, my friend, and life is always clearer when you look back. There, lord, a chestnut-haired woman from Wales is the one we seek."

Sam nodded, "A beautiful, hard-hearted woman."

A sudden memory came to me. At the time I had been too concerned with the criminal in the inn but Sam's words had made a memory surface from deep within me. "You are right and I remember her now. When we were in the alehouse we were fighting. It was the doxy tried to save One-Eyed Waller. Now that you have described the woman, I can see her too."

Sam said, "She was bonny. After we left London Harry told me that he wondered how such a monster as Waller could have had such a pretty piece on his arm. We might not have seen her but Harry did. Her face stayed with him and it did for him."

"And it got him killed." They were thinking that if young Harry had only mentioned it to one of the others then he might be alive. I was thinking that my son would still be walking the earth. "From now on if any sees one of the fugitives do nothing save find someone to tell. We know they are dangerous. This woman is a killer. She can look a man in the eyes and stab him. That is what they said in York. The guards she stabbed were stabbed in the front as she spoke to them. That takes a calculating woman. We know that Sir Jocelyn and his squire are ruthless and that they can deceive. Like us they will have discarded their surcoats and, I have no doubt, their names."

William said, "Then how do we find them?"

"By their faces and their voices. They can change their mail and their clothes. They can grow their beards and trim them differently but we know their eyes."

Padraig said, "With respect, lord, it is you who know their eyes. We saw their backs. I know how they ride. I saw their sword swings. If we see them in battle then I would know them but not their eyes."

I knew what he meant. I was the hunting hound. I would have to be the one to sniff them out. This would not be easy.

"So, father, when we land do we go north or south?"

"Neither, we head east. We go to Paris." I saw the incredulous looks on their faces. I smiled, "It is the best place to begin. The French have a new boy King, Louis. All those who seek to have power will be gathered like bees around a hive. I saw this with King Henry. They will gather for the crumbs from his table and hope to take advantage of a naïve King. Sir Jocelyn is no fool and, as he showed in Wales, he knows how to ingratiate himself with a young King. He may not be there but we start at the heart of the land and, if we have to, work our way back to Normandy. Besides, as we travel east, we can ask about a chestnut-haired woman." I turned to Mordaf, "You have red hair."

"Aye, lord our mother was Irish. Gruffyd's daughter has auburn hair."

"Then you can ask about your sister."

He looked confused for he had no sister and then he smiled, "Aye lord. We can spin a tale about her running off with an English lord."

"Then you and Dick can ride ahead of us and when you find an inn you two get rooms first. It will look suspicious if ten of us arrive together."

Padraig nodded, "It would be better, lord, if some of us camped in the woods and made hovels."

He was right. "Until we reach large towns, we can do that. We have a plan. As for the King's mission, we keep our ears open. We seek employment. We failed to find work in England and look for any master who will pay for our hire."

By the time we landed we had our stories and we had our line of march planned. While the horses were walked to give them their land legs, I went to the town square, ostensibly to drink some wine, but in reality, to gather intelligence. I learned much which would aid the King. There were lords and barons who wished England to rule them again but their motives were not pure. They sought more land in Normandy. Their cooperation would come at a price.

With Mordaf and Dick a mile ahead we rode the main road to Paris. I had learned that all the most senior French lords were gathered in Paris. The young King had not been given a council of regents and all those who wished power were gathered there. They were seeking to ingratiate themselves with the young King. I now understood why the Duke of Brittany had asked King Henry to attack. Normandy could easily fall. I was told that men such as myself would be welcomed for the French were seeking mercenaries to fight their war for them. The journey to Paris took us three days. We learned nothing to help us in our quest but much to aid King Henry in his decision making. For the first two days we had no news of our prey but our last night, in the town of Pontoise, yielded results. It was not the result I had expected.

Pontoise had a castle and the town was surrounded by a strong wall. Guarding a crossing of the Seine it was an important stronghold. It was the first place where we all stayed in the same inn. It was busy. We were lucky that it was such a large inn. The number of people there helped us to disguise the fact that we knew each other.

We watched Mordaf and Dick as they spoke with the owner. When I saw nods and smiles then I knew that they had learned something. However, that had to wait as two liveried sergeants approached William and me. "You are to come with us!"

I saw my men's hands, at the next table, go to their weapons. I gave the slightest shake of the head, "Why? I am just a weary traveller and I have not committed a crime."

"The Count wishes to speak with you." The sergeant who spoke looked belligerent. He had huge fists which were bunching even as he loomed above me.

His companion smiled, "There is no cause for alarm. The Count does the same with all knights who pass through his manor. We are the gateway to Paris and the seigneur is loyal to the young King. He is careful about who he allows through his land."

I nodded, "Very well." We stood. I saw my men watching. I smiled to show that there was nothing to fear.

The castle was a strong one. The barbican had double gates and murder holes. Once we passed through it to the inner ward, I saw that it had a large square keep. I would not have relished trying to take it. We were taken to an ante chamber. The less belligerent sergeant nodded to the sentry who went inside, "If you wait here the Count will speak with you."

Left alone I saw that William was about to speak. I shook my head and said, "Pretend that you are simple. Just answer questions. Leave the talking to me."

The doors opened and we were admitted. The Count was aware of his position as guardian of the gateway to Paris. His chair was more like a throne and was mounted on a dais. He had six heavily armed and mailed men behind him. There were pages and squires who were in attendance as well as two priests. I saw that he was slightly younger than me. The rings on his fingers and the quality of his clothes told me that this was a rich lord who liked to show his power.

The Count gestured for us to advance. "I am Raymond, Count of Pontoise, and you have come into my town unbidden. Who are you and what is your business?"

I feigned innocence. "I am Thomas of Kastelholm in Sweden. I am a sword for hire and seek employment. I have done nothing wrong."

The Count nodded. He waved over one of the priests and spoke in his ear. The priest hurried away. "Employment?"

"We have been in the Baltic on crusade. I swore that I would serve God for five years. I have served God and slain the

20

unbelievers. I need to have an income for my son and I. I heard that France had a new king and that he might hire my sword."

The priest returned with a book. He opened it and pointed. The Count nodded and the priest hurried away with the book. "Sweden is far to the north. Surely there were places you passed where you might have been hired. England for example."

I nodded, "We tried there. We travelled to my homeland, England, first, but there was no work to be had and we were sent hither. There were no places which needed my services. Perhaps we should try Toulouse."

He shook his head, "That crusade is almost over." He stood and came over to me. He studied my cloak with the sword upon it. He held out his hand, "Let me see your blade. For your surcoat is the plainest I have ever seen. It tells me nothing about you. Let me study your sword so that I may judge better."

I had a good sword. It was well made and balanced. It had a simple pommel and guard. It was as long as my body from my hip to my foot. It was the sort of sword only a warrior would wield. A man had to be strong to use it for any length of time. He balanced it and tossed it from hand to hand. The Count knew weapons. He swung it and then handed it back to me. "Your sword tells me that you are a warrior. Perhaps I might employ you."

"I had planned on going to Paris."

"Your choice, Sir Thomas, is either to serve me or head back west from whence you came. I rule the Vexin and I am charged with protecting Paris. I answer only to the King." He gave me a thin smile.

I nodded and smiled back at him, "It seems that I have little choice in the matter for I need pay but I need to tell you that I have a retinue of eight warriors. They are all that is left to me from those who followed me to the Baltic."

"Men at arms?"

"And men at arms who can use a bow."

"Then you are even more valuable. Would you accept my offer of service?"

"And if I do not then my passage to Paris will be barred?"

He smiled, "I can see that those grey hairs you wear in your beard have been well earned. You serve me or head back to England. Do not worry, you shall see Paris. I travel there in a month's time. Your men are good warriors?" I nodded. "What say you?"

"We have not discussed terms."

"Four sou a week for you and two sou for your men?"

I feigned ignorance. If I had come from the Baltic then I would not have known the currency. "Sou?"

"It is the equivalent of three English shillings."

"Then we are happy."

"Bring your men tomorrow to the gate. My Captain, Sir Guy de Senonche, will show your men where they are to leave their war gear. You have horses?"

"Aye we do. They belong to my men. If they are lost…"

"Then I will replace them." He smiled, "I can see that you truly know the business of war. I look forward to speaking to you about fighting heathens. I have only fought Normans, Gascons and the beef eaters." He seemed to see William for the first time. "And your squire can have a sou a day. Let us hope he is worth it. He looks simple to me."

As we headed back to the inn, I said, "You did well. You could be a mummer."

"I was studying the faces. After Sir Jocelyn I will not take anyone for granted. I trust no-one save those we bring with us."

"You have wisdom beyond your years, my son." We neared the inn, "I could do without this distraction but it may serve us. Keep playing the same part. It is a pity you cannot speak Swedish. I can talk with the other men and no-one will know what we say." Even as we entered the inn I came up with a plan. I sat next to Padraig and Richard Red Leg. They had the best Swedish out of any of my men. "William is playing the part of a simpleton. I would have you two play the part of Swedes who cannot speak French. I am hoping that when you are apart from us then some of the Count's men may be indiscreet. Can you do this?"

Padraig grinned and said, "Javisst!"

William gave me a quizzical look. I said, "He said *'yes.'*"

"We stay the night here and tomorrow we join the Count and his men. Spread the word and let the others know that the two of you are now Swedes."

William and I were seated in a quiet area. The ones close to us were all French. They looked like merchants on their way to

Paris. Mordaf and Dick came towards us and sat behind us. Mordaf spoke quietly. "Morag did pass through here some three months since. She was dressed as a lady and had two female servants. She did not look like a doxy but her hair marked her and her beauty. She was with a knight and four other men. I am guessing the knight was Sir Jocelyn."

"Did you get a name?"

"Sorry lord, they only stayed here for a meal and then they moved on."

William asked, "Why did the Count not question them?"

Mordaf answered, "I think, lord, that he was in the south of the country around Toulouse. He was on the crusade there against the Cathars. It is only since he returned that he has begun to question all. The inn keeper does not like it for people avoid this place and he loses trade. Our arrival has boosted his business. It is why he was so pleased when we arrived."

"You have done well. Padraig and Richard Red Leg will pretend to be Swedes. We want them to think they cannot speak French."

"If my brother was here, we could have done the same with Welsh."

"I wanted single men, Mordaf." He nodded.

My men had their own coin which I had given them and they all paid for their own meals. I was quiet as I ate mine. I now had to get to Paris. I could not suddenly abandon the Count. He would be suspicious. I doubted that the fugitives would leave Paris quickly. They had money from somewhere and Sir Jocelyn was clever enough to secure them a position in the house of a great lord. It was what he had done in Wales first with de Braose and then with the King. He had not yet finished his work. I was gambling that the Count would not stay away from Paris for too long. He struck me as a man who liked and needed power. I would just have to ensure that I was not recognised by Sir Jocelyn. I rubbed my top lip. If I shaved my moustache off then it might change my appearance. William had already changed dramatically. He was almost unrecognisable as the callow youth who had been ridden down by the renegade's horse. Since his brother's death he had broadened out and begun a beard. He had started to shave it but I would tell him to grow it and to cut his hair short in the Norman style. I would do the same. They were subtle changes but they might deceive Sir Jocelyn.

The next day we were greeted by the Count's Captain. Sir Guy de Senonche was not a pleasant man. He was a knight and yet the Captain of the Guard. I wondered what his story was. He looked like a brute. When I pointed out that two of my men were Swedes and could not speak French he reddened and said, "Then what use are they to me?"

I smiled, "I can speak with them and the Count did not ask about their linguistic skills, only their skills as warriors." I pointed to Mordaf, "He is Welsh and I doubt that you will understand his accent. Not to worry, Captain, I will be with my men when they need orders. Until then they are clever and can follow what the others do. Of course, if the Count thinks it is too much trouble then we will leave and continue to Paris. No coin has changed hands yet."

He was beaten and he knew it. "You and your squire can go to the Great Hall; the Count is there with his other household knights."

The hall was full when we arrived and I had to stand behind two other knights. The sentry closed the doors behind me when we entered. The Count had been seated and he stood. "Now that we are all here, I can give you your instructions."

I frowned. He had not said anything when I had met him the previous day. Was this why he had threatened me? Did he need me so badly?

"It has come to my attention that the Count of Évreux is stirring up trouble for King Louis. He is demanding that the County of Normandy is returned to English rule. We are going to discourage him." Now I saw why he had been so aggressive towards me. He needed as many men as he could muster and hired swords were always useful. This I did not like. I could not fight against one of King Henry's supporters. We would have to slip away and disappear. I would not fight those supporting King Henry. The King's command had made life difficult for me. "We ride in two days' time. I wish us to ride quickly. You all have men to summon. Go." He peered across the room and spied me, "Sir Thomas."

I approached him, "My lord?"

He waved a hand at my face, "What is this?"

I shrugged, "I have worn my hair and beard in the Swedish style. I thought to make a change."

He nodded, "I barely recognised you. You and your men have fought against heathens who attack from cover?"

I nodded, "Many times."

"Then you and your men will ride a mile ahead of us. I would have you warn us of any ambush."

"Of course."

He picked up a purse, "And here is the pay for the first week. I will decide, at the end of seven days, if you are worth the pay."

We left for Normandy. We were scouting which was strange because we rode down roads which were unfamiliar to us in the van of an army of our enemies. Once I knew of our intention, I had written a letter to the Count of Évreux. I had not signed it but I intended to deliver it so that he would have warning of the Count's attack. We had barely fifty miles to travel. After speaking to other knights, I discovered that Évreux was a formidable castle. With luck the Count of Pontoise would realise that he could not defeat the castle by siege. I waited until we were just ten miles from the castle before I rode ahead, with William. There was a church at Cherisy just a few miles from the castle. Hooded, we went inside. I had not sealed the letter but carried it under my cloak. The priest was at the altar. William and I knelt and said a prayer. I dropped the letter where the priest would be bound to find it and we slipped out. I had done all that I could. I knew not if he would act on what I had written but it was all that I could do. We would now have to find a way to escape and disappear in Paris. We headed back to the main column and I reported that we had reached Cherisy.

"And you met no armed men?" I could answer truthfully for we had not. "Good, then we camp there and your scouting days will have ended. When I deliver my ultimatum, we will discover just how good you and your men are at fighting."

I hoped it would not come down to fighting.

Our good work had earned me a place around the Count's fire. It was there I learned of his enemies. He had many. The house of Burgundy also had a new young Duke, Hugh. His uncle, Raoul de Lusignan was trying to control both the king and the young Duke.

Raoul de Lusignan was also Count d'Eu. That county lay to the north of Normandy and brought the two counts into conflict. There was rivalry as both men sought to influence the young king. I was learning valuable information for King Henry.

When we reached the village, it was deserted. The priest had gone and he had taken his flock with him. The Count turned to me and snapped, "I should have told you to take the village!"

I shook my head, "Lord, I do not make war on priests nor poor folk. My men and I are more than happy to fight any of your enemies so long as they are warriors."

He nodded, "You ae a rarity, a mercenary with honour. Next time take them. You are my men now and I pay you!"

The next day we rode to the castle. I was not worried about being recognised. I had an anonymous grey livery and a simple helmet. I was just twenty paces behind the Count with the other knights when he made his ultimatum. "Surrender to me or we will besiege you."

The Count of Évreux shouted back, "You are not my liege lord and I do not trust you, Raymond of Pontoise. Bring me my King and I will open the gates and gladly meet with him and discuss my grievances. I mean no treason."

"So be it!" Turning he said, "Make our camp here. Baron Geoffrey, take half of the men and make a camp at the far side of Évreux."

As we settled into the routine of manning the siege lines and digging trenches I wondered if I ought to slip away in the night with my men. My prey was getting further from me and I was not learning much to aid King Henry. Fate intervened on the third day of the siege. A rider, a pursuivant by his dress, galloped in. I saw the fleur de lys and knew he was King Louis' man. He dismounted and handed the Count a document. The Count read it and then turned to his squire who sounded the horn for a counsel of war. I joined the other knights.

"It seems the Count of Évreux sent a rider to Paris before we reached him. I am summoned there to answer charges from the King." He thumped one fist into the other. "I see Burgundy's hand all over this." He smiled, "I am summoned but not my men. Sir Geoffrey, take command of the siege. Captain Guy choose ten good men for my escort and I will take Sir Thomas and his men.

You will lead my men. Sir Thomas' men proved effective scouts."

Captain Guy glowered at me, "I could give you twenty men, lord, and then you would be safer!"

"I will be safe. Something tells me that Sir Thomas and his men will not allow me to fall into the Duke's hands. I am his paymaster and he has yet to be paid for this week's work." He laughed, "I am like a walking war chest. Sir Thomas, we ride in an hour. You will get to see Paris, as you wished."

The men at arms we took were solid men. I saw that all were veterans. Sir Guy de Senonche might not like me but he had chosen the best at his disposal to guard his lord. I had my men at arms lead the horses at the rear while I rode with my four archers. I had my helmet hanging from my cantle and my ventail about my shoulders. I had not forgotten how to scout. We stopped for the night at Montigny-le-Bretonneaux. It was a small manor with just a hall. The old baron who lived there was one of the oldest men I had ever met. His servants told me that he was over seventy years old. He was sad for he had no children. His sons had died and his daughters, when they had married, had left him. He did not seem to know where he was. What made it worse was the way the Count treated him. It was almost as though he was there to serve the Count. Count Raymond was typical of many men who ruled petty fiefdoms in both France and England. They thought that as they only answer to a King and then God that made them like God and they acted accordingly.

As I was the only other knight the Count was forced to speak with me, "Tomorrow you will see a snake in human form. I have no doubt that Raoul de Lusignan is behind this. He hovers close to the King manipulating the young man. The dowager Queen, Blanche of Castile, appears to be under his sway. I would not put it past him to try to marry the Queen and take France that way!"

"Surely that could not happen, lord." Even as I said it, I realised that this was a possibility. King Henry's mother was now married into the Lusignan family and they had their eyes on the English crown.

"Not so long as I live. Tomorrow we ride through a forest. There are bandits and brigands there. Your men need to be alert."

I nodded, "In Sweden there were many such forests. My men are like hounds and can sniff out an enemy."

"I have noticed that they stay close together. Was it the crusade bonded them?"

"They have served me a long time lord. I was a young man when I met some of them."

"Your service to the cross does you credit, Sir Thomas, but I fear it has done little for your personal well-being. A man of your age who has served God should have a castle, a wife, a family and armour and horse which reflects that."

"Blaze is a good horse, lord."

"But no courser. If we have to fight other knights then I fear your service to me will be brief."

I decided that I had not played the mercenary well enough. I said, "Speaking of which, lord, my men are now owed their next pay. Paris will be a place to spend money."

"Aye and to run. I am afraid your men will have to wait for their coin until we are back in Pontoise. I will not risk them, or you, running!"

That night as I curled up in the bed the baron had provided, I reflected that I had managed to deceive the Count. If he had suspected me of deception then he would not have been so open. I heeded his words, however. Forests were the best place for an ambush. The next day, as we left, I warned my archers and they strung their bows. Thus far they had carried them in their bow sheaths. They jammed half a dozen war arrows in their belts and, like me, they rode bare headed. I wore my shield around my back. My sword had been sharpened. If trouble came then we would be ready. We had a bare sixteen miles to go to reach Paris but the vast forest was a favourite hunting ground of the French kings. Although a trail went through the heart of it the rest was left wild for animals to enjoy. That made for good ambush country. Despite his words about bandits the Count and his squires appeared at ease as we entered the huge forest.

I rode with the archers forty paces ahead of the Count. We were a mile or so inside the forest when we found trouble. Mordaf did not rein in he merely slowed his horse and said, quietly, "Lord, there are men ahead. I can smell them."

I sniffed the air. The wind was coming from the east and it carried, not the smell of animals but men. Had this been a road then that might have been expected but there was no sound of horses or people moving. Men were still and waiting. I had learned to be decisive many years earlier. Hesitation could cost lives. I said, "Ride left and right! Find them. William with me!" I whirled my horse and we galloped back down the trail. The crossbow bolt thudded into the shield about my back. I felt the thump as it struck. The crossbow had been loosed from less than two hundred paces. It still had power. "Ambush!" I pulled my mail coif over my head and slipped on my helmet.

We whirled around and the Count said, "How many are there?"

"I know not but my archers will try to flush them."

He nodded, "And now you earn your coin. Take your men and six of my men at arms."

"Padraig, leave the horses and come with me." I pointed to the first five of the Count's men, "You men, draw your weapons and follow me!" William pulled the bolt from my shield and I pulled it around. Drawing my sword, I spurred Blaze. I waved my sword to the right, "Take your men right. Padraig, left! William keep behind me! No risks!"

"Aye lord!"

I had barely pulled my shield up when crossbows thudded into it. One almost hit Blaze. From ahead I heard the cries of men struck by arrows. My archers would be afoot and stalking the ambushers through the forest. We had set off the ambush and now horsemen rode towards us. The dense undergrowth made it hard to estimate numbers. The men wore conical helmets and had shields with red and blue diagonal bands on them. The Count had told me that was the livery of Burgundy.

The ambush sprung, they charged at us from cover. It was thickly wooded and I had no idea of numbers. I saw a crossbow aimed at me. I held my shield tightly peering over the top. Suddenly an arrow head sprouted from the crossbowman's chest as one of my archers hit him in the back. Two men at arms rode at me. William was, I hoped, behind me. He had improved his skills but killers such as these were too much for him to handle alone. At best he might distract them. The two of us, until my men at arms joined us, were alone. The two men at arms who charged me had different weapons. One had a sword and the other a spear. The spear would hit me first and that rider was to my left. The two men were both experienced and they came at me together. My eyes could only watch one of them. I braced myself for the spear as I prepared to swash my sword blindly at the swordsman. The spear hit me and he punched hard. My shield was driven into my shoulder. My sword failed to block his for he had not swung it but lunged. It tore into my cheek below the right eye. I was lucky that the tip caught on my coif or I would have been dead. As it was, I knew that I had a serious wound for I felt the blood pouring down my face.

The swordsman gave an elated roar. I swung my sword and hacked across his back as he passed me. I risked watching him for the spearman would have to turn his horse. William had taken advantage of the swordsman's movement and his sword had hacked across his chest. Wounded, he wheeled his horse away and I turned Blaze to face the spearman. He had already turned but I now had just one opponent. I saw the Count bringing the rest of his men to my aid. They were not galloping. He had paid me to defend him and he would have his money's worth.

This time when the spearman thrust I used my shield offensively and hit the spear head with my shield. At the same time I hacked across his left arm above his shield. The blood and the wound told me that he was incapacitated. He wheeled his horse away and galloped after the other failed ambushers. As my men at arms and the Count's men attacked the enemy I heard a horn and the ambushers fled. I heard cries in the woods as the last of the crossbowmen fell. William rode up to me. "Father, your cheek!"

I looked around for enemies and there were none. I took off the helmet and slipped the coif from my head. If I had worn my own helmet and mail, I would not have been harmed. My helmet had a mask and it had a ventail. Sheathing his sword, William reached into his saddlebag and pulled out a cloth. He handed it to me and I pressed it to the wound. The Count rode up. He nodded, "You did well and you and your men have courage. It is a pity you did not take one of the shields." He turned to one of his men, Stephen, "Go and see if any of the crossbowmen have livery. We need proof for the King. This attack will be the undoing of the Burgundians!"

I saw the look of disgust on William's face. The Count was unconcerned about my wound. Padraig galloped up. He threw himself from his horse, "My lord, dismount! That is a bad wound."

I did as I was bid for, in truth, I felt a little woozy. Padraig tended to our horses when they were wounded and to the men too. He took his ale skin and, after removing the cloth poured ale on the wound. "Master William, hold the cloth in place. I will sew him. You need to wash as much blood away as you can."

"Aye, Padraig."

"Lord, have a good drink. This will hurt. I will try to keep the stitches neat but you need the wound sealing."

My archers led their horses from the wood. I saw the Count looking bemused. Stephen rode up. "Nothing on them my lord save Burgundian and French coins. They were from Burgundy. One spoke to me before he died. He asked me to give his cross to his mother in Lyon."

The Count shook his head, "That is not evidence. Come, we have wasted enough time here. Sir Thomas, you and your men follow when you can. We will be at the Palais de la Cité. Find your men accommodation where you can but you and your squire come to the Palais. I need your testimony for the King." With that he galloped off.

Padraig shook his head, "If you ask me, lord, we should head back to England! There is no gratitude."

I smiled and regretted it instantly for it hurt. "Remember why we are here, Padraig, we seek my son's killers. The Count is a means to an end. So long as he gets us into the city then I am satisfied. Either we find them in Paris or we find their trail. We are getting closer."

"Hold still, lord."

Richard Red Leg said, "We will fetch the horses."

Padraig began to sew. I had endured such things before. The hardest part was when the sharp bone needle first entered my flesh. Afer that it was endurable. I forced myself to plan how we would find the fugitives. We now had more information. There were more of them. They would find it harder to hide. They had

31

money from somewhere. I suspected that it was Sir Hugh of Craven's coin. They were travelling as lords and ladies. They would be remembered, especially with a beauty such as Morag. When I had seen her in the inn in London I had been preoccupied. She had been dirty then. I wondered if she and Sir Jocelyn had known each other before she had murdered Harry.

Padraig wrapped a bandage around my head. I could only see clearly out of one eye. "There, lord, it is all done. Have some ale now and then we will head to Paris. I would like a real healer to look at it. It is a nasty wound."

My men rode protectively close to me as we headed to Paris. My archers had taken coins from the dead and they shared them out. Mordaf asked, "When the fugitives are found do we head home?"

"We still have a job to do for the King but we can do that amongst our own folk if you baulk at serving the French."

"I do, lord. I have spent too long killing them to fight alongside them. When we slew the crossbowmen, it would have been easy to do the same to the Count's men. They are unpleasant!"

I laughed for that was quite mild from Mordaf.

# Chapter 3
# King Louis of France

Paris, like London, sprawled out from the centre. In Paris' case the centre was the Ile de la Cité. We would cross by the bridge which was close to St. Severin. We saw the Palais de la Cité ahead of us. There was a formidable barbican. We reined in before we crossed the bridge. "We will have to find lodgings close by." I threw a purse to Richard Red Leg. "When you have found some then have one of the men wait here to guide us to them."

"Aye, lord, do you need one of us with you as well?"

I said, "No, William here has been blooded. All will be well." We rode over the wooden bridge. The sentries looked up at me. My bandage was more than a little bloody.

"Yes lord?"

"We are men of the Count of Pontoise. I believe he is expecting us."

One of them nodded, "Yes, lord. If you and your squire would go to the inner ward there will be a page waiting for you."

We dismounted and walked our horses. I saw the page waiting for us. I handed my reins to William. "You had better wait here. Keep your eyes and ears open."

"Aye lord."

We entered the palace and walked down a corridor. I saw many guards there. They all wore royal livery. By contrast King Henry was barely guarded at all! As we neared a double sentried door, I heard raised voices from within. The page said, "Wait here, my lord." He slipped inside and I heard shouts. The two sentries exchanged a knowing look. The door opened and the page beckoned me forth.

Inside I saw that the hall was filled. There were courtiers and clerics, lords and knights. On a throne sat the diminutive figure of King Louis. He was the King of the country I had fought against for most of my life. He was slight and looked as though a good wind would blow him over but, after meeting him, I found that I liked him. From his speech and his actions when I was with him, I gained a favourable impression and all that he did in his relatively short life showed that he was a good king. He truly deserved his canonization. That moment, however, was long in the future and, as I entered the room fell silent and all eyes were drawn to me. I only had eyes for the King. I knew that I had to show him obeisance and so I dropped one knee.

His voice was stronger than I would have expected from one so slight. "Rise. The Count has spoken of you. From your wound you must be Sir Thomas."

"I am, King Louis."

The Count of Pontoise stepped forward, "And this, Your Majesty, is an example of the treachery of Raoul de Lusignan! Sir Thomas has been scarred for life by the killers that were sent by this noble to end my life. But for the courage of Sir Thomas and his men I would be dead."

A wall of noise rose until a bishop banged his staff on the wooden floor, "Silence, King Louis would speak!"

"Tell us, Sir Thomas, what happened. The Count has told us of what he saw but you were the one who was attacked."

"We were traveling through the forest west of here when we spied men about to ambush us. My shield was struck by a crossbow bolt. Men with red and blue diagonally striped bands ambushed us. I was attacked by two of them. Thanks to my squire I drove them off."

The King smiled, "Well?" He looked at the Count d'Eu.

The uncle of the Duke of Burgundy stepped forward, "Your Majesty I protest. My nephew is at home in Lyon. He could have had nothing to do with this attack."

The Count of Pontoise waved a dismissive arm. "No, Lusignan, he could not and I did not accuse the Duke of Burgundy. I accused his uncle. I accused you. I just said that the men were Burgundian."

Raoul de Lusignan affected a sly smile, "Did you draw your sword, Count?"

"No. Sir Thomas of Kastelholm and his men were the ones who led my men at arms."

"Then the only noble who can actually verify if the men were Burgundian is this knight." He turned his hawk like gaze on me, "Are you French, Sir Thomas?"

I shook my head, "No, lord, I was born in England."

"Where did you ply your trade as a mercenary before joining the Count?"

"Sweden in the Baltic Crusade."

Raoul de Lusignan adopted a perplexed look, "I am not arguing with the Count, Your Majesty, I do not doubt that the Count was attacked. He has many enemies and I confess I am no friend of his but there is no proof of any Burgundian involvement. I have been here at court for the last ten days. I put it you that Sir Thomas was mistaken. Perhaps the blow to his head made him misremember."

The King looked from the Count to the Burgundian and back. He said, "I fear there is no accurate way to settle this. Had there been clearer evidence I might have judged. Sir Thomas, you were attacked in a royal forest. For that I apologise. Guy, take this knight to Brother Paul. He is a skilled healer. Bring him back when you are done as I would speak with him about his experiences on Crusade."

I bowed and turned to follow the page. It was as I did so that I spied Sir Jocelyn and his squire. They were in the hall. Neither were looking at me but were talking to a tall knight. He had a blue and white horizontally striped surcoat. It was surmounted by a red rampant lion. As I recalled it was the livery of the house of Lusignan. He knew Sir Jocelyn. I was actually grateful to the man who had wounded me. My bandage disguised me. I had an advantage now. I knew where to find Sir Jocelyn but he was unaware that I was on his trail. I almost rushed out to fetch my men but, instead, I followed the page.

Brother Paul was an old priest without a hair on his head. He made up for that with the longest and whitest beard I had seen. The page said, "Brother Paul, the King would have you look at the wound of this knight."

The page went to leave but the priest said, "Not so fast!" To me he said, "How did you earn this wound? Duelling?"

"I was escorting the Count of Toulouse to visit with the King and we were ambushed."

The priest nodded and waved to the page, "Go!"

He washed his hands in some scented water. He carefully removed the bandage and then held a candle close to the wound so that he could examine it. "Who stitched you?"

"One of my men."

"It is not a bad job but I must undo his work and ensure that there are no evil humours left in the wound. Lie down. I will fetch you a draught."

I lay down but said, "I can bear the pain, Brother."

He laughed, "I care not. I want you immobile for my own safety and health. I swear the draught will just allow you to sleep briefly for I must cleanse the wound."

I nodded. I had little choice. I drank the draught and soon found myself slowly falling asleep. I seemed to go around and around. I was heading for the bottom of a pit. I did not reach it. I smelled rosemary and opened my eyes. The priest smiled at me as he dried his hands. "I commend your man. He did a good job. The blade which sliced you was not clean and I have removed the impurities I found in your cheek. You were lucky, the blade missed the bone by the smallest of margins. I am not certain they would have killed you but better to be certain. I used more stitches than your fellow. They are smaller. When they are removed, in a month, there will be no scar."

He held a mirror up so that I could see the wound.

"Who will remove them? I am here but briefly."

He smiled, "Your fellow looks to have skills. Have him use a sharp blade which has been seared in heat." After bandaging my face, he handed me a small pot jug. "Here is a draught. If the pain is too severe then take it and you will sleep like a babe. I have done all that I can for you." He waved a hand to dismiss me.

I had no intention of putting myself to sleep. I would take the jug with the sleeping potion. Who knew when it might come in handy? As I left, I put my hand to my face. It was heavily bandaged and I could not see out of my right eye. If Sir Jocelyn had not recognised me before he had no chance now. The page was waiting for me. "The King would have you dine with him this night. I have sent a message to your squire to fetch clean clothes for these are bloody, lord, and not fit for the King's presence. He said he would have to find your men. I will take you to a chamber where you can wait until he returns."

As I sat in the small, cell like room I began to fret and worry. What if Sir Jocelyn had spotted my son? He had seen him and although my son had changed, he was still recognizable. I had my prey under the same roof and I could do nothing about it. If he fled then I would have to begin my search again but this time my prey would know that he was being hunted. It seemed to take forever but, eventually, the door opened and William stood there with a clean, plain tunic. I had much grander ones at home but this would confirm my disguise. As I changed, I quickly told William all that I had learned. "When you leave with my bloody clothes put the hood of your cloak up and keep your eyes down. Have one of the men watch the gate for Sir Jocelyn. If he leaves then I would know."

"What do we do if he leaves?"

"Follow him. Do no more. We have been given a golden opportunity and I would not squander it."

The page came for me and escorted me to the feasting hall. I wondered why I had been invited. I was unimportant. I began to worry that someone had recognised me but then I dismissed the idea. The bandage made it hard to recognise me. The page escorted me directly to the young King. I saw that there was a space at the table next to him. The Archbishop of Paris was on one side of him and his mother, the widow of King Louis, on the other. The Counts of Eu and Pontoise were as far apart as was possible. There was no sign of Sir Jocelyn.

The King waved me towards the empty seat next to him. "Sit, Sir Thomas. I am most interested in your Baltic exploits. I would hear all about them."

A servant poured some wine and I saw that the Queen and the Archbishop were both listening intently. I raised my goblet to the King and, after sipping it, said, "What would you like to know, King Louis?"

"We have heard that Bishop Albert converts many heathens. How does he do that? I would take the cross when I am older but

I have heard that the Muslims do not convert. In fact, it is Franks who become Turcopoles!"

The Archbishop made the sign of the cross, "They are bewitched and enchanted. True Christians will never become heathens."

"Well Sir Thomas?"

"In the Baltic the heathens are forcibly converted. They have no choice and most do so to ensure that they live. Bishop Albert has his Livonian knights and they enforce his will."

"Were you one such knight?"

"No, majesty, my men and I served Birger Brosa." I was glad that I had taken a story which was based on truth. I was deceiving the King but I was not lying to him.

I was asked detailed questions about the battles we had fought and the arms and skills of our enemies. The meal was almost ended by the time he seemed satisfied. "And now you are reduced to selling your sword. Why did you not stay in Sweden?"

I hesitated and then gave a plausible answer, "In truth, majesty, I tired of the cold and the Bishop has almost won. I am a knight and I was no longer slaying other knights but the peasants and the poor."

He gave me an astute look, "Yet here you must fight for a lord with whom you might not agree."

I shrugged, "I did not say it was a perfect world. I have a handful of men and a squire. I must feed them."

The Queen leaned over, "Beware the Count of Pontoise, Sir Thomas. I can see that you are a true knight and the Count is a man with ambition."

"The Count forced me to join his ranks, majesty. I was told that if I did not join then I would not be allowed to travel to Paris."

For the first time I saw anger and shock on the King's face. He began to rise but his mother put her hand upon his, "This is not the time, my son." He sat. "Sir Thomas, would you return here on the morrow for I think my son would like further conference with you?" She smiled, "You are a pawn being used by others and it is not right but allow us to play the game a little longer I pray you. I promise that you will not lose out."

"Of course, Your Majesty. I am a guest in your country."

The King smiled, "And one who has enlivened our meal. I have learned much in your talk. There were things unsaid which I heard. You had other reasons for leaving Sweden." He held up his hand. "I do not pry. You are a noble knight and I respect your privacy. I am outraged at the behaviour of the Count of Pontoise. He and the Count d'Eu seem to think that because I am young, I can be moulded. They are wrong but until I reach my majority, I must curb my ambitions. I would rule a land which was at peace and where the people prospered."

I enjoyed the meal but I felt guilty about the deception. When the King rose to retire, I took my leave. They offered me a room but I declined. "I must share the lodgings with my men. They have followed me and it is the least that I owe them."

The King shook his head, "You are a throwback Sir Thomas, a true knight. Most knights these days are self-serving. God speed and we will see you on the morrow."

I had almost made the barbican when one of the Count's men hurried to stop me, "The Count has sent me to find you."

I looked at him, "And you have done so, well done!" I began to turn and he grabbed my right arm. "I may be wounded, my friend, but unless you remove your hand from me then you will feel my steel in your guts." I had slipped my bodkin dagger into my left arm and it was pressed against his middle. He released me.

"He just wishes to know what the King said to you. You are his man."

I shook my head, "He has paid for my sword and not the man who wields it. What is said to me by the King and others who seek my opinion remains with me. Had I sworn an oath it would be different. Tell him that I go to my lodgings and I will see him in the morning." I smiled although with the bandage across half of my face only I knew I was smiling, "The pay he gave us ran out five days ago. As he is in arrears it appears he does not even have my sword."

I turned and left. I was aware of smirks from the two sentries who had heard all. My buskins clattered on the wood as I walked to the end of the bridge. I spied Cedric Warbow. He looked relieved to see me. "I am sorry you have had to wait so long, Cedric."

He smiled, "We took it in turns. We each did an hour. The inn is a little way from here. Padraig chose it as it could accommodate the horses and it is quiet." He led me through the streets to an inn with a low doorway. I had to bend to enter. My men all looked when I entered.

"Good to see you, my lord."

"And you, too, Padraig. The King's healer said that you did a good job with my face."

He beamed, "Just what I was telling these fellows. When I cease being a warrior, I might become a healer. The pay is better and the work safer."

I looked around and saw that we were alone in the room. There was ale and wine on the table. William said, "The landlord is in the back room if you need aught, father."

I shook my head, "I have feasted well and I have to meet with the King on the morrow. Sir Jocelyn?"

William smiled, "You mean Sir Hugh of Newport? Mordaf followed them when they emerged. Sir Jocelyn has his squire and he has hired two men at arms. They strolled out of the castle as though they owned it." I was relieved. They had not fled. They had not seen William.

Richard Red Leg said, "They look handy, lord."

"They are staying at a house just a mile or two from here. It is on the road north and belongs to the Count d'Eu."

"You have done well. Dick and Cedric, ride before dawn and watch the house. If they leave then I would know where. I cannot avoid meeting the King but I will speak with the Count of Pontoise and seek permission to leave his service."

William asked, "And if he does not agree?"

"Then we will run. But let us cross that bridge when we come to it. We have found Sir Jocelyn, or as he is now known, Sir Hugh. We have to find a way to bring him to justice. Did you see the woman?"

Mordaf nodded, "I caught a flash of her hair when the door opened and they entered the fortified hall. She was there."

I was weary and my face had begun to hurt. Whatever the healer had given me had worn off. William saw my pained expression. "Sleep, father. Your wound was deep. I saw it when Padraig stitched it. You were lucky!"

I nodded, "And it has shown me that you, also, need a better helmet. That could have been you."

"We need to keep up the pretence, father. I will buy a ventail. They are old fashioned but it will keep my face both hidden and protected."

"Buy one?"

He smiled, "There is a weaponsmith down the street. Mordaf spotted it when he returned from his quest. I will go when first it opens." I took out my purse and threw it to him. "I will buy one for you too."

My son was growing. It was in his eyes and in his voice, I heard the new-found maturity. A knight was more than a mailed man who rode with sword in hand. A good knight had to think and my son was doing just that. I would worry less about him.

When I woke, I was not alone in the room. Padraig shook me awake. "Lord, it is daylight. There is hot food and your son has gone to the weaponsmith."

"Alone?"

"No, lord, Richard Red Leg went with him. He will not be robbed. Cedric and Dick have gone to watch the fugitives. You said you wanted to be awake early."

I nodded. It was a mistake for my head hurt. I went to the bowl and washed my hands and the half of my face not covered by a bandage. "We must be ready to move quickly. Help me take off my belt." Padraig unfastened the belt when I lifted my tunic. We laid it on the bed and I took out more of the coins I had secreted there. "Here is money for the inn. Pay what we owe and tell the inn keeper that we may be staying longer."

"Aye lord. Where do you think they will go when they leave the hall?"

"The Counts of Eu have their lands north of Dieppe. They are well placed to take ship for England. I do not trust this Count d'Eu. He seems to me to have influence over the Duke of Burgundy in the east of this land and he is related to the Lusignans in Poitou. That is where King Henry's mother lives. I fear a plot! If our prey heads west then he means to do harm to King Henry. The doxy, Morag, has already shown us that she knows how to kill and we know how poorly the King is guarded. When we move, we will have to move quickly."

I left alone and walked back across the bridge to the Palais de la Cité. I was expected for one of the sentries escorted me to the royal chambers where the same page who had fetched me the night before waited for me. The King, his mother and the Archbishop had broken their fast and were eating. The King nodded, "It was good of you to come. Firstly, now that we are alone, were the shields of the men who attacked you those of Burgundy?"

I nodded, "They were and one of the warriors confessed that he came from Lyons before he died. The fact that they had Burgundian shields does not mean that they came from the Duke, Your Majesty. Men can adopt disguises and motives can be hard to fathom."

"You are wise, Sir Thomas. I believe you." He pointed behind him, "If you would wait over there, Sir Thomas, behind the tapestry." A large tapestry depicting St. Denis hid a table with goblets and platters. He smiled, "I would speak with the Count of Pontoise and the Count d'Eu. I will call for you when I need you. I too am capable of deception. I do what I do for France and for God."

"Yes, King Louis."

I stood and waited. The three of them chatted but it was not idle chatter to fill a silence. Nor was it matters of state. They spoke of whom they could trust. I heard names mentioned such as Hugh de Lusignan and the Duke of Brittany. There were other names I did not know. I felt guilty for I was there under false pretences. They trusted me because of my service in the Baltic. I would not betray the French King, even though I had sworn no oath, but I was honour bound to protect the interests of King Henry. I was treading a narrow and difficult path! A short while later I heard the doors open and there was a hubbub of chatter. I knew the voices now and could identify the speakers.

The King said, "So, Count Raymond, could you tell us more about the Count d'Évreux."

"I believe that he is consorting with your enemies, Your Majesty. He and other Norman barons are seeking help from the English King! The English King is no war leader. His father was a weak king who allowed his lords too much power and these Norman barons just seek independence."

"And what have you done about it?"

"I have the castle besieged. The Count had the audacity to say that he would only speak with you!"

The King's voice was filled with reason, "I can understand the Count. I am the King and new to all of my barons. I will be happy to speak with the Count."

"But, Your Majesty, if you go out of your way to speak with all of those who question your authority..."

"I will be behaving as a King. It will be good to ride to Évreux. The County of Normandy has only recently become part of my French family. It will be good to speak with them. I, for one, do not want a war with the English. If I can solve this situation by peaceful means then so much the better. And you, Count Raoul, your lands are the closest to England; you too are Norman and related to the wife of King John. Do you wish the English to reclaim their lands?"

For a twelve-year-old he was showing great maturity. "Of course not! I am loyal."

There was silence. Then the King spoke, "I am young. I cannot help that. However, I believe that the two of you are trying to take advantage of me and of France. You seek to gain power at my expense; at France's expense! Do not speak. You have had your chance and now it is mine! Count Raoul, the men who attacked the Count of Pontoise were sent by you. I know not if you thought to cause trouble with our cousin the Duke of Burgundy but it has failed."

"I protest!"

"I demand silence! And you, Count Raymond, need not look so happy. You have tried to start a war with the Count of Évreux. You have acted like a robber baron stopping any from passing through your town. I have allowed you free rein because of your Uncle, Hugh de Poitou. He has done France a service but you have abused your position."

"Your Majesty!"

"You deny it?"

"Of course."

"Sir Thomas!" I stepped out from behind the tapestry. "And now Count, would you like to reconsider your words?"

"I do not know what you mean!"

"Sir Thomas, why do you serve the Count of Pontoise?"

"He would not let me pass through his lands. The choice was to join him or return west." I looked at the Count. He was beginning to open his mouth. "Of course, you need not take my word. There are many in his town, those who run inns and the like, they would confirm it. Fewer knights and warriors now travel through Pontoise." I saw, from his face, that the Count was beaten.

The King nodded and smiled, "Count Raymond, you hired Sir Thomas and his men. They are due pay. After that they enjoy my protection. If they are harmed then those who do so will answer to me. Understand!" He nodded. "And both of you will cease this petty feuding or I will use the power of the crown to do something about it."

They both nodded. Their eyes were filled with hate. I had made enemies. Count Raymond said, "Where are you staying? I will send the money you are due there."

I told him and then turned to the King. "I hope I have been of service, Your Majesty, and now I must take my leave."

He waved over a page and said, "Guy will bring you a royal warrant to facilitate your journey through my realm. It is the least I can do for a crusader."

I left but I was aware of daggers in my back. I had made a friend in the King but in the grand scheme of things, as I was in disguise, that would not help me. I was pleased that I had met him. Somehow, I felt better. If such a young man could be so level headed then there was hope for King Henry. I believed that I had learned enough now to return to England. If there was a rebellion brewing then it would soon be snuffed out by the King. I did not detect any desire to increase his lands. In fact, there was more danger from the Lusignans. The Count d'Eu had shown me just how far the web of that family stretched. They were in the east, south and north west of his land.

When I reached the inn, I told the innkeeper and my men that we would be leaving that day. I was anxious to resume my mission and catch the fugitives. The Count's man and Guy the page arrived at the same time. The Count's man's face told me what he thought of me. We had, in his opinion, betrayed his master. I did not care. He handed me the money we were owed and the page gave me what was, in effect, a royal warrant.

Cedric arrived back just as we had paid our bill and loaded the sumpters. "They have not left yet, lord, but a rider came from Paris and seemed to cause some debate."

I nodded. That would have been the King's ultimatum. My arrival in France had been like a stone thrown into a pond. The ripples were spreading out. Sir Jocelyn's master was giving him orders to move! What was their plan? "We will ride with you and watch this hall. Could we take them in the hall?"

He shook his head. "There are twenty men at arms, at least, and we have seen four banners. I think we would have more than forty men to fight. We are good, lord, but not that good."

I trusted my men, "Then we follow and look for the chance to ambush." I proffered the King's warrant. "This should keep us safe. Let us ride."

# Chapter 4
# Traitor's Road

It was dark by the time we reached the hall. Dick had found a good place from which to watch. My archers could hide in the small orchard which lay across from the entrance. If Sir Jocelyn, or Sir Hugh as he now styled himself, tried to leave, we would see him. Once I was confident that our prey could not escape undetected, we returned along the road to the outskirts of Paris. I had to remain hidden. My bandages marked me. If I was seen there would be suspicion. People would remember the wounded knight. Instead William and I stayed in an inn on the Paris road. None were suspicious for I used the excuse that my face was healing and I needed somewhere quiet to recuperate. William was the go between for my men. I spent most of each day in the room used by travellers. This was on the Paris road and the prices were lower than in Paris itself. There was a great deal of trade both ways.

I learned much. The baron who was sheltering Sir Jocelyn was Gaston d'Eu. He was a cousin of Raoul de Lusignan, Count d'Eu. The landlord knew little about him save that he had only arrived in the last year. That coincided with what I had learned about the Count. It now became obvious that Sir Jocelyn had met up with the Count and his cousin in Eu. The landlord would know no more as the baron never used the inn.

I learned more from the other travellers about the state of France and the lands of Poitou, Normandy, Anjou and Gascony. The French King was not the cause of the trouble. It was dissident nobles. The two young kings of England and France were seen as an opportunity for other families with claims to the titles of Normandy, Gascony and Poitou to make a bid for them. After three days of hearing the same names, most of them Lusignan, I realised that a perfect solution would be for the two young kings to meet. I was in a unique position. I had met them both. A war was unnecessary. If they spoke with each other then both kings would strengthen their position. King Louis' father had given Poitou to Hugh de Lusignan. From my talk with King Louis I learned that the Count of Poitou, Hugh de Lusignan, had ambitions to take Anjou. King Louis was unhappy with the decision taken by his own father.

The strange customs of Brittany had given King Henry a potential ally. The Duke of Brittany was John but he was a minor. His father, who had a vague claim to the French throne, Peter Mauclerc, still styled himself Duke and was the regent. As Earl of Richmond, he had a great income from England. It was he who had invited King Henry to come to France and reclaim his lands. I now saw the reason for the invitation. Peter Mauclerc saw a chance to win the crown. Despite myself I had learned all that I needed to return to England and speak with King Henry. I could now offer him solid and sage advice. His real enemy was not France but the Lusignan faction. If he travelled to south west France, he could take back Poitou. Hugh de Lusignan had been given Poitou. He had not had to fight for it.

Three days after we arrived at the inn Mordaf rode in. My men had taken it in turns to come to the inn. They came, ostensibly as travellers. The inn was busy and as I was known, by the landlord, to be a curious man it was not considered strange that I speak with them.

"Lord, they are preparing to move." I nodded for him to continue. "They have been preparing horses and Padraig thinks that they will leave soon."

"Then we will pay our bill and join you at dawn." I scratched at my bandage. "We will remove this bandage and let the good air cleanse the wound. I now have a ventail so that my face will be hidden. Take a couple of flagons of ale for the men."

Mordaf shook his head, "With respect, lord, wine would be better. The French ale is better than their water and that is about all I can say about it."

I smiled and handed him some coins, "Whatever they need."

After we had eaten our evening meal and paid the bill we retired to our room. We had paid extra for good quality candles rather than the tallow ones most customers used. They burned brighter and were less smoky. William unwrapped my bandages. The inn did not have a mirror but I saw, from my son's face, that the wound was ugly and angry. "Sniff the wound, William. I think the healer cleansed it but your nose would be better than mine."

He sniffed the wound. "There is no smell of putrefaction, father. There is redness along the stitches."

"That is to be expected. In three weeks' time Padraig can remove them." I gently ran my hand over my face. The area I had shaved and that the healer had also shaved had begun to grow. I had an irregular beard. That too would aid my disguise but Sir Jocelyn would still know me.

We reached my men just as dawn broke. We could hear, from the nearby hall, the sounds of horses being saddled. Their hooves clattered as they were brought out of the stables and gathered on the cobbles of the yard. "How did you know that they were leaving today, Padraig?"

"They shoed their horses yesterday and we saw John, Sir Jocelyn's squire walking a horse."

When they had fled York they had had to leave their own horses. The ones they had must have been bought in France. A good squire had to ensure that his master's mounts were in good condition. John was a killer but in the time his master had served with us in Wales I had seen that he was a good squire.

We were south of the hall on the road to Paris. We stayed in the woods which lay fifty paces from the road. The vegetation hid us. If they headed to Paris we would not be seen. If they headed north, then we would hear them. It was fortunate that they had chosen dawn to travel. There were few other travellers heading out of Paris. Later the road would be busier and that would help to disguise us. I hid behind a poplar to watch them as they emerged. I recognised the livery of Gaston d'Eu. Sir Jocelyn now wore a white surcoat with blue diagonal stripes. There were ten men who followed the two knights and then a closed carriage. That had to contain Morag. Finally, came four more men at arms and six servants with their horses. It was a sizeable caravan. They headed north.

We knew that there was no crossroads for ten miles and we allowed them a head start. We waited until two riders galloped from Paris along the road before we emerged. William of Lincoln rode after the two men. We would follow at a steady pace. William would ride to the crossroads and wait for us there. We headed up the road and passed the hall. The gates were barred and there was no standard flying from the hall. They were not returning for a while.

We soon passed wagons and men heading to Paris. I saw the horror on some of their faces as they spied my scar. I would no longer be hidden. The two counts whom I had offended would hear that I was heading on the road to the coast. I was going towards the lands of the Count d'Eu. It could not be helped. When we reached William of Lincoln, we discovered that the caravan had headed north. He confirmed that Morag and two women were in the wagon for they had emerged to make water. It seemed likely now that they were heading for Eu. It was clear that they were taking a route which would keep them far from Pontoise and the Vexin. We had a hundred miles to travel and, with a carriage, the journey would take us three days. That meant we had three days in which to find somewhere to ambush them. The closer to Eu we were then the harder it would be. They would be in the Count's territory.

The caravan stayed in the small town of Boran-sur-Oise that first night and we slept rough. I sent Mordaf and Cedric out before dawn to find somewhere we could ambush them. The second night our prey stayed in Berthecourt in the hall of the local baron. I began to fear that we would not find anywhere suitable. I could see why my men had not returned to tell us of a suitable place to ambush, for the roads had been open on both sides. Sir Jocelyn was a cunning enemy. He would not need to identify us when he saw us in the distance. He would be wary of any mounted men. We were in the woods which lay half a mile from the road when my men rode in.

"Lord, we have found somewhere. Seven miles up the road there is a village. It is where two rivers meet; the Thérain and the Avelon. We found an inn and spoke with the innkeeper. There is no lord there. The caravan will have to stop at the inn to water the horses and when it crosses the bridge it will have to rise through a wood. The road is steep and wends up through the woods. We could ambush them there."

"You have done well. We sleep for an hour and then leave at moonrise."

Our early departure saw us pass through the village at dawn. Only William and I rode through the village. The rest of my men forded the river upstream and awaited us at the woods. We watered our horses in the river. William asked, "How can we take more than twenty-two men? We will lose men before we can get to Sir Jocelyn."

"There are sixteen armed men and there are ten of us. We have four archers and they will be the difference. I intend to stop them with four of us and rely on our archers deciding the outcome. I am not certain that this Gaston d'Eu will relish losing men to defend Sir Jocelyn."

As we climbed the slope to the woods, I realised that the carriage would struggle up the slope. My men were waiting for me. "Tether the horses. Dick, have the archers wait in the woods. Sam and William, you two be ready to secure the carriage. The rest of us will wait here at the top. We step out on my command. If we can avoid hurting the Normans then so much the better but do not risk your lives!"

We took our horses into the woods. Then we prepared. I donned my coif and ventail. I put on my helmet and tied the side of the ventail which covered my scar. I took my shield and drew my sword. I waited with William on the west side of the road. Padraig and Richard stood on the east. I could see neither my archers nor my other men at arms. Part of this would be bluff.

Padraig must have had good ears for he said, "I can hear horses, lord, and a wheeled vehicle."

"On my command!"

I heard the horses now as they clip-clopped slowly up the steep hill. There was a buzz of conversation too. I had chosen a tree with a branch at head height. The leaves afforded me cover and yet allowed me to see down the road. They had kept the same formation and forty paces covered them from front to back. John, Sir Jocelyn's squire, and Gaston d'Eu's squire followed their masters. It had been the squire who had laid low my son and he would pay. I waited until the two knights were less than ten paces from us. Even before I stepped out the two coursers sensed us and neighed.

"Halt!" The knights and their men at arms' hands went to their weapons. "Draw your weapons and you die!" I saw Sir Jocelyn frown. The ventail had disguised my voice a little and I saw him puzzling to identify me.

Gaston d'Eu shouted, "How dare you! My cousin is the Count d'Eu. You will pay for this."

"My lord, you and your men may pass. It is Sir Jocelyn and his woman I wish to speak to."

"Sir Jocelyn?"

"The man you know as Sir Hugh is wanted by King Henry of England for the crime of murder. I am here to take him back; dead or alive."

Sir Jocelyn realised who I was and shouted, "This is a lie! They are murderers!"

"If we were murderers then you would be dead now."

The Norman said, "There are four of you only."

"There are four that you can see. Sir Jocelyn knows how good are my archers." The murderer could not resist looking around. It confirmed his identity. He did not know how many men I had brought with me. It was the squire, John, who made the fatal mistake. He drew his sword and spurred his horse. Two arrows struck him in his back and he fell from his horse which galloped off down the road. "My lord, take your men and continue to Eu. I mean you no harm and I would not shed more blood than is necessary."

The Norman looked down at the dead squire. He looked at the woods and saw no one. "Who are you?"

"I am Sir Thomas of Stockton, the Earl of Cleveland. When this is over if you would have satisfaction then seek me out and I will oblige."

He looked at Sir Jocelyn, "I am sorry, my friend. We have walked into an ambush but I fear you have been less than truthful. My cousin will be disappointed." He turned back to me. "You give your word we will not be attacked?"

"You have seen how accurate are my men. What do you think?

Nodding he turned in his saddle, "Men of Eu, follow me."

Sir Jocelyn looked horrified, "You cannot leave me! I am innocent!"

The fourteen men at arms followed their knight and squire leaving Sir Jocelyn and the wagon driver. Padraig turned to watch the Normans as they headed down the road. We stood in silence. I saw Morag and her women appear from the carriage. She looked around, seeking sight of my men. They were well hidden. Padraig said, when the Normans had disappeared out of sight, "They are gone."

"Sir Jocelyn, dismount."

He looked around as though he might flee. Padraig walked up in two strides, grabbed the knight's left arm and dragged him from his horse. "My lord said to dismount!" The women with Morag screamed. Padraig held his sword at the knight's throat.

"Get him to his feet." I walked down to the wagon. "Sam, William!" My two men at arms emerged from the woods. "Watch the women." I looked up at the carriage driver. "You may leave now. Walk down the road and you will not be harmed." He started to dismount. The other men who remained on their horses were Sir Jocelyn's servants. They were an unknown element. Had they been paid enough to try to fight us? The driver climbed down and began to run down the slope towards the distant village.

There must have been a signal for suddenly the men on their horses and the three women all drew weapons. Two of the women lunged at me with long knives. Morag turned and slashed the throat of William of Lincoln. Sam rammed his blade through her body but she managed to score a line from his eye to his chin with her dagger. I swung my sword and held my shield at the same time. The two women's knives clattered against them as my archers sent their arrows into the horsemen. Richard Red Leg swung his sword at the one horseman who was not struck by an arrow and hacked through his leg. His other leg was held by his stirrup and the horse galloped off with the corpse bouncing from the road. Padraig hacked into the back of one of the two women and then he did the same for the other. One of the servants rode at me. He was no man at arms and I ducked to his left and hacked him across the middle. The two women were still stabbing at me as three arrows ended their lives.

Suddenly Sam Strongarm began frothing at the mouth. He sank to his knees. I knelt next to him. Dying, he shook his head, "The bitch has poisoned me but Harry is avenged." Sam Strongarm had been my bodyguard with Robert of Newton. Robert was dead and now my other loyal warrior lay dying in my arms. I wanted vengeance.

His eyes glazed over. I turned and walked back to Sir Jocelyn. He was the only one left alive. I pulled back my arm to skewer him but William stepped before me, "No father. We take him back for King Henry's justice. He is not worth it."

My sword was pointed at Sir Jocelyn's eye. I saw a puddle appear as he wet himself. My son was right. He was not worth it. "Padraig, bind him and tie him to his horse. Gag him. I would hear none of his words." My archers emerged from the woods and looked at the bodies of my two men at arms. "We will bury our comrades in the woods. See if there are tools in the carriage." As they hurried off, I said, "William watch Sir Jocelyn. Padraig bring the squire's body." I looked in the carriage and found a chest. When I opened it, I found coins and jewels. This explained how they had been able to hire men. This was the last of Sir Hugh's treasure. There was nothing else inside. I picked up the body of Morag and put it in the carriage. We did the same with the others. Padraig unhitched the horses. Before we left, we would burn the carriage and the bodies.

Padraig and I carried our comrades' bodies to their graves in the woods. This was not the funeral I would have wished for them but they were warriors. We buried them with their swords. I said prayers and we covered the graves with soil and leaves. Hopefully they would rest in peace. They had given their lives for me but their friend had been avenged and we had begun to extract retribution for my son.

We now had spare horses. After I had fired the carriage, we took off along the road riding the new mounts`.

The men were sombre. Cedric and Dick rode on either side of our prisoner. He would not escape. Padraig said, "You know the Normans will come for us, lord."

"And that is why we leave this road at the next crossroads and head north to Boulogne. The fire will draw the Normans thence. Their hooves will muddy our tracks. We have a hundred miles to go and spare horses. We ride the borrowed horses to exhaustion and then change to our own. I hope to make Boulogne in two days. We will camp at night. I want to use the lesser byways and trails. I would have us disappear. Once we are in Flanders then we assume once more my livery. Sir Thomas of Kastelholm will cease to exist."

We did not stop until we had passed the Somme. The horses we had acquired were ruined but they had helped to hide us. We made camp and although we took Sir Jocelyn's gag from him and untied his hands, we shackled his ankles. He would not run. The fact that we had not killed him seemed to embolden the traitor. He grew in confidence, "You cannot get away with this you know? How will you get me back to England? You cannot transport me from this land!"

"Then you will die in Flanders. I will lose no sleep in ending your life but my son is right. I am not a cold-blooded killer. Besides, the King will need to ask you about your masters."

"My masters?" He suddenly looked worried.

"You sought vengeance against me but you were plotting against the King." I had a stab in the dark. "You were heading to Eu so that you could continue your plotting while you worked for the Lusignans!"

I had found the mark. He recoiled. "The Lusignan family is too powerful for King Henry. He is doomed!"

I wondered now about this so-called killer. From what I had seen it was his squire and his woman who had been the deadlier killers. Sir Jocelyn was the knight who fronted them. He was the one with the plans but they were the ruthless ones. The use of the poisoned blade confirmed this. The chest of coins had been in the carriage with the women. What I had taken for ladies, by their dress, were obviously not. They had handled their weapons well. I was lucky. I now believed that they had had poisoned blades too.

I turned to Richard, "Feed him. I would not have him deny the executioner."

"I know much! If I tell the King then he may let me live!"

There was a worry that he might but if that happened then I would end his life myself. One of us stayed awake all night. I did not trust Sir Jocelyn. He was more cowardly than I had expected him to be but he was desperate.

The next day we rode north through Flanders. This was not France but neither was it England. If we were stopped then I would have to try to talk our way out of it. We stopped on the cliffs overlooking the harbour. Once more we had our prisoner bound. "Watch him and I will try to get us a berth on a ship."

"You will never take me aboard a ship! I will shout and draw attention to you. You will be arrested. The Count will be on your trail already."

I smiled less these days for it hurt my face. The smile was in my eyes. "Let me worry about that, traitor. Come William." Now dressed in my proper surcoat and with William behind me I headed down the road into Boulogne. Flanders had been an ally to England. Indeed, Stephen of Blois' son had been Count of Flanders. However, the proximity of France made the County more pragmatic. As we neared the port, I saw that there were a number of ships in port. The problem would be the horses. So long as we could take the eight best horses home, we would sell the rest. I sought an English ship. I wandered along the quay. Not all ships had their names on them. I listened for English voices. I heard English voices and found a ship but it did not look big enough.

"Here is a likely one, William."

"It looks to me like the only one but is she big enough?"

"If we have to leave all of the horses here so be it."

The Captain was leaning on the stern rail watching the next ship being loaded. The Captain spoke to his first mate who knuckled his forehead and walked down the gangplank. He spoke English. The Captain had skin which looked like tanned leather and his knotted muscles told me that he was not averse to hauling on a sail. I did not board but, instead, stood and spoke from the quay, "Hello Captain, may we come aboard?"

He saw my spurs, "Aye my lord."

"I am the Earl of Cleveland and this is my son William. We seek passage to England."

He brightened immediately, "I am Captain Michael of Kingston. I have been waiting for a cargo to take to England. This is most opportune. What is the cargo?"

Sometimes you look into a man's eyes and know that you can trust him. "It will be passengers and their horses. There will be nine of us but one will be a prisoner we are taking back to England for King Henry's judgement."

"What is his offence, my lord?"

"Murder and treason."

"I worry not for myself but my men. I have my grandson with me. He is cabin boy. Will the prisoner be safe?"

"Trust me, Captain, the man will be bound and as I only need passage to Dover there will be no time for him to cause trouble."

He looked relieved, "If I can serve the King then so much the better. How many horses will you take?"

"We have many but if we have to leave some then we shall. We have some already that we intend to sell before we leave."

"I can manage up to twelve for such a short voyage. And now the cost…" Before he could name a price, I reached for my coins. I had a purse already on me. It was some of the gold I had taken from the carriage. I counted out five gold pounds. It was far more than the voyage should have cost but I wanted discretion. I needed to be able to bring the prisoner on board unseen. He shook his head, "This is a king's ransom."

"And I pay it for a king. I will arrive just before the watch is set. The fewer who see him the better."

"We will be ready."

When I reached my men, it was already coming on to dark. We did not have long to wait. I could see that they had been discussing what to do with the traitor when Richard Red Leg said, "Do we tap him on the head, lord?"

The knight recoiled, "You cannot do that!"

Padraig fetched him a clout and said. "Quiet traitor. Three of my friends lie dead and it is down to you and your whores. I am happy to slit your throat."

"And that will not be necessary. Padraig, hold his head. Richard, open his mouth." Sir Jocelyn tried to wriggle but with his hands bound he could do nothing. I took out the pot jug with the medicine that the healer had given me. "William hold his nose while I tip this down his throat." I poured half of the jug's contents down his throat. Richard closed his mouth to stop him spitting it out. He wriggled but when William released his nose he had to swallow.

"You have no honour!"

It was the last thing he said before he fell asleep.

"Put him on his horse and let us go." We could now return to England.

# Chapter 5
# King Henry

We reached Westminster two days after landing at Dover. It had been a short voyage and the money we had obtained for the horses we had sold had offset the cost of the passage. Our prisoner had been unconscious until we were within sight of Dover harbour, nestling beneath the most powerful fortress on the south coast. When the Constable of the castle saw armed men disembarking, he sent men down to question us. Although my livery was recognised, I was interrogated until they were satisfied with my story. Sir Jocelyn was gagged and the sergeant who led the constable's men had asked, "Why the gag, my lord?"

"He is a royal prisoner. The King must judge him."

As we approached London, we had removed his gag. Too many other people had asked questions of us seeing that he was gagged. He must have realised the futility of complaining for he rode sullenly on his horse.

The King was not in the palace. He was hunting but Hubert de Burgh was there. He looked in horror at my face. The swelling had gone but there was still bruising and the stitches, whilst small, looked alarmingly painful. "It seems, Sir Thomas, that you have had an interesting time."

I nodded, "And this prisoner needs locking up until the King can judge him. This is Sir Jocelyn."

"I protest my lord, Sir Thomas has abducted me."

For the first time since I had known him Hubert de Burgh was sympathetic to me. He pointed a finger at Sir Jocelyn, "You are a murderer and a traitor. I am just amazed that Sir Thomas brought you back to receive the King's judgement. I expected summary justice. None would have blamed him had he slit your throat."

"It is not merely for the justice, lord, the man was plotting with the Count d'Eu. His treachery is not yet finished."

Sir Hubert waved over two guards. "Put him in the cellar. Shackle him to the wall."

"Aye," I said, "And make it secure. He is slippery. We have searched him for blades but let none speak with him. He has a golden tongue and lies like Satan himself."

With only six men accompanying me there were enough beds in the warrior hall and William and I were given a chamber close to the King. I enjoyed a hot bath. The King had one for his guests and I took full advantage of it. I felt cleaner and, somehow, healthier. I knew that there were many men who did not bathe but the Holy Land and then the Baltic had given me an appreciation of such treats.

When I joined the King and his Justiciar I felt like a new man. It was as though I had shed a burden. I told them first of the people I had met and what I had learned. I was aware that much of it was opinion but all men knew that I was truthful. For once Hubert de Burgh and the King were both interested in what we had to tell them.

When I had finished it had a different effect on each of them. King Henry said, "From what you say, Sir Thomas, King Louis is not my enemy." The Justiciar looked sceptical. I had learned that Hubert de Burgh had allies in France. From what I had seen the Lusignans were ambitious too. Did they have designs on the French throne as well as the English one?

"I believe he is not an enemy, lord. He is as pious as you. He has attained the crown at a young age and is surrounded by enemies. You have much in common. I think it is your enemies who seek to put barriers between you. I believe that if you spoke with each other then war and bloodshed might be avoided."

"But Normandy!"

"Normandy is a nest of vipers, my liege. The Count d'Eu is not the only one who seeks power there. The Duke of Brittany does not act in your interests but his own. I believe that the Lusignans pose the greatest threat. Sir Jocelyn was being brought to Eu for a reason. Knowing that he associates with killers I dread to think his purpose."

Hubert de Burgh said, "I have men who know how to extract information. We will discover the truth tomorrow." He turned to me, "You think that Poitou sides with France now?"

"I think that Hugh, the Count of Poitou, sees an opportunity to sever links now that he has married your mother, the Queen. The crown of England lies tantalizingly close."

I saw that Henry was worried. He was unmarried and had no children. "What can we do, Sir Hubert?

Hubert de Burgh smiled, "We have more than forty thousand pounds raised to fight a war with France. I do not think that is enough to hire men to take on the might that is France but we could re-establish your authority in Poitou. What say you, Earl?"

"I think it is essential that we save Poitou for the King's lands in Gascony would be in danger too."

"And then we could retake Normandy! At last I will be able to show England that I am a King who can lead his men in war. With you at my side, Earl, we can retake that which is ours!" I had talked myself into a war! "You will need to send for your knights and men at arms."

"Not all of them, my liege. When we take men from the border then it encourages the Scots. You have men enough in the south who can follow your banner."

"Very well." His face became a mask of ice, "Here is my judgement. Sir Jocelyn is guilty of crimes against England, our person and Sir Thomas of Cleveland. The punishment is death. No matter what he tells us he will be executed at the end. Sir Hubert, I leave it to you to extract every piece of information from Sir Jocelyn."

"Do not worry, my liege, when my men have finished with him, he will have told all and beg for death."

As the Justiciar of England left us I felt nothing but distaste. Hubert de Burgh was not a warrior, he was a counter of money and yet he could torture another man. Perhaps that was a flaw in me that I could not do so.

King Henry came to look at my scar. He shook his head as he ran his finger down the stitches. "You are disfigured! How can you bear it?"

"I am a warrior, King Henry. This is but one of many scars I bear. Most are hidden but all are a reminder of how close I came to death. I took too many chances this time and I have learned my lesson." He nodded and sat down. he waved for me to join him. "Majesty, is it wise for you to lead your armies?"

"Wise?" His eyes narrowed.

"May I be blunt?" he nodded, "You have not led armies before and you will have men's lives in your hands."

"God will guide me."

I sighed.

He smiled, "And you will be close at hand."

"I have fought in battles, King Henry, and I have led parts of them but I have never commanded one."

"Yet the Earl Marshal felt that you were the man to guide my hand. I trust his judgement. You are tired and your wounds are yet to heal. After you have eaten with me, retire and have a good night's sleep. Tomorrow, after noon, we will study maps and begin to plan this campaign for it will take a month or two to assemble an army. Hubert de Burgh may not be a warrior but he knows how to count and to organize. He will arrange a fleet to take us to Bordeaux. By then we will have a plan and we will have prayed to God to help us."

I was dismissed and I went to the warrior hall. "The King needs my men, Padraig. I would have you take Richard Red Leg on the morrow and ride to my home. I will give you letters for my wife and Sir Edward. You will need to ensure that David of Wales has enough arrows." I handed him a large purse of coins I had taken from Sir Jocelyn's chest. "Here is for your journey and in case Ridley the Giant and David of Wales need to make any purchases for my men. Have Father Harold say prayers for Sam Strongarm and William of Lincoln."

"Aye lord."

"Take the sumpters with you but we shall need the rest."

Once back in the room I sent William for parchment and pen. As I took off the belt with the coins, I felt relief. I would no longer be encumbered by the weight around the middle. When next we went into danger we would be in the heart of the King's army. After I had written the letters, I had William read them back to me. I signed and sealed them. I would send for just four of my knights: Sir Edward, Sir Fótr, Sir Peter and Sir William of Hartburn. I would leave my daughter's husband, Sir Geoffrey

FitzUrse to watch my valley. He had enough knights to forestall any Scottish incursion; at least for a while.

We had some time before the meal. I sat and spoke with my son. "When we go to Gascony and Poitou I will have to watch and guide the King closely. You are new to this position of squire, especially in war. Do not be afraid to ask for help from the other squires."

He smiled, "Father, I have seen more battles in recent time than Henry, John, Robert or Sir Peter's brother Henry. They have not had to play the simpleton nor hide in plain sight. I am not Alfred, my brother, but I can aspire to be him. Fear not, father, I will not let you down."

"I never thought for a moment that you would. I was more worried that I might let you down by having to watch over a King who has yet to lead men into battle."

After Padraig had left us to return to Stockton, I realised that my stitches would need to be removed soon. I sought the King's doctor, Atticus of Corinth. "The healer in France who stitched me said that these stitches should be removed soon. Would you look at the wound for me? My face has been itching for many days and I was told that was a sign of healing."

"Of course, my lord." He was Greek and had an accent. He smiled. "The King spoke to me this morning and asked me to look at your wound." He lit a candle and turned my face so that he could see the wound better. "These are fine stitches. Was it a priest who sewed you?"

"It was."

"They are very neat and precise men." He ran his fingers over the wound and then sniffed it. His hair was perfumed. He sat back, "I think it is healed. I can remove them now if you wish. I have a salve which will make the scar less noticeable, although I fear it will never be truly hidden. Your beard will cover much of it but the blade came perilously close to your eye."

He was remarkably gentle. He used a very sharp blade and I barely felt it. He had a mirror and when he had done, he held it before me. The wound was red but I knew the redness would fade. The stubble which had grown since the priest had stitched it would soon grow back and become a beard but the doctor was correct. There was now a line which led to just below my eye. God had, indeed, been watching over me.

When I joined the King he smiled, "That looks better. Was the doctor optimistic?"

"There will be a scar but I am of an age, my liege, where I am less concerned with my looks and more concerned with my health. It will not impair my ability to fight and that is my prime concern.

Hubert de Burgh took until the middle of the afternoon before his work was done. "The prisoner has died, King Henry."

The King looked cross, "Was he executed as I commanded?"

"He was hung and drawn but he died before he could be quartered."

The King seemed satisfied, "And what did we learn?"

"The Earl was right. There is a deep conspiracy. Sir Jocelyn, it appears, had decided that as his birth father had been so badly treated by England he would become a hired sword working for any who was an enemy to England. As the Earl was close to you, King Henry, the knight chose to work for your enemies. Hugh de Lusignan, it seems, bears a grudge against your father. It might explain why he married your mother. I know not how his mind works. He has entered into an alliance with King Louis and will rule Poitou as his own fiefdom."

They both looked at me, "I know nothing of this but I confess that I am surprised. King Louis struck me as a pious young man."

King Henry said, "He may well be but he is a king and just as I wish the return of Normandy, he may wish to strengthen his defences to the south. Do not berate yourself. Go on, Justiciar."

"The Count now casts his eye upon Gascony. Sir Jocelyn and his killers, had Sir Thomas not apprehended them, would have sailed into Bordeaux and played the part of warriors seeking to serve the Constable. They would have murdered him and the other leaders. With England so far away then the Count of Poitou would have succeeded before we could have done anything,"

"Then my idea to retake Poitou is a good one."

"Aye majesty. I am unsure of how deep the treachery runs. There may be other men already in Bordeaux and ready to aid the Count of Poitou. Sir Jocelyn knew his part and the rest he conjectured. He did not die well."

King Henry was all business. He rubbed his hands, "Come Sir Thomas, let us look at the maps and plan how we can bring Poitou back under my hand."

He was becoming a King before my eyes. Soon he would no longer need the regency that was Hubert de Burgh. I saw the glimmer of greatness as he questioned both the Justiciar and myself. He knew what he wanted. He quickly grasped the Justiciar's understanding of numbers and from me of strategy and using archers, men at arms and knights successfully. He sent for his other knights and they arrived two days later. Bohun, de Clare and the Bigod clan were all there. It was an enthusiastic gathering of military minds. The problem we had was that we did not know enough about the strongholds in Poitou. The knights who had become the King's inner circle were either too young or had only fought in the Welsh wars. William de Vesci, Gilbert de Clare and his son Richard, the Earl of Norfolk and his sons Hugh and Roger were all good men and I did not doubt their loyalty but I was the only one who knew of the lands around the Loire and that was because I had lived, albeit briefly, at La Flèche.

The strategy which emerged, after three days, was to strike north from Bordeaux and secure the coast, gradually working inland. Niort, Chauray, Apremont and La Roche sur Yon were all our targets. Of those Apremont had the hardest castle to take. It was decided that we would use my mounted men at arms and archers to be a strike force to ride quickly through the rebellious lands and prevent the rebels from reinforcing their strongholds.

The Justiciar left to organize the ships and the inner circle of knights left to fetch their retinues. William and I were left to enjoy London. The pleasure did not last long as I found the city expensive and dirty. It always struck me that the people in the city were self-serving and could change their loyalties in an instant. Perhaps much of that dislike came from the Warlord. He had always been bitter that London had chosen to support Stephen and not Matilda. What disturbed me, as we wandered the streets, was the news that de Burgh was taking the manors of the Poitevin lords and giving them to his supporters. I blamed myself for I had told the King and de Burgh about the Lusignan plot. I approached the King but he seemed unbothered. He thought that the Poitevin deserved to lose coin for their treachery. I was not so sure.

I had begun to worry about my men when they had not arrived five days after the Justiciar had left for Southampton. The King had also begun to fret. When they did arrive, I was relieved. I now had my own men around me. We had fewer knights than many expected but they were of the greatest quality. The King greeted them like old friends for they had served him before.

Sir Peter's squire was Henry, his younger brother. Possibly because of the name the King was fond of the squire. He had grown since last he had seen the King and was now as tall as his brother. Their father, Ridley the Giant, had passed on his height to his sons. "You have grown young Henry. You are a head taller now than your king."

"I am sorry, Your Majesty! It just happened."

The King laughed, "I was not criticising. Are you ready to become a knight?"

He looked nervously at me, "When the Earl deems it judicious to dub me then I will be ready."

The King's mouth dropped open, "Your sovereign offers you a knighthood and you defer to the Earl?

Sir Peter intervened, "The Earl is like our father, King Henry. It is generous of you to offer a knighthood but Henry is not quite ready. Perhaps this campaign will see him earn the honour. Besides, I have no replacement for him yet."

When my knights and their squires went to their chambers the King said, "When will I inspire such loyalty amongst my men, Sir Thomas?"

"In truth I know not. Sir Peter's father served with me in the Baltic. The boys grew up in my army. Sir Peter, when he was Petr, was my squire. My world is the only world they have known. I am honoured to be their leader."

Two days later we were ready to head to Southampton. The pace we moved at was slower than the one we would adopt in Poitou. I rode with my knights and two captains, Ridley and David of Wales. As I looked at Edward, I saw that his hair, which had been flecked with grey, was now white flecked with strands of brown. He was getting old. When the doctor had shown me my reflection, I had seen that I, too, was getting old. We all were. Even Ridley had aged.

Sir Edward gestured behind us with his thumb, "Do we travel at the pace of the rest of the army when we are in France, lord?"

"I hope not. We are the ones who will ride ahead. We will not be besieging castles. Our task will be to seize bridges and ensure that help does not reach isolated castles."

Sir Fótr asked, "And treasure?"

I smiled, "As the King does not pay us then we need to earn coin in Poitou." The smiles and nods showed that all approved of that.

"And who are our enemies? Whom do we fight?"

"The Lusignan clan and their French allies. There may still be loyal Poitevin but I suspect that in the early days they will sit and watch our new King. This is his first campaign!"

Sir Edward said, "I should warn you, lord, that Sir Geoffrey, back in the valley, may well have his hands full. We had word from the north that the Scots had begun cattle raids. The Constable of Norham was fully stretched trying to prevent incursions. The Bishop was mobilising his men."

The Scots often crossed the border to raid for cattle and captives. It was usually small scale and the perpetrators were often caught before they crossed back into Scotland. "What is the new Bishop like?"

Sir William said, "He is keen but he is a churchman. He has spent much of his time building a cathedral at Salisbury. Fighting cunning Scots is not something for which he was prepared."

"Then the sooner we can reclaim Poitou the better!"

The town of Southampton was totally full. My men and knights were forced to camp in a field but, as one of the King's advisers, I was given a small chamber in the castle. That first night, as we feasted, I met the former Count of Poitiers. He was one of King Henry's supporters but had been ousted by Hugh de Lusignan. He was bitter. That evening as we ate, he bordered on the insolent when he spoke with the King. It culminated when, after a few too many goblets of wine, he burst out, "King Henry, your mother has given her new husband the land of Poitou. We were abandoned by your father and, thus far, the loyal Poitevin have been treated badly."

I saw the King colour. He turned to Hubert de Burgh and said, loudly, "I do not wonder that some lords feel abandoned when they have the audacity to speak to a king as though he is an equal." He turned his back on the Count.

The Count made to rise and I restrained him, "Count, the King is young and you do him a disservice. He has barely managed to claim his own kingdom. He has not yet achieved his majority. Do you blame him for the sins of his father?"

"His father was a bad king!"

I looked at him and said, mildly, "Do you think I do not know that? I had my lands taken from me by King John."

He seemed to see me for the first time. "And yet you remained loyal and you did not join the rebellion."

"I may not have liked the King but I loved the country. Remember, Count, when my men and knights fight and bleed in Poitou, they do it for you and not their country. They will gain nothing from this campaign."

"But can you retake our land? We lost it because of treachery. There are strong castles. My own in Poitiers is almost impossible to take."

"What of the ones by the coast?"

He had drunk too much and he was not thinking clearly, "They are too small and inconsequential! We need to take the larger castles."

I waited until his rant had ended, "Think about this, Count, if we attack the smaller places the lords there either defend or flee. We have an army which is more than big enough to take any of the smaller estates. Each castle and estate feeds us and gives us shelter. Each castle we take makes more mouths for Hugh de Lusignan to feed and less food to do so. His allies, the French, will soon tire of subsidising him. The Norman barons, like the Duke of Évreux, are already unhappy with the new French King. Any success we have will embolden them. You do not start a landslide by dislodging the biggest rock. You find small ones which roll and collect others. Once there are enough stones then no matter how big the stronghold, it will fall."

He pushed his goblet away, "Your idea might work. It would be easier for individual knights and barons to return to the English fold if they are isolated."

I leaned in and said quietly, "And better to be humbled before the King and retrieve your lands than have a stiff neck and receive nothing."

He nodded and approached King Henry who had been speaking with Hugh de Burgh all the time I had counselled the Count, "Your Majesty, I apologise for my tongue. I am afraid I forgot myself. It will not happen again."

The King glanced at me and then smiled at us both, "Of course! I know what it is like to lose something precious. With such noble lords we will triumph. Of that I am certain."

On that uplifting note we were ready to leave England. We were ready to take on the French and the Poitevin rebels!

# Chapter 6
# Chevauchée in Poitou

My men sailed in three ships. I had a knight on each of them. Ridley and his sons sailed with me. I saw that the six I had taken with me to seek Sir Jocelyn travelled together and they gathered at the prow of my vessel. We had left two of our number in France and it both bound us and gave us a common enemy. It had been the Lusignans who had hired the killers. They had yet to be punished.

Sir Peter had already identified a new squire. One of the workers on his estate at Whorlton had a son who did not wish to be a shepherd. He had expressed a wish to be a warrior. My former squire knew that this would be a chance for the son of two peasants to become a lord. It had happened to him and he was ready to help another. I promised Henry that when we returned, he would be dubbed. I knew, of course, that a promise such as that would have an effect on my own son. That day would soon be upon us and my wife would be unhappy about that.

I also spoke with Ridley. He had accompanied Sir Edward when he had ridden to the lands of the Palatinate to confer with the Bishop. He was a huge warrior and men often thought such size precluded intelligence. Ridley had as sharp a mind as I had ever known. He and I stood at the prow looking at the coast of France off the larboard bow, "The problem, lord, is that there is no lord north of the Tyne who will take on the Scots. The Bishop is new. He has a good constable in Norham but he needs a landowner who will grasp the nettle that is the Scots. Alnwick is a fine castle but it is owned by the Bishop and he has a constable commanding there. If that was your castle then I know you would prosecute the defence of England vigorously. King Alexander knows that he and his border raiders can steal from England and all that they will receive is a rap on the knuckles."

"You are right. My family has ever made sacrifices for the Bishop and the Palatinate. My late aunt, Ruth, lost her husband there and what was gained for us? Nothing. Perhaps I will ask for an estate for one of my knights. When I knight Henry, I will need a manor. Sir William could manage a castle like Alnwick or Norham and keep the land safe. Your second son could learn how to be a lord at Hartburn."

"And that would please his mother too."

We had plans. We had ideas but first we had a land to regain.

We landed not at Bordeaux but on the north bank of the Gironde River at an English controlled port called Royan. After my chat with the Count of Poitiers he had become much more positive and it was he suggested the port. He had told the King that while it was small it would save having to cross the river and we would be closer to our foes. We would not have far to march to reach our first target. We had chosen La Rochelle for the first attack. It was well defended from the sea but when the French had captured it five years earlier many of the defences had been damaged and had yet to be repaired. We had a different task. We were to ride towards Surgères. It was a powerful stronghold which had been fortified by King Henry II. It was highly unlikely that my one hundred and twenty men could take it but the French and the rebels might think that we were the vanguard of the whole army. King Henry could then approach La Rochelle unseen. Once we had drawn our enemies away from the King, we were to head north and east. We would, in effect, be a chevauchée.

We had twenty sumpters for we would be self-sufficient. Those men who had served with Sir William when he had been lord of La Lude were the scouts. They spoke the language and they knew the land. We left before most of the army had disembarked. We headed for Saintes. This had been an old Roman town. The walls of the Roman town had been robbed out and used for other buildings. It was situated on the left bank of the Charente and the Count of Poitiers told us that it was held by a French supporter. He was a minor member of the Lusignan clan, Geoffrey de Lusignan. The town had been taken from its rightful owner. I hoped that the inhabitants would resent their new lord. We reached the outskirts an hour before dark. We watched the town from the cover of a small wood a mile from the town. Hamlin the Archer and Griff Jameson had both lived in the land and they went with four other archers to scout it out. My men assigned horse holders for our sumpters and the rest of us waited. Darkness had fallen and I wondered if anything had happened to the scouts when they ghosted up out of the dark.

"Lord, they keep no watch on the city. There are just four men guarding the bridge. We slipped into the town. There is a hall and there are mailed men on guard there."

Griff nodded, "Hamlin is right, lord. We could take it easily."

I said nothing. Sir Edward grunted, "I have slept for ten days on a ship! I do not want to spend my first night ashore on the cold hard ground, lord. Let us take it and shift some fat burghers from their beds!"

I had already decided to take the town. My silence had merely been to help me to think. "Sir Fótr take your men and ride around the town. Enter from the east. You may have to ride for a while in the river. Hold the bridge for us. Sir Peter take your men to the south. Sir William, take yours to the north. Sir Edward, you will bring your men with mine and we will come from the west. You three ride now. We will give you the count of two hundred and then we will follow. Spare those who do not resist. If men draw swords then they die!"

I walked to my horse, Blaze. My courser was with the servants and sumpters. This was not the time to risk my best horse. I tightened the girth and then mounted. I had said the count of two hundred. It was an estimate only. I just needed them in place when we galloped into the town. This was one time when my archers would not need to string their bows. Night time was not the time for my most potent weapon. They were all skilled with sword and buckler. More importantly they were supremely clever men. Riding without mail meant that they were quicker and lighter than my men at arms. I did not bother slinging my shield. I drew my sword and, after ensuring that all of my men were ready, I dug my heels into Blaze's flanks and galloped down the road. For the first time in a long time I was riding next to Sir Edward. He was the most reliable warrior who had ever protected my left side. It was like old times. We had eight men at the fore. When we reached the town that would reduce to six to enable us to ride down their streets. Six mailed men riding big horses would intimidate anyone.

As we neared the town the thunder of our hooves alerted the occupants. As I had hoped they were drawn to the sound. I saw, in the light from an open door, the glint of metal as mailed men ran to block the entrance to the town. The town should have had a gate and a wall but it did not. The rebels had taken it because the town had no gate and now the rebels would pay the same price. The men in the entrance had spears and pikes. They lunged at us. I leaned forward to hack across the shaft just a handspan behind the head. The man was left holding a stick until Blaze's shoulder barrelled him to the ground and Ridley the Giant's horse crushed his chest.

I heard the town bell ringing. People rushed from their houses. I ignored all except those with weapons. I did not care if people fled. If they did then I would be drawing more rebels to us and not to the King. If we held La Rochelle then we controlled the coast.

We neared the town square and the cathedral. There was the sound of hooves ahead of us and a mob of men ran towards us. There were mailed men mixed with ordinary folk wielding whatever they had as weapons. I saw three men on horses and one looked like a knight. Were we going to have worthy opponents to fight? As the mob came towards us, to my dismay, I saw two of the horsemen gallop away from us towards the north side of the town. They were trying to escape. They might bring help. The press of men before us was too great to allow us to get close to them. The mob flailed and swashed their weapons at us. My mail and my armour were too well made for me to be harmed. My helmet, ventail and coif protected my face. I turned my sword sideways and smacked it into the side of the head of the warrior who ran at me with his sledgehammer. Had he hit me he would have broken limbs. I was above him and he was too slow to swing it forward. The flat of my sword hit him on the side of the head. His helmet was ill fitting. He was not wearing an arming cap. The sledgehammer dropped to the ground and he fell in a heap next to it. The last mounted man rode towards me. He had a shield and he held a spear. It was foolish. There were simply too many men between us for him to gain any speed. Sir Edward, fighting next to me, was not as merciful as I had been. A man with helmet, sword and shield ran at him swinging his sword. Sir Edward brought his sword from on high and struck at the unprotected shoulder before the rebel's sword could get close to my knight. He clutched the savage wound with his left hand as he dropped to the ground. He crawled away to an empty doorway.

I spurred Blaze and my horse took advantage of the two falling men to trot towards the Poitevin horseman. He stabbed at me, ineffectually, with his spear. His horse had not given him any impetus and the thrust was not powerful enough. I dropped my reins and, using my mailed left hand, pulled the spear across my body. I backhanded him across the upper arm with my blade and my sword grated off bone. The spear fell and he slumped over his cantle. The mob had now been broken. The wide expanse of the square had worked in the favour of my men. We drove the crowd back to the cathedral. I saw the bishop and his priests there.

"Hold!" My voice rang out and my men, all of them, stopped. There was the sound of wailing. Children cried. I saw the Bishop holding his crozier before him as though it was a weapon. "Surrender and you shall all live. Throw down your weapons." I took off my helmet. There were brands around the cathedral and as the helmet came off and I dropped my ventail a flare of light caught my scar. A woman screamed and the weapons dropped. I must have terrified them. Just then came the clattering of hooves as first Sir Peter, then Sir Fótr and finally Sir William appeared from the other sides of the square.

Sir Edward shouted, "Ridley, collect the weapons."

I stood in my stirrups. "You may return to your homes. Is there a mayor?"

The Bishop pointed to the horseman I had struck. "He is wounded."

"See to him, priests. I will speak with you," I looked around and saw the lord's hall from whence the horsemen had appeared, "there!"

Sir Edward shouted, "Sir Peter, find food. Sir Fótr, find the stables."

I looked at Sir William, "Did you slay or capture the two horsemen who rode north?"

He hung his head, "They slipped by us. I am sorry, lord."

I nodded, Men made mistakes. None was perfect, "I fear that might have been Geoffrey de Lusignan. We could have a more serious fight in the next couple of days." I dismounted and handed my reins to William. There was blood on his sword. Padraig and Richard Red Leg flanked me as I strode towards the hall. It was a stone building. Had they had time they could have defended it but our night time attack had caught them unawares. Servants cowered as we entered the feasting hall, "Fetch food and wine." They scurried off, grateful to have something to do and to still be alive. I put my helmet and sword on the table. I slung my cloak on the back of a chair and sat down.

Padraig and Richard had naked swords and stood behind me. The Bishop came in along with what looked like four merchants and three priests. "This is banditry, my lord!" The Bishop's voice lacked conviction. The servants scurried in and put wine, goblets and food on the table. I poured myself some wine and drank it slowly. It was good. I nodded to my men. They laid their swords on the table and poured themselves some wine.

"Bishop, it would have been banditry if we had come to take this town from its rightful owners but we have not. I am Thomas, Earl of Cleveland, and I serve King Henry, the rightful liege lord of this County. We are here to reclaim his land." His face told me that they had no idea that the English had landed. "Geoffrey de Lusignan showed what kind of man he was when he fled without trying to protect the town he had just stolen." I took my dagger and cut a slice from the ham the servants had brought. I ate it and then poured some more wine. "This is what will happen, Bishop. Any who swear loyalty to King Henry can stay here in the town. They will do so tomorrow in the cathedral. God will judge. Any who do not swear may leave."

I saw puzzlement on his face, "You do not wish ransom or treasure? You will not ransack the cathedral?"

I leaned back, "Were you not listening? This town is now King Henry's once more. Why should I steal my own King's coin?

His shoulders sagged and he nodded, "Aye, lord. You are a clever man. You have taken a town and we can do naught about it."

The next morning the cathedral was packed with all of the men of the town. We waited only long enough to hear the oaths being taken before we rode north. We had not taken from the town but when Geoffrey de Lusignan returned, he would find that his personal treasure, weapons, mail, horses and jewels had disappeared.

Sir William was keen to make amends for his mistake and he and his men were the van guard. We rode north along the road to Surgères. This was rich farmland and it was flat country. According to the Count of Poitiers there were no strongholds close by but there were others further east. The road we took headed north and east and although we only had twenty-eight miles to go I still worried that we might be found. The fields had been harvested of their summer crops. Stubble lay in them. Some farms had pigs rooting in them. If this had been a true chevauchée we would have taken them but we were bait. We were drawing all Poitevin rebel eyes towards us. We were between Poitiers and La Rochelle. King Henry and the rest of the army would, even now, be besieging the port.

I had men to the east and men to the west as a screen of scouts. The ones to the east were the ones who had the most important job. If Hugh de Lusignan sent men then Sir William and his retinue would see them. It was Leofric of Elton and Egbert son of Tam who were the scouts to the west. They galloped towards us with a pair of horses. There was blood on the saddles. "Lord we spied two messengers heading east. We were able to bring them down with our bows."

Sir Edward said, "Then the King is at La Rochelle. These were messengers summoning aid."

I nodded. "Take the horses to the baggage train and then return west. There may be others." They galloped off and I looked up at the sun. "It is gone noon. Let us find somewhere to rest the horses."

This land through which we rode was low lying and filled with small streams and tiny rivers. The Lustrum, back in Stockton, was a river compared with some of them. It meant there was plenty of water for our horses. We were just four miles from Surgères when we stopped. The Romans had made most of the roads in this land and they had, obligingly, left markers.

I waved over Gruffyd and his brother, Mordaf, "When your horses are watered I would have you head north with half a dozen archers. Surgères should be four miles in that direction. Scout it out for us." I had been told by the Count that this was a strong town. I did not expect to take it but a threat might draw Hugh de Lusignan towards us and then we could rejoin the King.

They rode off and we mounted. We rode with arming caps and our coif and ventails hanging from our shoulders. With shields at our sides we were ready to fight. Our squires rode behind us with our spears and lances. I had chosen a formation which kept us close together. I did not want us strung out across the land. The archers rode in two columns on the east and west of the road. The men at arms rode along the road. Four archers, along with Roger of Hauxley and Ralph of Appleby brought up the rear. In all there was just two hundred paces between me and Ralph.

It was the middle of the afternoon when Sir William's squire, Robert of Hartburn, rode in, "My lord there are horsemen approaching from the south and east. My father is keeping their scouts occupied."

"How many are there?"

"We counted twenty banners. I recognised one as the man who evaded us at Saintes."

I turned to Sir Edward, "That would be Geoffrey de Lusignan. Robert, ride to your father and tell him to pull back." He galloped off, "William, have the baggage train move to the field to the west of us. Gilles, fetch back the van guard!" As the three squires rode off, I shouted, "Form line on me facing south and west. David of Wales, dismount the archers and form two blocks on the flanks." We were just forty paces from the nearest ditch and low hedge.

While I waited for William and my spear, I pulled up my coif and donned my helmet. I left my ventail unfastened. I still had orders to give. We had forty-six men at arms. Sir William had a further four with him and four archers. When Sir Peter and Sir Fótr arrived, they placed themselves next to Sir Edward. Sir William would be to my right. Ridley the Giant was on the other side. Robert and William returned and handed us our spears. I dismounted Blaze and mounted the courser William had brought from the baggage train. Lion was a chestnut with a golden mane. He was a magnificent horse but it had been some time since I had ridden him. My time in the Holy Land and the Baltic had made me into a good rider; I would not have a problem adjusting. I mounted and patted his neck, "Good boy." I turned to William, "You and the squires guard the baggage train. This will need one spear and then it will be sword work." I knew that the squires would resent the task I had given them but they would obey.

Sir William and his men rode in from the south and west. I counted them and they were intact although Robert of Hartburn's horse had been struck with a bolt. Sir William put his horse next to mine and shouted, "Robert, ride to the baggage train and see to your horse." He shook his head, "His mother would skin me alive if she knew how close he came to death." He pointed to the advancing banners. "There are two hundred or so of them. Gurth of Oxbridge rode close to count them. They are all mounted. Thirty have crossbows. There are twenty-two knights. Fifty are sergeants and the rest are light horsemen."

I had enough information now. I shouted, "We let them charge. David of Wales, they have crossbows. If they are foolish enough to advance their crossbows then kill them, otherwise concentrate your arrows on their horsemen."

He shouted, "Aye lord. You heard the Earl! You do not need telling twice. Wait for me to release first!"

The enemy had seen our line. I saw at least one French banner amongst them. There were three or four standards of the Lusignan family. I did not see Hugh de Lusignan's. They approached to within four hundred paces of our defences. There were fields between us. Some had low hedges and others had ditches. When they struck us, they would not be travelling as fast as they might have liked. I saw the crossbowmen scurrying forward. They used the ditches and the low hedges for cover. A crossbow is cumbersome to carry and you cannot run with it loaded. I saw them reach arrow range. David of Wales did not release an arrow. He waited until they were at the hedge and ditch which was two hundred paces from us. I tied my ventail and swung up my shield. Even as they began to load their bolts David sent his first arrow. The others followed quickly. The first man to rise with his crossbow lifted his head just as David's arrow plunged down. It pierced his cap and skull. The other arrows descended on men who were vulnerable to an arrow storm from above. Four bolts came flying across the field towards us but they hit helmets and shields. The men were too panicked to try to hit our horses. No more crossbowmen risked raising their heads. There must have been survivors but they wisely stayed in the ditch.

A horn sounded and the horsemen came towards us. I estimated that they had fifty men in their front rank. They managed to keep a good formation until they reached the first low hedge and ditch. The better horsemen cleared it easily and landed ahead of the others. The better riders, the senior knights, were in the centre and so the line became an arrow head. The weaker riders took the jump more cautiously. David of Wales did not waste an arrow. He waited until they reached the second field boundary and, as the horses rose to clear it, arrows fell amongst them. One horse was struck and, landing badly, broke its neck. It made the other riders swerve to avoid them and the line became strung out. They no longer had cohesion. There were gaps between horses and men. The next fifty paces were a killing ground for our archers.

I raised my spear. While many of my knights and men at arms chose lances, I preferred the slightly shorter spear. I shouted, "Forward!"

I nudged Lion and he began to move towards the enemy. They were still galloping as best they could. The uneven line was closer to my knights in the centre. David and his archers would concentrate on the men on the flanks once we began our advance. My aim was to hit them as they landed. There were many things for a knight to think about when he was jumping. I saw that the centre of our line, ten horsemen wide, would be facing the arrow tip that was the enemy knights. We would be facing seven of them and they were not all close together. I had been fighting in such battles for over twenty years. I had learned to judge distance and to time my attack well. I pulled back my arm when I was twenty paces from the hedge. As we closed, I saw the enemy horses rise. It had to be Geoffrey de Lusignan whom I faced. I recognised the livery. He had a lance. There was no way in which he could control the lance as he first rose and then fell. He was too concerned with staying in the saddle and holding on to the reins. In contrast I just had to punch up towards him as his horse descended. Our lines closed. His horse tried to turn its head and merely succeeded in running into Sir William's spear. My spear hit Sir Geoffrey in the chest. He had good mail but his weight and momentum drove him on to my spear. His falling horse dragged him to the side and my spear ripped into his left shoulder. He tumbled from the horse.

"Hold here!"

All along our line the enemy horsemen were suffering the same fate. A horn sounded and the rebels and their French allies reformed. Even as they did so David of Wales and his archers began to pick off men. They were using bodkin arrows. They could penetrate mail. As riders and horses began to be hit a horn sounded and the enemy retreated.

"After them!" Now that there was no one to dispute the hedge we could jump it. I backed Lion up five paces and then spurred him. He cleared it easily. We did not need cohesion. We were running down those that had fled. Now the crossbowmen began to flee and, as we jumped the second hedge it was the crossbowmen that we first slew. They had no mail and their padded jackets did not stop a sharpened spear. The men with their baggage train saw the line of over fifty warriors and, leaping on to the best of the horses, they galloped off. There was little point in exhausting our horses and so, when we reached their abandoned baggage, I raised my spear and shouted, "Halt!"

I took off my helmet and lowered my ventail. It made it easier to see and I was not as hot. The Lusignans had left sumpters. They were laden with spare spears, crossbow bolts and weapons. I turned to Ridley, "Take these animals back to the baggage train."

"Aye lord. A good victory. I do not think we lost above four men."

"Aye, Ridley, but that is four men too many."

We rode back across the fields. The archers were stripping the dead of boots, belts, mail and weapons. They knew where to find the purses. They would share what they had taken with the men at arms. Other bands did not do this but mine understood that we each played a part in every battle. None would be robbed; none save the dead.

Padraig was tending to the wounds of Geoffrey de Lusignan. It was not an act of mercy but economics. He could be ransomed and that meant money for all of us. I dismounted and let Lion graze. Geoffrey de Lusignan was not a young man. I know not why but I had expected him to be. He looked to be in his thirties. He looked up as Padraig began to stich his wound. "Is your man any good?"

I pointed to my scar, "He did this."

Suddenly he stared at me, "You are the grey knight! You are the one my cousin spoke of!" He shook his head, "Now it makes sense. You were a spy! Have you no honour?" He winced as Padraig pulled the thread tight. I suspected my man at arms did so deliberately. "Of course, you have no honour! You are Thomas of Stockton and you murdered a priest."

I smiled. It no longer hurt to do so, "And I need you for ransom. That is the only reason you live. Curb your tongue or you will be treated as a man at arms!" He opened his mouth and then thought better of it. "Padraig, when he is ready take him and the other prisoners to the King. You know where to join us tomorrow."

He nodded, "Aye lord. Come my lord, you are  healed as much as I can manage. You had better pray that there is a doctor with the King or you will not sleep this night."

I waved over Mordaf and Gruffyd. They had just returned from the north, "Did you manage to reach the town?"

"Aye lord. There is a small castle but we only counted twenty or so men on their walls."

The Count had been wrong or perhaps he underestimated our skill. A small castle would not stop us. I turned to Sir Edward, "Should we stay here or push on to the town?"

"Push on to the town, Sir Thomas. We know that there is no help coming and we can sleep safer in their houses with hot food in our bellies."

He was right, "Prepare to move! Squires!" Our squires galloped up. I handed my spear to William. "The squires will be needed with the baggage train."

His shoulders slumped as he took the spear from me, "Yes, lord." He was disappointed.

This time, when we moved, we stayed closer together. I needed numbers to intimidate those in the town of Surgères. We had the bodies of our dead with us and they would be buried at Surgères. There was a church there and a priest. The enemy dead had been left in the fields where they had fallen. We had no time to observe the niceties. These were rebels and such was the fate of rebels. It was getting on to dusk as we approached the small town. My archers rode with strung bows. If there was opposition then their arrows would clear any human obstacle. The light behind us and the sun setting in the west glinted from our helmets and mail. We were easily seen. The farms and homes which lay along the road suddenly disgorged people as they headed for the safety of the walls of the castle. We did not hurry. The more who crammed into the small castle the sooner would they sue for terms. Even as we entered the town the gates were slammed shut and men appeared on the walls. The people who did not gain entry ran to the church which lay outside the castle walls. I waved for my men to surround the castle. I did not need to tell them to keep beyond missile range. I rode, with my knights, toward the church which nestled just forty paces from the walls. The people who had been denied entry now packed the church and three priests stood before the door. They held their crosses as though to ward off evil.

I dismounted and handed my reins to Edward. I took off my helmet and slipped the coif over my back.

The priest held his cross before him as though to ward off evil. "These people have claimed sanctuary. You cannot harm them!"

I smiled, "Nor would I wish to. I am Sir Thomas of Cleveland and I am here to reclaim the lands which have rebelled against King Henry. Who is the lord of Surgères?"

The priest looked confused at my reasonable and calm argument, "Baron Richard of Gynes."

I nodded, "Would you come with me while I speak with him?"

"Aye, lord, but I do not know what good it will do."

"I can but try to avoid bloodshed. Surely you approve?"

"I do but you ride here armed and with bloody surcoats."

"Aye that is because we fought a battle this day with Geoffrey de Lusignan." I paused and looked the priest in the eye so that he could see the truth which lay there, "He is defeated and now resides in La Rochelle at the pleasure of King Henry!"

"The King is come?"

"This is his fiefdom, of course he has come. I am merely an emissary, my men are outriders for the main army."

One of his priests came with him as did Sir Edward and Sir Fótr. Sir Peter and Sir William waited with the rest of my men.

We reached the gate. I saw that there was a bridge over the ditch. The walls were wooden although the keep, which I could see in the distance, was made of stone. I looked up and saw knights wearing helmets. Crossbows were aimed at us. I shouted, "Lower the crossbows or my archers will clear the walls!"

An English voice shouted, "Idle threats!"

I said, over my shoulder, "Show him David!" An arrow flew and struck a crossbowman in the hand. The arrow pinned his hand to the weapon. Other crossbowmen hurried to his side to remove the missile. "That was a warning. The next one will be deadlier."

The English voice shouted, "Lower your weapons!" I saw the crossbows withdrawn. "What is it that you want?"

"I am the Earl of Cleveland. King Henry is come to France and he would know why you have rebelled against him. If you have not then open your gate and welcome us as friends."

"King Henry is here?"

"He is close."

"How do I know that you speak the truth?"

"Because I am Sir Thomas of Stockton and I am never foresworn."

The knight took off his helmet, "King Henry abandoned us!"

"King Henry fought his enemies at home. Now he comes to do the same here in the land of his grandmother."

"Geoffrey of Lusignan will come. He will bring men!"

"He has come and he did bring men!" I paused, "The blood I wear is his and the wounded warrior now resides with King Henry. If you are hoping for help then I fear none is forthcoming."

He looked at the knights close to him for help. Then he said, "I need to speak with my people."

I shrugged, "As more than half are in your church, I fear it will be a short conversation. My men and I are tired. You have the night to consider my proposal. My men need full bellies before they sack a town!"

I turned my back on him. The priest said, "And what of us?"

"The people may return to their homes if they wish. You have my word that they will not be harmed but if they try to leave Surgères I will have them bound."

He nodded, "Thank you lord. When we saw your banners, we expected the worst."

I smiled, "No, father, the worst will come if the baron decides to fight me!"

# Chapter 7
# The Lord of Chauray

My men found a pig and two sheep which were grazing in a small holding. The owner must have been in the castle for none objected when my men slaughtered and then began to cook the animals. We had sentries set to watch the gates into the castle and my men watched the roads but I did not think that any would run.

William took my sword to the smithy and sharpened it. He brought it back to me, "Why did you give them the time to debate, father? They may plot!"

Sir Edward laughed, "Plot? What can they do? We have better men and if they try to break out then they will be slaughtered. The lord inside hopes that your father lies. He is counting on Sir Geoffrey arriving with banners and men. While we enjoy his animals, they will be on short rations. Tomorrow they will surrender."

William turned to me, "And if not?"

I shrugged, "They have wooden walls and we have archers aplenty. There is wood to burn and half of the town are within. If they do fight then it will not be for long."

I was not worried about Surgères. It was what happened next. The initial plan had been for us to come here and draw the enemy from the west. It looked likely that we would achieve that objective easily. The King would, if he managed to capture La Rochelle, be moving up the coast subjugating the towns as he went. There were few large and defensible strongholds until Apremont. I would continue to move north. We had to keep enemies from attacking his flank. If we continued to lose men then that would not be easy. I walked my lines after I had eaten. I had learned that a few words with each group of men made their confidence increase. I liked to do it, especially after a battle. I only ever saw the battle before me. I gained a better picture of the whole battle after talking to them. We had men at arms who had been wounded and I needed to ascertain their fitness to fight. It was not a surprise that men had been wounded. They had been fighting knights who had better horses and wore better mail.

James son of John said, "The knight I fought escaped, lord, only because he wore a breastplate beneath his surcoat. My spear thrust was a good one and he was knocked back but I did not penetrate his mail and he was able to wheel around and ride away."

His brother, John, said, "I struck the helmet of my opponent but he had a full face mask and although his head was driven back, he was not hurt."

The enemy had not been better fighters, they were just better protected. We would need to find a way around these new defences. Back at the hall we had commandeered I spoke with Edward. He nodded, "That surprised me too, lord. Sir Geoffrey was not wearing the good armour. Perhaps that is only worn by the French knights. When we were on the ship the captain told me that France was a much richer country now that she has the revenues of Normandy, Maine, Touraine and Blois.. Our arrival here is timely else they would have had Poitou's coin too. Do not worry, lord. I will back our men at arms and their skill against any knight no matter how well armed."

I did not worry about my men just the lack of numbers. We had been lucky. Although outnumbered, nature and my archers had come to our aid but I could not rely on that in every future battle.

The next morning Padraig and Richard rode in at dawn. "The King has captured La Rochelle, my lord. We found the bodies of the two men slain by Leofric and Egbert. We took their bloody tunics to the King. He is quick thinking, lord. He took the tunics and Sir Geoffrey to the walls. He told the constable that we had defeated the army coming to their aid. The garrison surrendered. He took La Rochelle without losing a man!" I could tell that my men liked King Henry and his clever mind. "He is staying in La Rochelle for two days. He sent to Royan for the ships. He has this idea of using them to keep us supplied as the army moves up the coast. It will mean he can do without a baggage train and move that much faster."

I felt much better after speaking with my two men at arms. The King was making wise decisions. Hubert de Burgh was still a worry. I feared he was working with others for he seemed determined to slow down the King. I went, with my knights, to the gate. "Well, castellan? Do you yield or do we begin to hack at your walls? Shall I unleash my dogs of war? It is your decision. King Henry will soon retake Poitou. You can take my word for that. If you ally yourself with Hugh de Lusignan then you will suffer for it."

He nodded and his dead voice displayed the disappointment he felt, "I will surrender my castle to King Henry."

"And any French knights will be surrendered to me."

He looked down and frowned. He was close enough for me to read the surprise on his face. "Frenchmen?"

"I know there are French knights within. They will come with me!"

He looked surprised, "You do not stay?"

"I am part of King Henry's army and I have my part to play. You will give your word to hold this town for the King and I will leave."

"You would trust me?"

"Of course, for if you break your word then I will bring my avenging angels back and your town will be a blackened ruin full of widows. Now open your gates and let me in so that I may speak with your French knights!"

There were four French knights who emerged from the castle. All were young men. I took them to the commandeered hall to question them. They were inexperienced and, I think, a little intimidated by the looming presence of Ridley the Giant and Sir Edward. Even though my two men did not speak, the four French knights kept glancing nervously at them. They were a physical threat. I first had their word that they had surrendered. Once that was done, I made it clear that they would be taken to La Rochelle and enjoy the King's company. That was the lure to make them speak. The sooner they had answered my questions the sooner they would be away from the two warriors who looked as though they would be able to pick the knights up and chew them! I suspect my scarred face made me look more intimidating than I actually was. I also put them at their ease by asking questions which appeared to be harmless. I asked where we should send for ransom; the names of their fathers and families. I asked them about the retainers they had brought. When I sent Ridley for wine for them then they visibly relaxed. They opened up even more and began to talk as though we were friends. I sent them, after noon, with an escort of men at arms, to the King. I learned a great deal about the opposition and the conspiracy which became clearer by the moment. Once they had gone, I led my column north and west. We were heading for Apremont and a meeting with the King but, along the way, I knew that we would have to fight more rebels.

Sir William and my other knights had not been present and I told them what I had learned. "All of the knights served the Count d'Eu. That lord has a web which goes from Normandy to Burgundy and across here to Poitou. He looks to have gathered your unattached knights from all of his lands and sent them to Poitou. If I were Hugh de Lusignan I would fear him more than I would fear an external enemy. The Count has seeded the garrisons with his own knights."

Sir Peter asked, "They know of their lord's plans?"

I shook my head, "They are all young and more than a little naïve. They believe they have been sent on the business of the King of France. I know, for I met the King in Paris, that this is not true. The Count is not working for the King but for himself. It seems to me that he is using his young knights to be hidden in plain view so that when he makes his bid for power his men will already be in place."

"But how does this help us, lord?"

"The King needs to wrest back control of this land. Whether we like it or not the Lusignan family controls Poitou. If King Henry can persuade Hugh de Lusignan that it is in his interests to have England as a protector then it will be one less worry for England. By revealing the Count d'Eu's plot, we gain the trust of the Lusignan family. The dowager Queen still has a part to play but first we must secure the west of this land before we advance to Poitiers. We fight skirmishes until then."

Poitiers lay well to the north and east of us. For that reason, I kept my screen of archers and Sir Fótr a mile to the east of us. The lord of Surgères had sworn an oath but he had not said that he would not inform his lord of the situation. Hugh de Lusignan would know where we were. He would gather his forces and send them after us but it would take time to gather them. We found a small, inconsequential village as dusk approached. There was a hall but it was not fortified. As we neared the hall a knight, flanked by his squires and four retainers, appeared. They were armed but their weapons were not drawn.

"I am Baron Robert Thierry. What do you wish here?"

I dismounted, "I am Thomas Earl of Cleveland. King Henry of England has returned to reclaim the lands which were stolen by Hugh de Lusignan. To whom do you owe your allegiance, Baron?"

He smiled and spread his hands, "As you can see, Earl, I have a handful of retainers. I am loyal to whoever controls this land." He was a pragmatic man.

I sympathised with him but I had a job to do. "Then I will ask you to swear allegiance to King Henry."

"The King is young."

"Yet he is older now than when we first began the conversation. He has taken La Rochelle. We have captured Surgères and I have defeated Geoffrey de Lusignan. We will win."

He nodded, "Your name is not unknown to me. I remember when you were the lord of La Flèche. I will so swear."

This time we did not take animals from the fields for the baron fed and housed us. When we left the next day, I was more confident than I had been for some time. We captured another small manor before my men at arms caught up with us. They had with them a conroi of knights. The King had sent Sir Robert of Derby and eight other knights, along with forty men at arms to swell my numbers. It was a relief. My plan was working. We were taking smaller places and that reduced the number of rebels we might have to fight in the final battle.

We headed the next day further north towards Chauray. Here there was a castle and there were enemies. My archer scouts had had a brush with Poitevin riders. Their bows had driven off the riders but the Lord of Chauray knew that we were on his land. As we approached the walled town, he sent some men to watch our approach. He used a dozen knights, their squires and forty men at arms. They halted three hundred paces from us and three hundred from their own walls. This was a cautious baron. He wanted to scout us out before he reacted. I saw that his walls were manned but they looked to be manned by his people. They were interspersed with the helmets of warriors. I sent Sir Robert and his men to the east. "Find the other gate. Make a camp and keep watch."

"What will you do, my lord? You send the bulk of your knights away. You will be outnumbered."

"We will test the mettle of this baron and his men. I have my archers and men at arms. Keep a good watch."

A rider left the Poitevin horsemen as Sir Robert led his men away. I signalled for David of Wales. "Have your men form up behind us. I will advance as though we are going to charge. I will not. On my command send five flights in their direction."

"Aye lord."

I turned to my knights, "Have the men at arms form a long line as though we are going to charge." I pointed at the enemy. "They have sent roughly the same number of men at arms but three times our number of knights. He hopes we will charge. I intend to make him think that we will oblige him."

Sir Edward nodded and as the men began to form up said, "He will have sent a rider to Poitiers, lord."

"I know and the strategy is working. So long as we are the lure then the King has free rein in the west. He has taken La Rochelle. Let us see if he can capture St. Jean and St. Gilles. If he does then that leaves just Apremont, La Roche and Noirmoutier. Once we have taken Chauray, we head west to join him. We have pushed our luck long enough. The Lord of Poitou cannot afford to lose so much of his land. We have poked the dog enough. After this is the time for discretion."

We lined up and our squires brought our spears. They also brought our banners. It would clearly signal our intent. Our archers came on foot and were hidden from the enemy by us and our horses. David placed himself behind my horse. "Ready, my lord."

"I will halt just two hundred paces from them. Is that range sufficient for you to hurt them?"

"Aye lord. The men are well rested and we need the exercise."

"Advance!" A charge by heavy horse never begins quickly. It begins at a walk, then a trot and it was only the last forty or so paces where it would be at the gallop. We walked and then trotted. We kept perfect formation. I saw the enemy swing shields around and lower visors. They prepared their horses. In a perfect world they would charge and then we would be able to sweep them from the field. When we were two hundred paces from them, I shouted, "Halt!"

As soon as we stopped and before the enemy could react our archers sent the first of their five flights in the air. The enemy had their shields before them. The were expecting a charge. The first they knew of the arrow storm was when arrows plunged from the skies. I saw two horses struck. They reared and threw their riders. Three of the riders, men at arms, were hit as arrows tore through their mail and into their shoulders. The second flight had struck and the third flight was on its way before the leader sounded the horn for a retreat. The fourth flight stuck men's backs and horse's rumps. By the time the gates slammed shut they had left four dead men at arms, and two who had been wounded dragged themselves towards the closed gates. We let them go. The two maddened horses my archers had first struck were being retrieved by three of my archers.

As crossbow bolts flew from the walls, I ordered my men to fall back out of range. "Make camp here. The siege has begun."

I rode with William to Sir Robert. The knight knew his business. His camp sat astride the road east and he had stakes around it making it into a small fortress. "Your task is to warn me of any who try to reinforce the town. There are too few of you to hold up a relieving army. Your purpose is to spread the guards along the walls so that we may try to attack tonight. If you hear my horn sound four times then it means we are inside and you may try this gate."

As we rode back to our main camp William asked, "Will we attack this night?"

"I will have men attack the walls under cover of darkness. First, however, I will try to speak with the lord as we did at Surgères. It cannot hurt." By the time we reached the gate the light was fading in the west. I took off my helmet. "William, take off your helmet and unfurl the banner." We rode close to the gate. I was aware of the crossbows pointed at me. I trusted that this knight was not only cautious but honourable. Why risk the wrath of a king?

The baron appeared. He was a greybeard. "I am Hugh de Chauray, what do you want?"

"I am Sir Thomas of Cleveland and I am here on behalf of the King. He would that his rebellious lords return to him. He forgives all who followed Hugh de Lusignan. They were misguided."

He laughed, "If this were any other than Sir Thomas of Stockton then I would say that he was a deluded hypocrite but I know that you speak that which you believe is the truth. King John abandoned us and I see no reason to support his idiot son! This is a strong town and you will need strong machines to take it." He swept a hand around us, "And I see pitifully few men to take us. King Henry has lost this land of Poitou. It is now ours. We will soon have even more land!"

"I implore you, baron, do not be so stiff necked. Listen to my words. You and I know that an army unleashed upon a town often forgets that they are men. Save the lives of those within these walls."

"You have to breach them first. I tire of this and I have a fine meal waiting. Enjoy the cold comfort of the siege!"

I rode back to my lines. The baron was a brave man. He was misguided but brave. "Sir Edward, have the men fed. When it is dark of night then you and I will lead a chosen band of men. We will take this burgh despite the baron's words."

"Aye lord."

"William, find me food. I have an appetite. David go and examine the defences. We will talk while we eat."

We took off our helmets and swords. We lit fires. We prepared food. We sat around the fire and ate. We were behaving exactly as the lord expected us to. His men would be able to see our camp and they would report our action to the baron. I explained my plan. I was counting on the fact that he would not expect us to attack immediately. He would assume we would dig ditches and build machines. The last thing that he would expect would be for us to scale his walls and open the gates. That was precisely what I planned.

"David, how many men are there at the gate?"

"There were ten but since dark there are just four. The wall is an irregular shape but they seem to have ten men who patrol. They each cover fifty paces of the wall."

"And is there a weak spot?"

He nodded. "There is a corner. The wall cuts in at right angles and then continues straight. We could use the corner for when the sentries patrol, they cannot see it."

"Then here is my plan. David of Wales and four archers will go with Ridley the Giant, Sir Peter and his squire." I saw Ridley grin. He would be with his sons. "They will use the corner of the wall to gain entry. The rest of us will wait close to the gate. As soon as the sentries are eliminated then the archers will cover the gatehouse and slay any sentry who moves or tries to sound the alarm. When the gate is opened then we enter. Sir Fótr, you take your men and open the other gate. Let in Sir Robert and his men."

It was a simple plan but it relied on my men achieving their objectives. It was why I had sent Sir Robert to the far gate. He just had to react. I did not know him well enough to entrust him with the task of scaling a wall and killing the guards upon its fighting platform. Once we had eaten then we moved around the camp and I explained what we were doing. The men banked up fires and made sleeping warriors of blankets, cloaks and logs. One by one they slipped away as though to make water or to check on horses. Instead of returning to the fires they crept closer to the walls of the town. Our servants moved around as though they were sentries. The sentries would see what they expected to see.

The sentries on the walls had brands burning on the walls. I knew not why. The area they lit was the top of the wall. The bottom lay in darkness. Worse the light made their night vision that much poorer. That gave us an advantage. We were not relying on helmets. We just had arming caps and coifs. We had swords and hand weapons. None of us approached the walls from the direction of the gate. We waited until the sentry who patrolled above us had his back to us and then moved closer. In that way we were able to make the base of the wall without being seen. There was a ditch but it was no longer an obstacle. It had filled with the detritus of the town. So long as a man was careful, he could step across it. In Stockton we had men cleaning the ditch each autumn. Leaves and branches were removed; the sides were sharpened. Here they were not so rigorous. Once in the shadow of the wall we were able to move along it towards the gatehouse. So long as we were silent then we would be invisible. Our shields were slung on our backs. Our swords were sheathed. Our coifs hung upon our shoulders and we were able to hear. I thought I heard the soft sigh of death from above me but that might have been my imagination. David and his archers were masters with a knife. They could move as silently as a hunting fox.

We reached the gate and I could hear the conversation from above. The night was so still that I could make out the words. The men were talking about the relief column coming to save them. They commented on the lack of wood to make siege engines and were confident that their crossbows could keep us from their walls. The men above were not the town watch. They were the men who served the Lord of Chauray. Then we heard a noise. We heard it because we were listening for it and it was not an alarming noise. It was the sound of feet moving on the fighting platform. It was the sound of surprise. The soft thump of a body hitting the wooden walkway as a sentry was slain was the sound of victory for it meant the gatehouse was cleared. I drew my sword and slid my shield around. The sword made no noise but there was a slight grating from the mail as the shield rasped around. When I heard feet on the steps inside the gate, I knew it was Ridley and his sons. My archers would be too silent. The bar across the gate was lifted. As the door creaked open, I saw Sir Peter and his squire, Henry. They were smiling. The opening of the gates was the signal for my archers to join us.

With Sir Edward and Sir William, I led my men at arms towards the hall where Hugh de Chauray would have his best men. I did not care if it was fortified for we had the town now. David of Wales and his men were on the fighting platform and they would have a good view and clear line of sight. Sir Fótr led his men through the small town to the other gate. My archers were racing around the walls. One sharp-eyed sentry spotted them.

"Alarm!"

Our luck ran out. However, we were inside the walls. We were armed and alert. Even as the town was awoken the ten sentries on the walls were dying or had been incapacitated. "William, sound the horn four times! Let us warn Sir Robert that we are inside the town." Behind me I heard grunts as men emerged from their homes and were struck by swords, shields and mailed fists. These were half awake burghers come to see what was the noise. Then I heard a horn and knew that the Lord of Chauray was awake and he was preparing to defend his town. It was what I would have done. Any sympathy I might have had for Lord Hugh de Chauray had disappeared when I gave him the chance to be loyal again. I remembered those lords who had opposed King John. Even when he had acceded to their demands some asked for more. This Hugh de Chauray was another such man. He was greedy.

I heard the clash of steel. Sir Fótr and his men had run while we had walked. They were already at the gate and soon we would be reinforced by Sir Robert and his men. Our horn must have told the baron where we were. He was a brave man for he led his men from his hall to meet us. He might have sat inside his walls. I suspect that he would have done that if it had been any other than myself. I had a reputation.

I heard his voice, "Shield wall! Take shelter in my hall!" They were two separate commands. One was for his warriors and the other was for his people.

The streets of the town were narrow. The houses were made of wood. He intended to block the roads leading to his hall with his men. I saw people rushing to get into the hall. I did not need to give a command. I was flanked by my knights and my men at arms. I locked my shield with Sir Edward and Sir William. Sir Peter and Ridley filled the gap to the buildings on either side of us. We emerged into the square before the hall. There was a line of shields and spears waiting for us. The Lord of Chauray was in the centre. He had some knights with him but it was mainly a line of men at arms. We would, in theory, be evenly matched. The edge my men had was their experience. They had fought in the frozen north and some had fought in the deserts of the Holy Land. They had fought wild Estonians and cunning Seljuk Turks. They had been ambushed by Welsh hill men and charged Scottish Highlanders. They would be prepared, no matter what the Lord of Chauray did.

We did not run to meet the line of spears. We advanced steadily. Lord Hugh did not know that Sir Fótr and Sir Robert were bringing more men to attack his right flank. The Poitevin lord thrust his spear at my head. I wore no helmet and I must have appeared an easy target. With no helmet I could see more easily than he could. It was dark and he was peering through the eyeholes of his helmet. He misjudged the strike. I blocked the thrust with my shield and lunged with the tip of my sword. He was not expecting it. His spear thrust had opened up his middle and my sword hit his mail. He had a breastplate over the mail but my sword tip hit him below it. He reeled backwards. My sword did not break his mail but it winded him.

Just then there was a shout from my left as Sir Robert led his men into the line of men at arms. The cohesion of the line disappeared in an instant. As the men at the extreme right of the Poitevin line were slain so the others turned. It allowed my men at arms to break through. Sir Edward and Sir William forced their way through the line and began to lay about them with their swords. I faced Sir Hugh, "Surrender lord, your defences are breached and you can save unnecessary slaughter!"

He thrust again with his spear but it had no power and I blocked it easily. "Fool! The Count d'Eu and the Count of Poitou are already on their way! By this time tomorrow you will be prisoners awaiting ransom!"

In answer I swung my sword, not at his shield but at his spear. I hacked through the shaft. I saw the knight whose back was against Lord Hugh's suddenly fall as Sir Edward hacked across his neck. The Lord of Chauray's head turned and it was enough. The tip of my sword was under his helmet and pricking his neck. "Surrender or die!" I am not sure what he might have decided to do had not there been a sudden flaring of flames from behind him and a scream.

The hall was on fire. It was naught to do with us although long afterwards men blamed the Earl of Cleveland. I guessed someone had been careless and knocked over a brazier. Whatever the reason the Lord of Chauray realised that his people were in grave danger and he nodded, "I surrender! Now stop the slaughter."

I shouted, "The Lord of Chauray has surrendered. Stop now. There are people who need our help!"

My men were well trained and they stopped but they kept their weapons pointed at the defenders. When the Poitevin saw that their lord had surrendered they laid down their weapons. The hall was on fire. Even though it was made of stone there was enough wood inside and on the towers for it to be a fire trap. It burned. We let the people pass but the flames defeated us. They spread to the nearby buildings. While my men helped the people from the town the Lord of Chauray and his men fought the flames. By mid-morning they had won but half the town was in ruins.

A weary and blackened Hugh de Chauray led his men from the ruins of his town and handed me his sword. He shook his head, "I have been betrayed. I was promised help and none came. I will swear allegiance to King Henry."

"You could have done that yesterday and saved the lives of many people. Your town would not need rebuilding."

"The Count d'Eu promised me aid and none was forthcoming."

I nodded, "Next time chose a better lord."

"And is King Henry a better king than his father?"

"Time will tell but I am hopeful." In that moment I believed what I said. I was not to know how events would turn out.

# Chapter 8
# King Henry's Victories

We stayed two days. That was partly to ensure that those who had survived the fire would be safe and partly in case the Count d'Eu came with the relief column. They did not. Sir Hugh, the lord of the manor, was very bitter. I had sent my archers ranging far to the east and they saw no sign of a relief column coming to the aid of their beleaguered castles. I wondered what the Poitevin leaders were thinking. Then the words of the Count of Pontoise came back to me. They thought that King Henry was a weak king with no military experience. They expected that he would fail. Hugh de Lusignan and the Count d'Eu were hoping that they would be able to walk in and accept the surrender of the King of England when he failed to take their castles. They would demand more land or coin. They had underestimated, not the King, but the men he led.

A rider arrived from the King. They had left La Rochelle and were advancing north towards La Roche-sur-Yon. I was ordered to meet him there. I was not happy about the order. Our plan was succeeding. We had eliminated two enemies and while the Poitevin vacillated we could take the rest of their coast. The town was inland. However, I realised that I probably had more information than the King. I had an idea of their strategy and he did not. The remainder of the army had just thirty-one miles to travel and we had more than forty. He would reach there first. We turned to head north and west.

The Viscount of Thouars had a castle at Bressuire. It was held for him by the lords of Beaumont. It was a strong castle built upon a rocky outcrop. One of the manors of the Beaumont family was La Châtaigneraie and it lay along our march. It was a small manor but they must have spied us as we approached. We stopped in the village to water our horses and to eat. I asked the locals if they supported King Henry. When they said they did then I paid for the food we took. I suspect, in light of later events, that they were lying. Since leaving Chauray I had kept Sir Fótr on our right flank. He paralleled our line of march. Robert of Wulfestun galloped in. "Lord, Sir Fótr sent me. There is a column of horsemen approaching. They have come from Bressuire. They have the double headed eagle on their standard."

I nodded, "And there is a castle there."

"Return to Sir Fótr and tell him to fall back here in good order." La Châtaigneraie was a small hamlet. There were, however, many small farms surrounding it. They were many field boundaries and there was little open land. This was not good country for horses. I turned to my men, "We fight on foot. David of Wales you will stop these horsemen."

"Aye lord." The squires and servants led our horses to the centre of the village. They would be safe there. I took off my cloak and picked up a couple of spears. I raised one to lead my men at arms and knights to the north east side of the village. We stopped at the edge of a field which had grown beans. Most of them had been cleared by pigs. With the village behind us I formed us into a double line. I rammed one spear into the soft soil. It was at an angle. Then I waited for the rest of my men to appear. We did not have enough spears for all of us to ram one into the ground before us but my men at arms improvised and used palings they took from gates and fences. It was a barrier. I hung my helmet from the spear.

Sir Edward had found a bean pod and he was eating the beans, "This means we will not join the King until the morrow."

"Perhaps this is for the best. If we can hurt the men of Bressuire then it might make that castle easier to take."

"This is not profitable yet, lord."

"We have a little ransom. Would you rather be at home?"

"I would rather be at home. If I am here in Poitou then I would rather be fighting for reward. It seems to me that fighting for a King is not as profitable as being a sword for hire."

Edward's words showed how far the royal family had fallen in the eyes of ordinary warriors. Edward had known King Henry II, his son, King Richard and King John. He knew good kings and, thus far, the King of England had not shown he came from the same blood as his grandfather.

"Give King Henry a chance. If he fails to capture Poitou then he may be judged."

"When we take Poitou, lord, that will be your doing."

The conversation was ended by the arrival of Sir Fótr and his men. He reined in while his men carried on to the village. "They come. There are over a hundred and twenty men. They are led by fifteen knights and their squires. They have neither crossbows nor archers."

"Take your horse to the others and then join us."

I saw the banners as they approached to within half a mile of us. They stopped. Their leader was assessing what he saw. He could not see the archers for they were behind our third rank. A horn sounded and they formed into a long double line. They held spears and lances. The horn sounded again and they charged. Here there were no hedges as boundaries. The land was divided by low mounds. Here they did not raise animals but crops. It meant that the horses could charge and gallop unchecked. Our squires were with us this time and they stood amongst the archers. Our banners fluttered behind us. They were a gauge for the archers and the strength of the wind. The enemy kept up a steady pace. With no obstacles before them and us static they could wait until the last forty paces before they spurred their horses.

I raised my spear, "Archers ready!

"Aye lord. Nock!"

I was estimating the range. "Prepare!"

"Draw!"

The horses were one hundred and fifty paces from us, "Now!"

"Release!" The goose fletched bodkins soared in the air. They made a whistling sound as they were released. They would not land together. Some archers were stronger than others. The slightest variation in the angle of the bow would also affect the flight. The second flight was in the air when the first flight struck. Some horsemen and their horses were hit at the same time while others escaped completely. David of Wales would have ordered his men to adjust for the closing range. The second flight struck and then a third. There were now gaps as horses were hit and fell. Riders were knocked from their saddles. A plunging arrow could be stopped by plate but not mail. Bodkin arrows drove deep into shoulders and arms. If they struck a helmet, they did not penetrate but the strike had the same effect as a sword blow. Still the horses came on. The lords who led them had mail plates on their horses' heads. The ten in the centre were still largely intact and they would strike at the centre of our line. That was good for it was where Sir Robert and the rest of my knights stood. We all had full face helmets. We had good mail and I had metal plates on my shoulders.

"Brace spears and lock shields." I held the spear against my right foot. I pushed my shield to touch Sir Edward's and Sir William's. Behind me I felt the shields of the second rank press reassuringly into my back. The horses were now being spurred by their riders. They came at us faster. David of Wales and his archers now used a flatter trajectory as they loosed over our heads. Sometimes luck was with the archers and one arrow, it had a green feather amongst the white, drove through the eye hole of the knight next to the leader. He tumbled backwards over his horse. His dying hands gripped the reins and he pulled the horse to the side. Although the other riders kept their saddles it spoiled the cohesion. Other horses were struck and fell. There were increasing numbers of gaps.

Then I had no time to watch for the leading lance came for me. I resisted the temptation to lift my shield. It was locked with two others and that was a stronger barrier. If the lance came for my head then I could always move my head out of the way. As the horsemen and his weapon closed with me, I saw that the lance would strike me on the shoulder or miss me completely. It slid and slipped over the metal plate on my shoulder. My spear gouged a line along his horse's flank. The horse tried to stop and turn at the same time. Its head hit my shield and Sir Edward's. I lifted my spear head, it was easier to do so than with a lance and I drove it up and over the cantle. The lord who faced me had a breastplate too but my punch and the horse's movement made the spear head gouge into his lance hand. The spear shaft caught between the cantle and his body. My spear snapped. I dropped the haft and drew my sword. The men behind would deal with the horse and the wounded knight. I hacked upwards into the throat of the next horse as its head passed me. I hit a vein and blood spurted. Already wounded and maddened it raised its forelegs to clatter into our shields. It was dying and the animal fell backwards. It trapped the leg of the lord who had the surcoat with the double headed eagle.

I took a chance. I stepped forward and on to the carcass of the dead horse. A man at arms from the second rank saw me and lunged with his spear. I deflected it with my shield and then hacked at his leg with my sword. I hit him below the hem of his hauberk and drew blood. The leader was lying beneath his horse. He was desperately trying to drag his leg free. I pressed my bloody sword against his throat, "Yield, seigneur, or die!" His head fell back and he raised his hands.

He was the one who commanded and the battle should have been over but the ones on the flank could not see the fate of their leader. They continued to fight on. The ones around me saw that he had surrendered and began to turn their horses to disengage. As soon as they turned their backs then my archers had easy targets. A horn sounded and the men of Bressuire fled. We had won. I looked down the line and saw four knights had surrendered. That would please Sir Edward. Four war horses wandered disconsolately over the field. They too would give us coin.

I sheathed my sword and held out my hand to the fallen knight. I helped to pull him from beneath the dead animal. He stood, somewhat unsteadily. I think the falling animal had hurt his knee. He took off his helmet.

"I am Baron William of Beaumont." He handed me his sword. I took the sword and then gave it back to him. The handing over of the sword was the sign that he had surrendered and would neither run nor fight until ransom was paid. "You must be Sir Thomas of Stockton."

"You have heard of me?"

"I heard of your exploits at La Flèche. I did not know that you were here. Had I known I would have used different tactics. Your archers have a reputation!"

I realised then that the longer we stayed in Poitou the less effective would be my archers. The rebels would prepare for them. I hoped that the King was still adhering to the plan. We stayed the night in the village and the wounded, of both sides, were tended to. There was a priest who had accompanied Baron Beaumont. I discovered, as I spoke to the Baron, that he was a very devout man. He had been considering taking the cross for some time. I told him of my experiences.

"I can see how that would make you bitter but to see the place our Lord lived and where he died…"

"If that is your intention Baron, then save yourself the journey. The Turks control those lands and they do not let pilgrims through."

"I hear that King Louis of France is considering a crusade."

I smiled, "I have met him and he is little more than a boy. He may well go on crusade but it will not be for some time." I liked the lord from Bressuire. He was a vassal of the Count of Thouars and had little choice in his affiliations. The Count of Thouars was opposed to England.

We reached La Roche-sur-Yon not long after noon. The town had welcomed King Henry as a liberator. We did not have to fight a battle. My scouts had arrived before we had and the King and Hubert be Burgh were waiting for us as we rode into the town. The King was only a couple of weeks older than the last time I had seen him but he appeared to be much more assured and confident. Victory did that to a man.

"More ransom! You have done well. We had an almost bloodless victory and there was no ransom to be had."

"I would rather a bloodless victory than the ransoms, my liege but I am pleased that we have had so many victories already. We need to keep our swords in the enemy's backs."

Hubert de Burgh shook his head as he led me into the hall of the castle. "We can continue to do as we have, Earl. Safe and sure is the way!"

I raised my voice, "No, Justiciar! God has presented us with a golden opportunity. Hugh de Lusignan and his allies believe that the King is too young to lead armies. They expect him to fail."

"Earl!"

"Sir Hubert, the King needs the truth from us!" I turned to the King. "I do not believe you are too young. Let them believe what they will, we keep on advancing. If we can secure this coastline then the only trade for Poitou will be from the east. We make them landlocked. Then their leaders will have to bring an army to fight us."

I saw that the King was struggling to understand the strategy.

"Chance all our gains on one battle! Earl that is too great a risk!" The caution of the Justiciar made me suspicious once more.

"I have fought three times since I landed. I have lost a handful of men despite fighting superior odds. I have done so with a handful of knights. Now we are together. We have an army which is whole. Our men are victorious and full of confidence!"

I knew I had won this battle when the King slapped his right fist into his left palm, "The Earl is correct. We leave tomorrow for Sables d'Olonne, St. Gilles Croix de Vie and the other west coast ports." He looked at me, "Does that satisfy you, Earl?"

I smiled, "It will take just days to subdue those and then we take Challans and Apremont. If that does not draw the Lusignans here then we might as well march on Poitiers for they will have lost the whole county!"

Hubert de Burgh did not like my victory. I could see that he was a cautious man. He was a merchant who wore armour. Either he did not understand war or he had ulterior motives. He could have been working with others, I knew not who. We stayed but one day in the newly captured town. The first of the ransoms arrived while we were there. Baron William and his men would remain at La Roche-sur-Yon while we headed west, to the sea.

Sir Edward, riding next to me and just behind King Henry and his household knights, shook his head, "This is not warfare lord. It is like a royal progress." He was right. None of the small towns resisted us. All swore to support the King and we moved on to the next one. After five days we reached the island of Noirmoutier. This was a different prospect. I did not relish an attack over the sea but our victories meant that the constable of the castle had little choice but to join us. With every port in Poitou now in our hands there was no way that they would survive. The King had a fleet of ships and they could blockade and starve the island fortress. We had taken the last stronghold without losing a man. That night, as we camped at Le Barre des Monts, we held our first counsel of war.

I addressed the counsel, "Challans is but fourteen miles away. They know where we are and they will be prepared. The castle at

Challans is not a big one but they have town walls and they will need to be assaulted." I paused.

The King asked, "You have a plan?"

"We attack at four different places at the same time. We have ladders built here. The walls are not high and they will have to spread out their better warriors. By making them spread themselves thinly we give ourselves the best opportuinity."

Hubert de Burgh said not a word. I think he hoped I would be defeated and that would end my influence on the young King. The King surprised him, "I would like to assault the walls!"

Sir Hubert's mouth opened and closed. I shook my head, "Very brave of you, my liege, but ill thought out." He frowned. "Firstly, you have never fought to the death. This would be such a fight. Climbing a ladder and fighting one handed is a difficult skill. Besides, we need you and your household knights to be ready to ride through the gates when we open them. We will be on foot and you and your knights will lead the charge!"

I could see that the idea of leading a charge of horses appealed. Of course, it would not come to that. If we were able to open the gates then we would have won. The men at arms and knights who climbed the ladders would have achieved the victory.

He beamed, "That is a fitting task for a King of England!"

There was plenty of timber and we spent some time building ladders. Hubert de Burgh was just grateful that his King would not be climbing the walls and he put his organisational skills to the task of building ladders and dividing the men into four groups. Leaving men to finish the ladders we moved to Challans. We surrounded the town with our tents and our fires. We dug ditches. It was a low-lying town and there was nowhere we could build a counter castle. I set my men to feign building a ram. They would expect that. The King, his herald, Sir Hubert and four priests rode to the gate of Challans. Sir Edward wondered why I did not go.

"The King and his Justiciar need to feel that they can beard the enemy. If they succeed then so much the better."

They returned having been given short shrift. The King was red in the face. "They will pay for their insults!"

I did not ask what insults he had endured but I guessed they would be to do with his age. "It is all part of the game they play, King Henry. They do not mean what they say. They hope to enrage you. We keep to our plan and our victory will be vengeance enough!"

He seemed mollified. "When do we attack?"

"The ladders will arrive in the morning. We will attack at dusk."

"Dusk?"

"I have my archers making fire arrows. They are an unpredictable weapon but they can cause fear in civilians. I have recently seen the effect of an accidental fire. Our deliberate fire may well win the battle for us. No matter what happens we will have a distraction when we attack. Darkness helps us."

We now had so many men that I was able to concentrate on the men I led. Robert of Derby had asked to assault with me and I was honoured. He had shown himself to be both reliable and able to think for himself. We had four ladders and I explained how we would use them. The attack would be begun when the archers sent their arrows into the roofs of the town. We would run to the walls. Two men would hold them and then we would attack. Ridley would lead the assault up one ladder and Sir Edward would take a second, Sir Robert and his men would have the other two. We were not attacking close to a gate. We did not need to. Once inside the sheep pen that was Challans then my wolves would soon reach and open the gates.

This time we did wear helmets. It would be impossible for almost five hundred men to advance in silence. We would try to get as close as we could before the inhabitants knew we were there but they would dispute the walls with us. Each group had two ladders and only one ladder was needed to reach the fighting platform. The difficulty would be in climbing up to the fighting platform. David of Wales commanded the archers. He would be the one who began the attack by using his fire arrows. Sir Hubert had been appalled that someone so low born should command. I did not comment on the irony of that. He had been born the son of a merchant and done little to merit his position save advising King John how to tax people.

We moved into position. Men at arms carried the ladders and we all carried our helmets. We wore our shields over our backs. The night was black as we closed to within thirty paces of the walls. The ground around the walls had once been open. It had given the defenders clear sight of any who attacked them. In the years since the wall had been built houses and out buildings had sprung up. The buildings gave us some cover. They were empty now and we rested close by a pig pen. The archers had advanced with us. Their fire was in a pot which they carried. The town was in darkness but we could see irregular shadows which were the tops of the buildings. We had seen how each town through which we had passed had buildings which were closely packed together. When the arrows fell they would be more likely to hit a building than not. Of course, fire arrows were notoriously unpredictable. Some would extinguish themselves when they struck wood. Others might not ignite the building they struck. We needed just twenty or so to start fires and that would aid us.

After donning my helmet, I nodded to David of Wales and tapped Ridley the Giant on the shoulder. We moved towards the walls. We had covered ten paces of open ground when a sentry spotted a movement. He shouted the alarm and we heard horns and bells begin to sound. It may not have been my men who were seen. It did not matter for the fire arrows soared from behind me. As soon as the first was launched then the sky was lit up as though filled with shooting stars. We hurried forward. They had crossbows on the walls but it takes time to load one. We had reached the walls before the first bolt struck Matty of Thornaby. My archers must have seen him fall for an arrow was sent to fell the crossbowman. It struck his padded jacket and the down inside flared like kindling. He screamed and ran down fighting platform. I looked up as the ladder was pressed to the wall and saw the crossbowman running towards the gatehouse like a human candle. It distracted the defenders. Ridley took full advantage and with William and Henry holding the bottom of the ladder securely, he and I climbed the ladder as quickly as we could. Flaming arrows were thudding into the buildings. I heard the hiss and crackle of fire. A spear was thrown at me and struck me in the side. It was like being punched but the head did not penetrate the mail and it clattered off the ladder to fall to earth. My sword was sheathed. I concentrated on using two hands to climb. With his great strength and height Ridley the Giant was able to use his sword. The walls were not as high as those on my castle and I heard steel on steel as Ridley reached the top. He was poised precariously with one foot on the stone crenulation and one on the ladder when I saw the spear dart out from the crenulations to impale him. I took another step and, while holding on with my left hand I pulled the spear down. The defender forgot to let go and he found himself flying through the air. I let go as soon as I saw his face begin to fall towards earth. His scream as he fell distracted Ridley's opponent enough to allow my Sergeant at Arms to smash his sword into the man's shoulder. Ridley jumped down to the fighting platform and I followed a heartbeat later.

A man ran at me with a spear. My sword was sheathed and my shield around my back. I grasped the shaft as the spear was thrust at me and I pulled it along my body. As the man's head drew closer to me, I pulled back my own and head butted him. He fell in a heap and I drew my sword. The wall was to my left and I left my shield where it was. I began to advance down the fighting platform. Ahead of me I saw Robert of Derby and his men as they tried to gain the top of the walls. Knowing that Sir Fótr would be behind me I advanced. Suddenly, to my right and about forty paces away, the roof of a building flared into the sky as the flames took hold. I ran towards the men who were attempting to deny Sir Robert the wall. The defenders who had been racing towards the wall to help the sentries now had a dilemma for the fires needed fighting. In war hesitation can be deadly.

I ran at the men who were hacking and stabbing at one of Sir Robert's men at arms. As the warrior was speared and tumbled to the ground, I swung my sword from the right. With no wall to hinder me I had a free swing and my sword hacked through the leather jerkin and into the side of the man. As I sawed out the blade he fell to the ground. I grabbed the helmet of the warrior whose back was to me and pulled him over the edge of the fighting platform so that he too fell to the ground.

Sir Robert, his helmet bloody from the blood of his man at arms, took full advantage to leap up to stand on the crenulations. I backhanded my sword across the throat of the warrior who tried to spear him as he stood there. Sir Fótr's sword took the arm of the man who had tried to sneak up on me and stab me. When Sir Robert landed on the fighting platform, I knew we had taken the walls. The fire had taken hold. As I looked around, I had a vision of what hell might be like. On the walls men were dying and they were the defenders. My men were better armed and mailed. The fire danced and sparkled below us. I shouted, "Sir Robert, clear the walls. Cleveland, with me!"

There was a set of stone steps just behind me. I swung my shield around as I descended. I saw that Sir Edward was leading more of my men along the wall to the south of me. When I reached the bottom, I turned to get my bearings. We had to get to the gate as soon as we could. The sound of horses galloping through the gate would end the battle of Challans. My slight hesitation almost cost me. From the dark a knight and four men at arms launched themselves at me. It was fortunate that I had swung my shield around or else my battle would have ended there. As it was the mighty blow from the war axe almost knocked me to the ground. I lunged upwards with my sword and it scraped across the helmet of the knight. Sir Fótr had been joined by Sir William and more of my men at arms but I had a battle with a knight to win.

My sword had not hurt the knight but it had shaken him and he stepped back to swing again. I did not want to risk another blow to my shield and so I backhanded my sword across his strike. I hit the haft of the axe and deflected it above my head. Some men wear plumes in their helmets. Had I done so then I would have lost my helmet. I punched, somewhat awkwardly, with my shield. It unbalanced him. An axe is a good weapon but it is not one which can be used quickly. My sword was a quick weapon. Even as his axe came down, I lunged at his middle. It struck metal. The knight was wearing a breastplate. The blow knocked him back and the fact that his axe was above his head gave me room. I was able to swing again. This time I aimed at his knee. He had chausse but the sword not only broke the mail and drew blood, the weight of the sword hurt his knee. I must have broken some bone. I raised my sword as he dropped to the ground. "Yield!"

His head came up as he tried to swing his axe, "Merde!" He was French and the axe was swinging towards my side. I drove my sword down between his neck and his shoulder. It was a quick death. I looked around. Tom son of Egbert had been wounded. Leaving Harry Archerson with him I ran with Sir Fótr and Sir William towards the gate. There should have been many men there for it was the key to the town. Our dual attack had split their defenders. Most were on the walls fighting our men at arms while the rest fought the fire. Sir Fótr reached the two gatemen first. He slew one and the second fled. While I watched the two of them lifted the bar. I stepped out of the way as the gates were quickly opened. King Henry, followed by his squires and household knights, with the royal banner fluttering galloped through them. Although the buildings on both sides of the main street were on fire the King did not hesitate and he led his forty men through an avenue of fire.

Sir William shook his head and said, "He is game, lord, but foolish!"

I nodded, "Aye let us save him from himself." Just then David of Wales and my archers appeared at the gate. They now had bodkin arrows nocked. "Come with me, let us save our King from himself." We hurried through the street aware of the heat from both sides. The side of the town nearest to my archers had suffered the worst damage. I could see that the far side of the town was relatively undamaged. The square around the hall was filled with those who had fled the attack and the fire.

King Henry and his knights had spread out and had lances and spears pointed at them. As we arrived, I heard him shout, "Lord Robert, your town is burning, surrender now or I will order all of your people slaughtered."

Just at that moment men arrived at the other sides of the square. The walls had fallen and with it the last chance for the people of Challans. I saw the Lord of Challans take off his helmet and then walk to the King to hand his sword over hilt first. The King retained it. He was making a point. We had won and my plan was succeeding. Any joy in our victory evaporated when William ran up to me, "Father, Sir Edward has been badly wounded. They have taken him to the King's healer. Come I beg of you for I fear he may not last." I heard the fear in his voice. I turned and ran through the burning town. Sir Edward, one of my most loyal of men, was in danger of losing his life and the King's victory seemed immaterial now!

# Chapter 9
# A Warrior's End

As soon as I saw that it was Atticus, the King's doctor, who tended to my knight my hopes rose once more. I saw that he had the clothes stripped from Sir Edward. A blade had almost severed his arm at the shoulder. I now knew why my son thought that my knight must die. I could see muscle and bone. It was hard to believe he was not dead already. Edward opened his eyes, "It seems, my lord, that my days of service to you are ended." Gilles, his squire, held his right hand.

I looked at Atticus. He said, "Do not consign yourself to the grave yet, Sir Edward. As the Earl knows I am not without skill." He turned to his assistant, "Administer the draught."

Sir Edward did not know doctors and he was suspicious. I saw the fear on his face. I smiled, "It will help you sleep, Edward. Fear not, when you awake Gilles and I will be at your side. Sleep and dream of your home."

He nodded and the assistant poured the potion down his throat. Atticus said, "And now leave me to work." I was about to protest until he said, "When I am done, I will send for you."

As I left the tent, I saw that dawn was breaking over the burning town. Sir Fótr, Sir Peter, Sir William and the rest of my men arrived. All looked concerned. "How is he?"

"Grievously wounded, Fótr, but you know Edward. He is made of English oak. I have hope. What does the King?"

Sir William said, "He is angry, lord. He has decided to punish the town. Their walls are to be razed to the ground and he has set a fortune for the ransom of Sir Robert of Challans."

In that moment I was distracted. I should have thought about the King's actions but I did not. I was too worried about Sir Edward. Sir Edward was but one man wounded and yet I forgot my duty to advise the King. Sir Hubert filled that gap. The King should have moved on. He should have headed to the next target and he did not. He vented his fury on the town. For the next few days as Sir Edward hovered between life and death, I was oblivious to the King and his decisions. The King set about destroying the town which had dared to challenge his authority. Had I been less worried about Sir Edward I might have urged him to move eleven miles down the road to the stronghold of Apremont. As it was, I spoke each day with Atticus and, when he allowed, I sat along with Gilles at Sir Edward's bedside.

On the third day I saw a little colour appear in my knight's cheeks and he asked for ale. He was asleep more than he was awake but that was as a result of the draughts Atticus gave him. The fact that he spoke raised my spirits. When I came out, leaving Giles and Sir Peter with him, I said to the doctor, "He is healed?"

"He will live if that is what you mean. That, in itself, is no mean achievement. If that had been me or the King or Sir Hubert then we would be dead, but he is a hard man and he fought for life. Healed? What do you mean by that question, Earl?"

"Will he be the same man he was before the wound?"

He shook his head, "You mean can he be a warrior?" I nodded. He shook his head. "He can never go to war again. He has no feeling at all in his left arm and shoulder. I saved his arm but it will just be a useless appendage. The muscles in his left side will atrophy and wither. His right will stay the same as it is now. Perhaps it might even grow stronger for it will have to do the work of two arms. He will grow more deformed year by year. But he will be alive. He has children?" I nodded. "Then he will be able to watch his grandchildren grow and reflect that God, and Atticus, saved him to enjoy an old age." He gave me a searching look, "That is not something you can guarantee is it, Earl?"

I smiled and gave the doctor a gold coin, "You are a wise man. Here is for your trouble."

"It was no trouble for I was doing my job but I will take it. A king's physician has an uncertain future."

"When can he travel?"

"He will go by ship?"

"Aye."

"Then another seven days but he will need company."

"Do not worry. He shall be well looked after."

There was little hurry for the King was still destroying Challans' walls three days later. I went to speak to Sir Edward and his squire. "Edward, you are to go home."

He shook his head, "When I am healed, I will return to your side. You need my right arm!"

It was bravado. Edward was no fool and he was putting on a brave face, He was deluding no one. "You are lucky to be alive. You can never use your left arm again and it will wither and hang useless from your body." I had to give him the cold truth.

"Then cut it off and strap a shield to me! Let me wear a French breastplate."

"The wound was to your upper body. You would die fighting a peasant armed with a bill hook! This is not a request. It is a command. I would have you and your men return to Stockton. I will go tomorrow and arrange a ship. You can leave your horses here for you will not need them." I turned to Gilles, "Your master is obstinate. I leave his passage in your hands."

Gilles nodded, "I will do as you say."

I nodded, "And Gilles."

"Aye, lord?"

"When I return to England you shall be dubbed. There will be a knight at Wulfestun."

When Edward smiled, I knew that he would obey me. He and Gilles had been together for some time. Edward wanted his squire to be knighted. "And my son, Henry, shall be your squire!"

I rode to St. Gilles Croix de Vie. It was a fishing port and I knew that there were no large ships there but I paid the captain of a fishing ship to sail to La Rochelle and acquire one for me. I rode back and sought out the King. He was in good humour.

"Well, Earl, we have almost finished here and then we can see about reducing Apremont." I did not think he would find it so easy for it would have been reinforced but I nodded. "And how is Sir Edward?"

"He can never fight again. I am sending him and his men home. I need a royal warrant from you, majesty, to pay for the ship."

He nodded, "See to it, de Burgh."

Hubert de Burgh was much happier as I had not been involved for some days. He actually smiled at me. He nodded, "We have made coin aplenty from the Lord of Challans. The other ransoms have arrived too."

The King seemed to approve of allowing Sir Edward's men to go home, "Good, they might as well return to England. If we can capture Apremont then we will have even more treasure."

"And this time, Earl, I will be involved in the attack."

I looked at Hubert de Burgh, he shook his head. I explained, "Perhaps, King Henry, although much of the work in a siege is done by men at arms, archers and miners."

He seemed to accept what I said although I was not sure he understood what I meant. I could see that he had yet to experience a siege. The King and his Justiciar did, at least, send half of the army to surround Apremont. We had waited longer than we had needed in my opinion, but it was too late to change things. By the time the men arrived the castle would be well stocked and defended. The ditches would have been cleared and the walls well manned.

The King's warrant helped us to pay for a good ship. It was only a few miles to the port but Sir Edward looked exhausted by the time we arrived. I slipped the captain of the vessel extra coins to ensure the comfort of my most loyal of knights. I made certain that he would be comfortable on the ship.

Sir Edward shook his head, "Lord, I am touched by this concern but I am a warrior. I must become accustomed to my wound. I am just sorry that I will no longer be able to guard your side. I have told Fótr to take on that role. He is a good knight."

I nodded, "Thank you. And I do not want you to worry about my land. If there is trouble then send to the Bishop of Durham. You and I have carried the Palatinate for many years."

"This feels like the end of a journey, lord."

"But it is not. There have been times when you have not ridden at my side. When we have conquered Poitou and Normandy then I will return home."

A frown creased his face, "You think they can be recaptured?"

"We have done well here in Poitou and Normandy is ripe for recapture. I believe I will be home by Christmas."

Sir Edward shook his head, "I doubt that, lord." His words were prophetic.

I clasped his arm for I could see that the captain was anxious to sail. I joined my men on the quay. Our servants were already moving to the new camp. I watched the cog edge out to sea and then, as the sail billowed and it headed north and west, I turned my horse and went back to the war.

As we headed north and east along the River Vie to Apremont there was a quiet air about my men. We were all close. Sir Edward had left his archers but his men at arms and his squire had been part of us. I felt emptiness as I know did my men. For myself, I had lost my Aunt and son. Edward had been one of the first men I had taken on when I had returned from the crusade. William sensed my mood. "Gilles is ready to be a knight. Alfred told me that." My head whipped around. The death of my son, although avenged, was still a raw wound. William saw my angry look and shrugged, "We should be able to talk about him. If we never mention his name then it is as though he did not exist. He did and he was a good knight. All of us miss him. I spoke to him often and he told me that Gilles ought to be a knight. Sir Edward was too comfortable with him to ask you to dub him. I do not criticise Sir Edward. It is just the way he is, sorry, was. Henry is more than ready to be a squire and Gilles will be a good teacher."

I nodded. William was right. I smiled to show that my anger was forgotten, "And is this your way of asking to be knighted?"

"I am too inexperienced for that. This campaign has shown me my shortcomings. I am getting better and I believe that before too long my sword and I will be used. My mettle will be tested. I am content." I could have knighted him there and then for his mature words showed me that he was ready.

I had known that Apremont would be a hard nut to crack. As we neared it the difficulty of an assault crystallised in my mind. The castle walls rose above the river on a rocky outcrop. Just ninety paces from the river there was no opportunity to use either a ram or to mine. Sir William had been lord of La Lude before he had come to England. He shook his head as we saw the walls, towers and turrets manned with armed men. "This will be a long siege, lord. How do we take it?"

"The hard way. The only flat ground is by the river. We have to build towers and drag them close to the walls."

Sir William pointed to the skies which threatened rain. "Soon the rains will come and we will not be able to push the towers into place."

I nodded glumly, "And that is why I wanted the King to come sooner." I spied the royal standard. He had occupied a farm which lay just four hundred paces to the west of the castle. He and his knights would be comfortable. They had a table outside the farm and were drinking the farmer's wine. They produced rough wine in this land but it was drinkable. I saw the Justiciar and his clerk going over parchments. Hubert de Burgh was no warrior but he could make numbers go to war!

The King greeted me, "Well Earl, what is your plan?"

I saw that his household knights and those closest to him, Gilbert de Clare and his son Richard, the Earl of Norfolk and his sons Hugh and Roger and Humphrey de Bohun all turned their gaze to me. It was as though I was some sort of lucky token. I sighed, "As you can see, King Henry, they have fortified their castle well. We will need to hew trees and build two towers there, by the base of the castle. I would build them here but the ground is too boggy. I will have to walk the ground to determine the best place to build them."

Richard de Clare said, "But the towers would be built within range of their crossbows."

"Aye, and to protect the builders we will need to build pavise. Those willows by the river's edge will be perfect."

Roger Bigod's face fell, "But that will take many days!"

I did not mention that the King and his army had sat and watched as Challans' walls were pulled down. They had wasted the days we might have used. The King asked, "What do my knights do while our men toil?"

The King still had much to learn. I saw Hubert de Burgh lift his head as the question was asked. I gave him an answer. "The land to the east of us is still full of Poitevin rebels. It seems to me, King Henry, that your knights could ride and subjugate them. I am guessing that the ones who vehemently oppose England will either be within Apremont's walls or with Hugh de Lusignan. If you and your knights could ensure the loyalty of those close to us then when the enemy brings his army west, we would have both warning and support."

Sir Hubert asked, "And you are convinced that he will come? So far he has not."

"Had we attacked Apremont sooner then he would have come already. This is his last western stronghold. Autumn is upon us and he needs the food that this region provides. He has no ports now to supply him with fish. He cannot trade without ports. He will come. First, King Henry, why not ask the lord of Apremont to surrender?"

The King laughed, "What would I do without you, Sir Thomas? Such an obvious strategy! After our victory at Challans then he may well be willing to surrender. Come, Sir Thomas, you and I will ride forth."

"Do you need me, my liege?"

"No, Sir Hubert. Count your numbers!" The King laughed as he spoke.

With our squires, banners and heralds we rode through the village to the gate. We had to ride up a cobbled road to reach the gatehouse. All the way we were under the gaze of the defenders. It would be impossible to attack and not suffer a large number of casualties. Even the King saw the dilemma. "This is a well-built castle."

"Aye lord. It might be possible to march the army all the way around the castle and attack the gatehouse but those towers," I pointed, as we approached them, "would be able to decimate the men we sent. We need to have men at arms and archers here to prevent a sortie but the two wooden towers would be the safest method of attack."

He nodded. We stopped before the gates and his herald shouted, "King Henry of England, the rightful lord of Poitou, demands to speak with the Lord of Apremont."

A figure appeared and took off his helmet. The knight had a grey beard. "I am Lord Fulk of Apremont. You have come a little late, King Henry. Had you come when the French first began to make their inroads into your land then I might have fought at your side. Now it is too little and too late. The French are here in our lands and they can bring greater numbers than you. England has civil disorder at home. Your borders are threatened. I am sorry, King Henry, but I must decline. Hugh de Lusignan is coming and he has an army which will sweep you back to the sea. I hope there is someone in England who can pay ransom for you!"

I saw the King colour. He did not like to be spoken to in this manner and yet the Lord of Apremont had spoken reasonably. He had not insulted as had the Lord of Challans. The King showed his immaturity by reacting. "You know what we did to Challans when it opposed us?"

He nodded and said, calmly, "Yes, King Henry, and we have many of those who fled Challans in these walls. They will fight even harder this time. The Earl of Cleveland will not be able to slip over these walls at night. Nor will you be able to pull down these walls. We are embedded in the rock of the land. We have a well and our cellars are full. Do your worst, King Henry, but we will not surrender."

As we rode back the King was despondent. I tried to put a brave face on it. "It was to be expected, King Henry and we learned much."

"Did we?"

"The Poitevin are coming. If you raid to the east you will find them but more disturbing was the comment about civil disorder and our borders. Are the Welsh and Scots taking advantage of your absence?"

He showed his naïvety in shaking his head and saying, "They would not dare!" There was little point in arguing with him.

While my knights and I, along with most of the men at arms, began to construct first pavise and then towers, Robert of Derby took his men and they camped close to the main gatehouse. The King and the rest of the knights rode forth each day. It was a glorified chevauchée. They rode as far north as the Loire. Brittany was an ally and King Henry returned feeling self-satisfied for all the manors he had passed had sworn allegiance to him. He rode east to Les Essarts and received the same welcome. Gradually, as September passed, he rode further afield and we toiled, building the towers. The other men at arms took their lead from my men. It was not glorious work but it was necessary. Our archers kept the crossbows on the walls silent and we worked each day, knights and men at arms to build the towers. I had walked the land, during the night, and realised that we would need to make a roadway of logs along which we could roll the towers so that they were close enough to the walls for an assault. I sent Sir Peter, along with his father, to ride further afield and hew logs.

I went, with Sir Fótr and Sir William, to scout out the land around Apremont. I did not ride as far as the King and his men but I looked at the ground. I was seeking a good site on which to fight a battle. The Lord of Poitou would come. We had bloodied his nose too many times for him to ignore us. I found what I was looking for on the second day. I stored the information. I returned to the siege. I made sure that I rode around the walls at least once a day to let them know I was still there. My name still induced fear and respect. The words of the Lord of Apremont told me that

We had two days of rain. The rain confirmed that the ground would be too wet to support the weight and movement of the two towers. I was glad that we had already cut the wood for the roadway. We had almost finished them by the time we were in the last week of September. We were heading back to the farm, having left men to watch the towers, when the King and his knights rode in. I saw that some of them sported wounds. What had happened?

Sir Hubert also looked concerned as the King threw himself from his horse. "Hugh de Lusignan comes! He has an army. We ran into his scouts and were bloodied!"

Gilbert de Clare shook his head, "Had we had scouts then we might not have lost Sir Ralph and Sir Harold!"

King Henry whipped his head around, "If I had had the men of Cleveland then we might have destroyed the enemy, Earl!" It was a petulant outburst which hearkened back to the old Henry.

"How many men do we face?" I saw that no one had thought to count for they all had the same blank look. "Where did you see them?"

Gilbert de Clare said, "On the road to Chantonnay, about eighteen to twenty miles from here."

I nodded, "They will camp. Mordaf!"

My archer ran up, "Aye lord?"

"Take your brother and four archers. Ride east until you see the campfires of the enemy. Discover their numbers. I need an accurate account!"

"Aye lord."

I turned to the King. I could see he was still thinking of the two lost knights. He needed to focus on the greater threat. "King Henry, we cannot fight the enemy here. We need to be between Apremont and the enemy. We need to choose the battlefield rather than allowing our enemies to do so."

"What? Yes, you are right. Where do you suggest?"

"North and east of here, about three miles from the gates of the castle, the Boulogne and Vie rivers meet. The ground is boggy there. The main road and the bridge from the east pass that place. We hold them there. One flank is protected by the river. We embed stakes on the other side. We can use the timber we cut to make the wooden road."

"But have we time?"

"If we leave now, we have. We leave some men watching the gate and the rest of the army moves to the confluence of the two rivers."

The Earl of Norfolk said, "Our men are tired, Your Majesty. Let us wait until the morning when they are fresh!"

The King looked at me and I answered for him, "If we wait until the morning then we lose the battle and we lose all that we have gained. We move now or we go home!"

The King nodded, "The Earl is right. Break camp and let us move!"

# Chapter 10
# The Battle of La Vie

The river was fuller than when I had last visited and the boggy area larger. The rains had done that. Nature was helping us. It was getting on for dark when we arrived but I had had all my archers and men at arms each carry two of the stakes. While the ground was soft, we drove them into the ground. We would have time enough on the next day to sharpen them. The King and his knights were slow to arrive. My men had chosen the best area for our camp. We were already cooking our food when they arrived. The King's tent had just been erected when Mordaf and his men rode in. They had with them six spare horses.

"Lord," they bowed to the King, "Your Majesty, there are four hundred knights just six miles east of here. They have with them over a thousand men."

I saw the King's face fall. I shook my head, "Many of those, King Henry, will be servants. They will be men without armour. Are there French knights with them, Mordaf?"

"I saw ten French banners, lord."

I nodded, "And scouts?"

He chuckled, "They sent ten men to scout the land to the west. The ten now lie dead. The four horses we could not recapture will have told the enemy that their scouts failed."

"And their purses?"

"Their livery and their purses told us that they were the men of Apremont and Poitiers."

Hubert de Burgh looked the most worried of all. He shook his head, "King Henry, those odds are too great. If we lose and you are captured then the ransom would lose us not only Poitou but Gascony too. It is not worth the risk."

I saw the King vacillating. The encounter with the advance guard of the Poitevin army had shaken his confidence. It had not surprised me. The advance guard would not be knights. They would be the hardened men at arms and mercenaries. Scouting was one of the things they did the best. "Sir Hubert, why do you think we cannot win?"

"They outnumber us!"

I nodded, "Mordaf, how many archers did you see?"

"Archers lord? Proper archers such as you command, none. They had some of the levy with hunting bows but not above twenty. The hundred crossbows they had were the only ones with missiles."

"There, King Henry, you know our archers. If the French advance with crossbows then my men will win the duel. If they bring their knights and men at arms then the ground, our stakes and our archers will thin them so that when we meet them, they will be defeated. We need courage and we need to fight dismounted at first. Let us make them waste their animals in a fruitless attack. When the time is ripe, we mount our animals and we charge. We will have fresh horses and unbroken spears."

While I was with the King, he was positive. When he was with Sir Hubert, he was hesitant. I won the day and he nodded. "We will fight as the Earl suggests and my banner shall be at the centre."

I called over Ridley. "Have stakes embedded before us. Seed the ground with caltrops but leave us four avenues for our men to use. I want to slow the enemy and not stop them. We will be using our horses when the enemy have tired."

"Aye lord."

I went to speak with the most important men who would be fighting the next day, the archers. David of Wales was the Captain of all of the archers. I took David and his lieutenants to the stakes. "This is where you will be. You will guard the flank and you will attack the enemy. If crossbows come, then kill them. If not then then take out their horsemen."

"Aye lord. We will sharpen the stakes and foul them too."

The last ones I visited were the squires and the servants. We had a large horse herd. to protect and the squires had to be ready to fetch our horses when I asked for them. I spoke directly to the squires, "My squire, William, will be the only squire on the battle line. Even the King's squires will be waiting with the horses. When I give the command then William will come to fetch you. The horses must be ready and saddled. Spears and lances must be brought with them. Once they are brought then the squires will form a third rank behind the men at arms. The squires will have to fight as men on the morrow." I looked at their eyes in the light from the camp fire. "Can you do this?"

They all shouted, "Aye lord!"

"And you servants will bear arms. If the enemy try to come to take our horses then it will be up to you to stop them! I promise you that when we win all of you will be rewarded. You have my word!" That brought another cheer.

As we headed to our tent William said, "Can you promise that, father?"

"I have said it and it will be so! If the coin counter objects then I will pay it from my own purse. All who fight for us should be rewarded. That is only right and proper."

Before I retired, I spoke with the King. He needed to know the whole plan. My three knights knew it but the others would have to wait until the battle began. I could tell that the King was still affected by the loss of his knights. "What if there is not a battle tomorrow, Earl?"

"If there is not then it means the Poitevin lords have accepted your rule and do not wish to dispute it."

He gave a sad smile, "And that will not happen."

"No. The rebels have been gathering their army so that when the battle came, they would win. They have gathered what they believe to be overwhelming numbers. They hope that overwhelming numbers will prevail. They will not. We must be steadfast tomorrow and endure their attack. We fight on foot. I wish them to think we doubt our horses. We do not!"

"I am resolved."

"One more thing, we plant our standards behind us. I need the squires to be ready to bring our horses."

"But that means we do not retreat."

"If we retreat, King Henry, then we have lost Poitou. If we flee then Lord Fulk will sally forth and we will be trapped. We throw the dice, Your Majesty. We win or we lose. There is nothing half way."

He nodded, "I guess that I now know what it is to be a King."

"It is what your uncle, grandfather and great grandfather did. It is what helped them to build an Empire."

"You did not mention my father."

I looked at him, "If you want lies then ask another to advise you. I cannot. I only know how to speak the truth. It may be unpalatable but that is my way."

"You are uncompromising."

"My liege I had everything taken from me by your father and I had to fight to regain it yet I never betrayed my king. How many other men may say the same?" I stood, "Now I must sleep and, King Henry, have both your sword and dagger sharpened for tomorrow. I would say spear too but I fear you have not yet learned that skill."

He smiled, "I thought I had learned all to be a knight but this campaign shows me that I am lacking many skills. It is good that you are by my side. I feel we can win so long as your hand is on the tiller!"

I knelt, that night, and said my prayers. The King had vacillated. Had he not done so then Apremont might now be in our hands and it would be the Lord of Poitou who would be having to waste men attacking a town's walls. When the people of Challans had fled to Apremont, that had been the time to attack when those inside would have been fearful. Hugh de Lusignan had sent a message to Lord Fulk and he knew that help was coming. On such knife edges are countries won and lost. I prayed for my King and I prayed for my own lands. I prayed that Sir Edward would arrive home safely and enjoy the peace he deserved with his family. I was not hopeful that my land would enjoy peace.

I was awake before dawn. I made water and then walked to the sentries. They bowed their heads, "Earl!"

"Any sign of the enemy?"

"No, lord." It was Will son of Robin who commanded the sentries. "They are confident; too confident. Mordaf told me that when he saw them, they were laughing and joking. They think we are led by an untried King and that we are few in number."

"You are not afraid?"

"Lord, you lead us! If I was the enemy, I would have already filled my breeks. We have arrows and the ground betwixt us is treacherous. They could have four times the number and I would not fear." I nodded, "But lord?"

"Yes Will?"

"I tire of this land. Let us defeat them and go home. I miss Brigid's ale!" I laughed. They were in good spirits.

I went to the knights of Chester. They were awake. I spoke with their leader, Sir Roger Montmorency. He was an experienced knight but he tended to look out for himself. "Earl, when we attack I would have you ride to my right and lead that half of the battle."

"Aye Sir Thomas."

"I wish you to restrain the King. He will be keen to get to grips with the enemy."

He shook his head, "They would chew him up and spit him out."

"I know. Let me hit the line first."

He nodded, "Rather you than me!" The knight was no coward but his avowed aim was self-preservation. On this day that would suit me.

I went to the fire and, while warming myself, took some stale bread and ham from Ridley the Giant. "Are you sure about just using knights, lord? I am unhappy that you are leaving us to hold the line."

"I am more worried about the lack of men at arms. You will protect the baggage and the horses. If my plan goes awry, we will have somewhere we can retreat to. You will be the wall of shields and spears upon which the enemy will break."

He nodded, "We will stand. I can swear to that."

"Get the men ready. We all know how slow lords are to rise!"

By dawn the men at arms and archers were in position. I had mounted Blaze and I had ridden, with William, to examine the ground over which the rebels and the French would come. It was muddy and slippery. The ground did not suck at their feet but they would not travel as fast as they might have liked. Had I had time I would have put logs in the river to dam it but I was content. They could not gallop and the canter would enable my archers to reap a happy harvest! I saw no sign of the enemy. Mordaf and his archers had made them overly cautious. When they arrived, the knights would discover that the ground was not as they might have hoped. Dawn broke over our backs as we passed through the safe avenues in the stakes. They were not a barrier. They were an inconvenience. Some knights would have little to slow them but others would and they would arrive piecemeal. That was what I wanted.

The King was ready and armed. Even Hubert de Burgh was ready but I could see, from his face, that he wished himself anywhere but here. "Have you eaten, my liege?"

"I am too excited!"

I shook my head and dismounted, "You must eat! Come I have had but a little to eat. If we are to hew Poitevin heads we need strength. Fetch us ale and meat. A man needs meat if he is to fight!"

I saw that Hubert de Burgh looked pale. It was good that I was with the King or else his counter of numbers would have found a reason to absent himself and the King! The King had eaten by the time William returned. He had spears with him. One was a thrusting spear and the other two were throwing spears. I had charged Estonians who liked to throw spears. They were an effective weapon against horses.

The King had chosen his coterie of household knights to surround himself. I was not offended. A man always fought better with men he was comfortable with. I had Ridley and his son, Sir Peter, on my left. Sir William and Sir Fótr were on my right. Padraig and the rest of my men at arms were also in the front rank. The second rank was made up of the men at arms of my knights. The squires were the third rank.

The enemy appeared at noon. They had waited. They were probably hoping that the ground would dry. They were mistaken. They did not come to talk. They came to fight. I saw the banner of the Count d'Eu. He and Hugh de Lusignan were coming for the King and I. I studied their battle line. They had compromised. Fifty crossbowmen preceded them. Had they sent them all then the end might have been different but fifty was too small number. I knew, without looking, that David of Wales would have readied his men. A crossbowman tells the world that he is about to release his weapon. He stops and he pulls back the string, slowly. As soon as they stopped and placed their feet on the crossbows to draw back the cord, I heard David shout, "Release!" Some of the crossbowmen were struck by three arrows. All were hit and either died or crawled back to the waiting knights. My men cheered. The men at arms began banging their shields. We had won the opening encounter.

Sir Fótr said, "Lord, what would you do in this situation?"

"You mean if I was the Lord of Poitou?"

"Aye lord."

"I would send men across the river and behind us." He nodded. "But if I led my men then I would send David of Wales and his archers. By now this would be a charnel house! I am just grateful they only have crossbows. Now that fifty lie dead and wounded the other crossbowmen will be reluctant to attack. We have a chance!"

The Lusignans began to form their men. They had dismounted men at arms. They formed a solid phalanx. I saw that they were making a mailed and shielded block to negate the effect of our arrows. The one hundred or so men began to march towards us. I saw that they would have few casualties. My archers' arrows found shields. One or two of the men at arms were hit and wounded but it would not stop them. However, the boots of so many men merely churned up the ground even more. The central pathway to our lines would be a muddy morass. A second disadvantage was that they only had a twenty-man frontage. They were coming for me! The knights would want to capture the King and hold England to ransom. Hugh de Lusignan would try to eliminate the Earl of Cleveland. The lords I had defeated would have told him of my prowess. By killing me he would make it easier for his knights to win the battle and the war.

"They come for us! The rest, hold your positions and do not get drawn in."

The King was young and if he and his youthful household knights attacked the enemy flank and lost their cohesion, then the Poitevin knights would attack them. I hefted the throwing spear. The solid block of mail could not negotiate the stakes easily. They had to break ranks. David of Wales and his archers hit and killed four men at arms who exposed their chests. Then the phalanx passed too close to us for the archers to have an effect. They resorted to sending arrows into the legs of the men at arms. I pulled back and threw my spear at the man at arms in the centre of the line. He had stepped to the side to go around the stake. My spear hit him in the side. Ridley the Giant did even better. He hurled his throwing spear so hard that the head was completely embedded in the body of a man at arms. He fell and exposed the man behind. Sir Peter's spear took him. For the Poitevin men at arms this was a disaster. It was like a piece of cloth which is torn. The split grew as men in the centre fell and more spears hit bodies. The twenty-man wide phalanx was now two smaller phalanxes and one was just six men wide. My second spear was thrown when they were ten paces from us and about to charge. The man had an open face helmet and my spear went into his mouth and emerged from the back of his head. He fell forward and I picked up my spear and braced it against my foot.

The line hit us piecemeal. The man I faced had an arrow in his leg. He must have been on the right flank of the phalanx. He lunged at me with his spear. I blocked it with my shield as a second man at arms fell against my spear head. I know not if he slipped, tripped or was pushed but the spear was driven into his side by the weight of the press of men. I dropped my spear and drew my sword. The man at arms I fought tried to pull his arm back to spear me but the press of men behind was too great. We were so close that my sword sawed across his open mouth. He tried to pull away but could not. I pushed harder and my edge caught an artery. Spouting blood, he fell backwards.

The phalanx was now just sixty or so men at arms trying to get at us over dead bodies and the bloody mud which had been trampled over by those who had already died. A man at arms held his thrusting spear overhand and threw it. Had it hit me then I would have been killed or badly wounded. I saw it coming and my shield came up to block it. The spear hit it and the missile fell to earth. He drew his sword and ran at me. A big man, he held his sword in the air to smite my head. I did the unexpected. I held up my shield and dropped to one knee. I drove my sword up and under his hauberk as his sword smashed into my shield. My blade drove deep inside his body. His feral scream filled the air. It was almost a signal for the others. They began to fall back. The men were professionals and held up their shields above their heads. David of Wales and his archers thinned their ranks so that only twenty odd men reached their own lines unscathed. The rest dragged their bodies back. The first attack had failed. I looked down the line. Walter son of Edwin lay dead. I saw that there were men at arms I did not know in the front rank. My men had suffered wounds.

I stepped forward to retrieve my spear. I lifted the mask on my helmet and shouted, "Now they will send their horses. Be steadfast! For God, King Henry and England!"

The cry was taken up along the line and amongst the squires and servants, "For God, King Henry and England!"

It must have reached the ears of the Lusignans. A horn sounded and the line of three hundred knights began to advance. I saw that the Count d'Eu and Hugh de Lusignan had retained the last one hundred knights as a reserve. The ones who advanced were led by a French standard. I vaguely recognised it as one I had seen in Paris. It was a quartered fleur de lys. As I had expected they came more cautiously for they had a littered battlefield to negotiate. The French knights who were in the front rank had horses with plate and mail. I had no doubt that some of the knights had breastplates too. They might well survive my archers' arrows. There were twenty dead men at arms before us. They were an obstacle. The King had no such obstacle before him. I saw that four of his young knights were protecting his front.

When the line was two hundred paces from us, they began to gallop. Despite the horse armour and the breastplates my archers were felling knights. Their thighs only had mail hauberks. Horses' legs had neither mail nor plate. When horses fell, they made others swerve. The line began to change into an arrow and it was aimed at the King. I had made all of the lords plant their standards. They could not flee. William was still behind me. I turned, "Watch the King and if he is danger then tell me!"

"Aye father."

I turned my attention back to the line. I saw that the knights who were heading for the King were from Poitou. We would face the French. They reached the first of the stakes and the horsemen successfully negotiated them. They had to slow slightly and I saw arrows blossom from shields, arms and legs. The horsemen came on. I saw that the knight with the quartered fleur de lys had his horse covered in mail. He was heading for Ridley the Giant who was also closer to the King than was I. The French knight who came at me had a mail hood on his horse. The chest was exposed. I saw the rider pull back his lance. This was what I had been trained to do all those years ago before I had gone on crusade. I had to do two things at once. My left arm and shield would block the lance while I drove the spear into the chest of the horse with the snapping jaws which was galloping towards me. The lance was longer than my spear and would hit me first. The punch was powerful. I was watching the horse and did not see the spear as it shattered and splintered on my shield. It drove my left arm back but I held. I lunged up and into the horse's chest. I missed the chest and struck the throat. The weight of the horse drove the spear into its skull and the beast died instantly. It fell backwards and toppled on to the legs of the French knight.

All around me my knights and men at arms were stabbing with spear and shield at the horses. Glancing towards the King I saw that Ridley the Giant was wielding a two-handed axe. He looked like a Viking of old. Even as I looked, I saw the axe head smash into the mail protecting the horse's skull. Even mail cannot stop an axe. The horse fell and Ridley, with the joy of battle upon him, leapt onto the dying horse and brought his axe across the knight's head. Beyond him I saw that two of the knights protecting the King had fallen but his banner stood and he was using his sword.

I stepped over the horse and placed my sword at the French knight's throat, "Yield or die!"

"I yield."

Ridley had picked up the head of the dead French knight. I recognised it as Guy de Senonche. It was the Count of Pontoise's Captain. I had last seen him in Évreux. Ridley roared a primeval scream and it had the effect of making the French knights stop. They saw the head of their leader and the rest of their dead comrades. They turned and fled. The Poitevin knights began to follow. We had broken their attack. As the horsemen streamed back to the Poitevin lines I said, "William, fetch the horses!" After he had run off, I shouted, "Ridley, you madman, regain your senses and take charge of the men at arms!"

He grinned and hurled the head towards the retreating horsemen, "Aye lord. The madness is gone!"

The squires had been ready with the horses and we were soon mounted. William handed me the spear and I moved into the muddy, staked ground. The retreating knights were approaching the standard of Hugh de Lusignan. We would be well outnumbered but I was counting on the fact that they would not expect us to charge. We passed through the safe avenues of the stakes. The King was surrounded by his household knights. I was pleased that de Clare and the Earl of Norfolk were with him. I would be leading the charge and I could not afford to worry about the King. My three knights appeared next to me and then Robert of Derby and his knights. We would be the front rank. I led my ragged line through the stakes and then formed up on the unencumbered ground. The Poitevin rebels had chosen a dry area upon which to form. It was uphill from us. The King and his knights formed to our right. I lifted my visor, "Your Majesty, place yourself in the second rank!"

He shook his head, "I will lead my men!"

I nudged Lion over towards him and spoke quietly, "King Henry, you have asked me to advise you. We are taking on more than twice our number. The men who are in the front rank need to be knights who have experience of a charge. Have you had experience?" He shook his head. "Then be led by me. I go to end this rebellion in one swift strike. I cannot be worrying about you. Follow the knights of Cheshire, they are steady."

"Very well, Sir Thomas."

I rode back. The knights had formed up. I saw that Hugh de Lusignan was busy trying to organize his men. He would have been better using his fresh knights to charge us. I pointed my spear and spurred Lion. The men of Cheshire and the King would have one flank protected by the river and the other by me. My archers would be moving up to give us support on my left. They were light on their feet and if the charge went badly, they could escape back to the thick line of stakes. When we were two hundred paces from them the enemy line began to move towards us. Some horses were fresh and some were blown. It was a ragged line. Riding fresh horses and with men who had fought together, the sixty knights I led were boot to boot. I saw that the standards of their leaders were not moving. They were awaiting the outcome. As we closed with the enemy line, I spurred Lion. He leapt forward. Sir William and my other two knights were a heartbeat behind. Now it did not matter for I was charging a fresh knight. He had been in the reserve. His horse was ahead of his peers. He had a lance and I could see that it was wavering. I held my spear a third of the way down. It moved less but he would have first strike. His spear shattered on my shield and I lunged with my spear. It slid over his cantle and below his shield. The spear broke his mail and entered his flesh. He started to tumble from his horse and I pulled my spear out before it could be dragged from my hand. I saw a gap ahead of me. Sir William speared one of the riders who was mounted on a blown horse and Sir Peter unhorsed another. With Sir Fótr, the four of us had broken through their line. I could leave Sir Robert to lead the rest of the knights.

I rode directly for leaders of the rebellion. William was still with me. He knew enough to keep well back. The three knights were surrounded by pages, squires and heralds. They were not warriors. They were so preoccupied with King Henry that they did not see us approaching until a squire shouted a warning. The three of them should have charged us but they did not. They turned to flee. Their squires and pages bravely rode towards us. They were riding palfreys and had no spears. I knocked a squire to the ground as Lion lunged at another squire's horse. It fled. Lion was a powerful horse and he had the smell of battle in his nostrils. He began to gain on the three knights. Behind me I heard the clash of steel as the battle raged on. I glanced around and saw William engaging another of the Poitevin squires. The Lusignan standard had fled the field and I knew that the heart would have been torn from the Poitevin knights and their allies. Hugh de Lusignan and the Count d'Eu headed due east and I followed them. I heard a horse behind me. At least one of my knights had kept close to me.

We had passed through the enemy camp. Already the servants were fleeing. They could see that the battle was lost. They would be pilfering from their lords and taking all that they could carry. I saw the Count d'Eu turn. He must have realised there were just two knights who were following him. He and Hugh de Lusignan turned and rode back towards us. I glanced behind and saw that Sir Peter was twenty paces from me and William was a further thirty paces back. The two leaders thought to defeat us piecemeal. I did not falter and rode directly at Hugh de Lusignan. His lance had a gonfanon on the end. Lion was still galloping and I held my shield across my body. I had to cover both lances. The gonfanon made it easy to see the end of the lance of Hugh de Lusignan. The Count de Eu rammed his lance at me. It glanced off the angle of the wood and slid up my shield. The lance broke as the wooden end broke off. The tip embedded itself in my shoulder. I ignored the pain as Hugh de Lusignan's lance hit my shield in the middle. It shattered and I hit his shield with my spear. The strike was so hard that my spear broke and I unhorsed the Poitevin leader. I was wheeling Lion around and drawing my sword even as the Count d'Eu turned to strike at my wounded left arm. Gritting my teeth, I brought up my shield. I could feel blood running down my arm. Sir Peter was almost with us. I brought my sword from on high and hit the Count's shield. I stood in my stirrups as he reeled from the blow and brought my sword down again. He must have feared Sir Peter arriving on his sword side for he tried to turn his horse. I managed to hit his back. It arced and he tumbled from his horse. I dismounted and ran to him as he lay on the ground. I lifted my face mask. "Surrender!"

He looked up at my face as I undid the ventail. His eyes widened, "You! You were a spy!"

"Do you yield or shall I kill you?"

"I yield!"

Sir Peter dismounted, "Watch this one." I hurried over to Hugh de Lusignan. He was still. I took his sword and then took off his helmet. His eyes opened, "You, my lord, are my prisoner! Your rebellion is over! You have lost!"

# Chapter 11
# Homecoming

My capture of the two leaders effectively ended the war. Apremont surrendered when we took the two of them to the castle. King Henry did not wait one day. He rode east, with the bulk of the army, to Poitiers. With so many prisoners there was no opposition left. We had captured over a hundred knights and he rode in triumph into the capital of Poitou. I saw nothing of this for I was left in Apremont with my knights and with the wounded. The splintered lance had given me a serious wound. Atticus spent almost half a day picking out the tiny shards and splinters of wood. I did not mind the time it took. I wanted to retain my arm.

Lord Fulk was a good host. I suspect part of it was that he knew they had lost and wished to have one less enemy. "I thought, Sir Thomas, that you would have been defeated. When I saw how few knights you had I expected the King to negotiate a surrender."

"My archers and men at arms are the equal of any knight."

He nodded, "And now the rebellion is over. What next for this young King whom we have underestimated?"

I did not answer. The King was keen to retake Normandy. We could take it but he would need to use the knights of Poitou and first they had to pay their ransom. The French knights would also need to be ransomed. All of that would take time. I doubted that we could begin the attack until December. While we might not campaign in England during December, this was France and we could. I would not be home for Christmas. I wondered how Sir Edward fared.

I was summoned ten days after the battle. I had healed and Atticus had left the wounded to return to the King's side. We rode through black rain clouds and an autumnal storm which reminded me of England. My men had all done well out of the battle. They did not have the ransom we knights enjoyed but the breastplates, mail, swords and helmets were all taken. Some would be sold and some would be used. Purses had been lifted. Coursers, destrier and palfreys had been taken. They were content. We had lost just two men killed although many had been wounded. I was pleased that we would not need to fight until December. My archers had recovered and repaired many arrows. We were still a potent force.

The victory had done wonders for the King. He looked more confident and he greeted me warmly. Even the Justiciar, Hubert de Burgh, looked pleased to see me. I was given a private audience with the two of them. The King looked pleased with himself, "Hugh de Lusignan has sworn not to rebel again. My mother has promised to watch over my interests too."

"Do you believe her?"

"She is my mother!"

"And she did nothing to stop her husband taking your land, King Henry. What makes you think she has changed? Until you marry and have children, King Henry, then the Lusignans will remain a threat."

He seemed to ignore my comment, "We have taken a great deal of ransom. You will be a rich man and the ransom will ensure that they do not rebel again."

I nodded, "That may be but you need to find employment for the swords of Poitou. Take Normandy now while victory is fresh in the nostrils of your men."

Hubert de Burgh shook his head, "Let us recover fully. The weather will be more clement in March. That is the season to campaign."

King Henry said, "Perhaps Sir Thomas is correct. The ransoms hurt the French knights more than the Poitevin." He laughed, "Raoul de Lusignan is less than happy with you, Sir Thomas. He says you lack honour for you went under a false name."

I shook my head, "I take that from no man. I will challenge him!"

"Too late, my lord, he had his ransom paid and he is now back in Eu."

"All the more reason to attack Normandy! He will help the Normans to resist us. We should strike now!"

"Perhaps in a week. By then all of the ransoms will have been paid." He saw my sling. "And how is the arm?"

"It aches but you have a good healer."

"I will think on these matters. I will make my decision in the next day or two."

I was dismissed and he and Hubert de Burgh returned to the finances of Poitou. The war had to be paid for and Poitou had lost. The land would pay. With little to do we purchased a wagon to take our treasure back to England when we returned. We had chests of coins, mail, weapons and armour. We would need to carry it with us or send it back to England. Richard son of Ralph would not be able to fight for some time. A sword had broken his leg. I planned on sending him back to England, with some servants.

As all of his knights were now in Poitiers the King held a celebratory feast. He called it the feast of peace and it was more about the reunification of his lands rather than our victory of arms. Hugh de Lusignan found time to speak with me. He and his wife, King Henry's mother, took me to one side as the table was laid with food and wine. The King was with his young knights, Hugh, Roger, Humphrey and Richard de Clare. They had grown closer as a result of the battle. "Sir Thomas, you are a fine leader. Would you accept the command of the armies of Poitou?"

"I am honoured that you would choose me, lord, but I only serve here until Normandy is in the King's hands."

"Then command them in Normandy." He shook his head, "Raoul thought he had the beating of you but you outwitted him. I would be happier if you commanded our warriors in Normandy. If we can regain that land then mine will be safer."

"In which case I will command but only until Normandy is in the King's hands once more."

They both looked relieved. The Queen said, "My son is lucky to have you at his side and I confess he has shown that he can be a leader. I feared that de Burgh and the papal delegate would rule the land and I did not want that. When he rid himself of our friend, des Roches the Bishop of Winchester, I feared the worst."

It crossed my mind that she had abandoned her son a little too hastily. I did not totally agree with the regents but at least they had stood by him. "He is learning and soon he will have attained his majority."

The Lord of Poitou put his arm around my shoulder, "Your strategy to take the coast and starve us was an act of genius. Where did you learn to lead?"

I told him of my life as a sword for hire. I saw that he was impressed. He looked at his wife and said, "Your husband received better service from his lord than the injustice he administered."

"John was like that. He could be petulant and petty. It is fortunate that you put England first."

Three days after the feast a rider came from Royan. He had a leather pouch with letters for the King. They came from Richard Marshal, the new Earl of Pembroke. When I was summoned within moments of the arrival of the messenger, I knew there was trouble at home. The King looked concerned, "The Welsh and the Scots have risen and decided to cause mischief along the borders. The Bishop of Durham and the Lord Marshal have asked for my help."

I nodded, "The absence of the English King normally makes our neighbours more active."

He nodded and looked at de Burgh, "My Justiciar and I are of the same mind. We would send Gilbert de Clare to aid Richard Marshal but I would have you rouse the north and send Alexander's dogs back home."

I was relieved and worried at the same time. I would be going home but what of the King? "And you, King Henry, what of you?"

"Now that I have the armies of Poitou, we will retake Normandy. I am confident that we have learned enough from you to be able to defeat the rebels. The Duke of Brittany is keen to help us. With three armies then the rebels will soon rejoin the fold."

I was not convinced, especially after what I had learned in Paris, but I could not leave the north to the wild Scots. "In which case, King Henry, we will leave immediately."

"I will send a royal warrant to you before you leave. I give you total power to do as you see fit. The north must be kept safe. Do not worry, Sir Thomas, the Justiciar and myself are more than capable of handling Normandy." I nodded. He turned to a servant and took out a locket. "It may be that you have to speak with King Alexander. If you do then give this to my little sister, Joan. Give her my best wishes."

I took the locket and left. I confess I was distracted. I worried more about my home than Normandy and, in the long run, that proved a mistake. I did what I felt was right.

My men did not take long to prepare to leave. Most had families at home and they were desperate to defend our land. I had read the letter from the Earl of Pembroke three or four times. It was annoyingly lacking in details. The Scots had a ninety-mile border. The Palatinate had castles along its length. Any one of them could have suffered an attack. I was just happy that I had left most of my knights in the valley. They would be safe from the ravaging Scots.

William showed his maturity. He had grown into the role of squire. He organized everything. He had servants for the horses and packed all of our treasures. Within a year or two he would be ready to dub. I would have to look around for a second squire. William had helped Alfred before I had given my eldest son his spurs. William even managed to purchase some firkins of wine. We had long ago lost our source of wine from La Flèche. Unlike Sir Edward we needed berths for our horses. That meant two ships. Had it not been for the royal warrant we might have struggled. The warrant greased the wheels of commerce. As we watched the animals being boarded, I spoke with the constable of Royan. He could not stop smiling. "I confess, Sir Thomas, that I feared our young King might not be able to handle the Poitevin but he has won a great victory. This bodes well for us. When he takes Normandy, we will prosper once more."

I nodded, "I hope so."

As we sailed to England, I reflected that all believed he had won a great victory. With a couple of skirmishes and one decisive battle King Henry had wrested back Poitou from the rebels. I remembered the barons I had met like the Counts of Pontoise and Eu. They would be seeking a way to stop King Henry. Both had a vested interest in keeping Normandy in French hands.

It was a dreadful voyage home. Autumn was never the best time to sail the Channel. We had storms all the way. Some of the waves towered over us like cliffs. We plunged into troughs so deep that I felt sure we would all be drowned. Our two captains handled it well. Most of my men at arms spent the voyage on their knees praying for God to save us. They had no fear in battle yet nature was another matter. The storms finally abated as we passed the Humber. The captain said, as we neared the mouth of the Tees, "I hope you have a shipyard in your port, Sir Thomas, for we will need to repair both ships."

I nodded, "We have but I would not dawdle over your repairs. The Tees often freezes at this time of year."

He shook his head, "Wet and windy, lord. No snow and ice yet. I have lived long enough to smell the white stuff when it is due!"

Despite the cut in the river it still took too long to reach my home. I saw the towers long before we reached the quay. We had to tack against the current and the wind. It was almost dark when we arrived. We had been seen by the sentries in the east tower. They did not know it was me but Sir Edward would have told them that I was due home by Christmas. We were greeted at the quay by Henry Youngblood, the captain of my Guard and Leofric my clerk.

"Her ladyship thought it might be you. She has sent a rider to Sir Edward to let him know of your arrival."

"It is good to be home, Leofric. Henry, did the Scots trouble us here?"

He shook his head as my men began to disembark. "They raided Sedgefield and took slaves and animals but none of your manors were hurt. Bishopton had sheep taken but the people there fled to Elton and Hartburn. They were safe. The lord of Sedgefield and his family were all slaughtered, lord." I shook my head, Sir Hugh Convaille was an old knight. He and his wife had had no children. Why had they been killed? The raiders had gained nothing from it. One of the guards had brought a torch to help us see our way into my castle. Henry frowned, "I see you have been in the wars lord."

I nodded, "Does it look bad?"

"Not to a warrior but I think her ladyship might be upset. I will stay and help Ridley and the others unload, my lord."

It was as I crossed beneath the gate that I realised there would be no Aunt Ruth to greet me. This was the first time since Alfred had been killed that I had returned from campaign and my aunt was now dead. It was a warning. I, too, was getting old. I knew I should enjoy my grandchildren but it was unlikely that I would be given the opportunity. When I had taken on the mantle of the Warlord, I should have realised the full ramifications. Isabelle ran to greet me as I entered my hall. She had been damaged by Sir Jocelyn. I prayed that she might find happiness but she had not yet recovered from her infatuation. She blamed herself a little for Alfred's death. Nothing we said could bring her comfort.

"It is good that you are home. I…" she suddenly saw my cheek. Softly touching my face she said, "More wounds… this is not right. Are there not others who can bear the brunt of the fighting?"

"Sir Edward has a worse injury."

She touched her cross, "Aye you are right." Brian, my servant, took my cloak as I entered. Isabelle looked beyond me, "And my little brother? How is he?"

"Your little brother is a head taller now! He is whole and soon he will be a knight. Your sister and my son's widow?"

"Matilda takes great comfort in her two children. Mother says that Henry Samuel is identical to Alfred when he was the same age and little Maud…it is good that there is a girl too. All will be pleased that you are home." My wife appeared and Isabelle reached up to kiss my cheek. "I will go and see William."

Margaret saw my wound instantly. The light in my hall was bright. I saw her put her hand to her mouth and then she smiled, bravely. She hugged me and she kissed me, "I have missed you. I care not what the Scots do. I would have you in my bed at night!"

I laughed, "And I would like nothing more too!" I knew I would have to leave soon enough and so I changed the subject, "Are the bairns in bed?"

"I am afraid so but you need a bath and a change of clothes anyway. Tomorrow will be time enough for you to see them. For tonight we will enjoy your company and that of my son. He is well?"

"He has no wounds if that is your question and he is grown somewhat. You may not recognise him."

"A mother would recognise her son no matter what changes have been wrought! Come let me bathe and change you. Matilda is putting the children to bed and you smell of the sea and sweat."

"Thank you for your kind words, my lady!" I laughed and let her lead me to the bath house. I knew that my knights would be desperate to get to their own homes. The married men, like Ridley and David of Wales, would also go to their families while those like Padraig and Richard Red Leg would spend some of their coin in the alehouse in Stockton.

Matilda was young but her experiences with Sir Hugh of Craven and then her husband's untimely death had aged her. There were flecks of grey in her hair and there should not have been. When she came into the feasting hall, she saw my face and, throwing herself into my arms, began to sob. I did not try to speak, I just held her and stroked her hair. William and Isabelle had come in and when they saw her in my arms my son put his arm around Isabelle's shoulders. When her sobs subsided, she pulled away and ran her finger down the scar, "You are a brave man, Earl. Your son would have been just like you, had he lived."

I nodded and put my arm around her shoulder to lead her to the table, "And I cannot wait to see my two grandchildren. I hope this ugly old face will not frighten them."

"They are of your blood. They are of the blood of the Warlord. It is not the face which matters but the heart which beats beneath."

As we ate, I learned that Rebekah's husband, Geoffrey FitzUrse, had kept a close watch on my land until Sir Edward had returned. It had been he who had deterred the Scots after they had raided Sedgefield and Bishopton. William showed his new maturity by asking the right questions. "Were there knights with them or were they just the border thieves who would rather thieve than toil?"

My mother shook her head. She would not have asked that question nor would Matilda. Isabelle said, "Sir Geoffrey said that there were warriors with spurs but they had no banners."

William looked at me, "Then they were not sanctioned by King Alexander."

"The King has a duty to control his own men. We will ride and speak with the King before we scour his lands for our enemies."

"Do we not simply find them and punish them?"

"You have learned much, my son. Here is another lesson for you. It may well be that King Alexander is innocent of any involvement in this mischief. However, it may be that he has set his men to raid us so that we will invade. Such an act would give him the opportunity to appeal to the Pope and his allies in France and Germany to make King Henry the aggressor. No, we shall do this properly."

"Father," I looked at Isabelle, "this is more than mischief. They took captives. They razed farms and they killed men. We were lucky hereabouts they just took animals. Tam the Hawker was sent by Sir Edward, after he returned, to see what the Scots had done. Even Tam was shocked by what he saw."

My wife squeezed my hand. She knew that I would be away again and soon. I picked up her hand and kissed it. "It will take time to rouse our men and prepare for a winter campaign. We have time for me to see my family and show my people that the old fox is not yet dead."

The next morning, I sent riders to summon my knights for a counsel of war three days hence. I sent William to Durham to speak with the Bishop. That done I was able to play with Henry Samuel. He could now talk, after a fashion, and he could not only walk, he could run. As much as I wished to cuddle my granddaughter I was forced to run after my grandson and prevent him from running into the walls or the edges of tables. Isabelle, my wife and Henry Samuel's mother laughed until the tears ran down their faces. When finally my grandson stopped to play with the scabbard of my dagger, I shook my head, "I had forgotten what it was like to have a boy who has just discovered his legs. Were William and Alfred like that?"

My wife looked sad, "You missed most of the years when they were. Your Aunt used to chase them. She said it kept her young."

I stroked Henry Samuel's head, "Aye it probably did." I looked over at Matilda, "And Alfred's untimely death probably broke her heart." I looked up at the ceiling and touched my cross, "I hope you are watching the bairns now, Aunt. We will tell them of you."

My grandson went to pull the dagger from my scabbard. His mother said, "Sam, no! Danger, danger!" He looked up at his mother and removed his hands from the hilt.

I said, "Sam?"

"It is his pet name. Henry Samuel sounds so formal." A shadow passed over her face. "My husband barely knew him. We picked two names for we liked them both." Her eyes welled up.

My wife said, "Sam suits him. When he is a man grown, we can give him his formal name. Come Sam, let your grandfather give Maud a cuddle."

"And Maud is what we call this beautiful bundle of joy?"

Matilda laughed, "Aye. I was always called Matilda. She is a Maud. I wanted to be a Maud, like the Empress."

Isabelle nodded, "Just as I was always Izzy when growing up and now I am a spinster I am Isabelle." I heard the regret in her words which were hidden by the smile on her lips.

"Come Maud, let me see those beautiful blue eyes." She was a chubby little baby and she was happy. As she saw me, she giggled and put her fingers in my beard. When she felt the hair, she laughed louder and squealed. "She has a powerful set of lungs on her!"

Matilda nodded, "Especially in the wee hours. I am just glad that Sam is a good and sound sleeper." Maud had pulled herself close to me and her mouth came open to bite my nose. "Be careful my lord, she now has a tooth."

I put my mouth to her neck and blew. It made a rasping sound and she squealed once more. This was a joy. This was what I had missed when my children were growing up. Now I would enjoy it as much as I could. I spent the morning playing with them until Maud went down for her nap. Wrapping a cloak around Sam I took him to walk my walls. Henry Youngblood was at the gatehouse. His warm smile showed that he knew Sam. "The little warrior is with the mighty lord. This is as it should be. It is good to see, Sir Thomas." He pointed down the road from the Oxbridge. "Sir Geoffrey and your daughter are come to visit."

I picked up Henry Samuel, "See, your aunt, uncle and cousin come."

My grandson chattered all the time. He was like a flock of magpies but they were not yet clear sentences which came from his mouth. There were words which you could make out. He pointed and said, clearly, "Alf!"

I smiled, "Aye, your cousin Alfred and when you are old enough, if God allows me to live that long, I will teach you all that I know to be a warrior."

My Captain of the Guard nodded, "Aye Master Henry and that will be a lesson from the best!"

My grandson insisted upon walking down the steps. He allowed me to hold his hand but I feared that he would slip. When we walked across the inner ward to the gate he marched. He frowned until I kept in step with him.

Rebekah's hug was heartfelt. She whispered in my ear, "Thank God that you are home and safe. Sir Edward told us of the dangers you faced!"

I stepped back, "And it is good to be home. Thank you, Sir Geoffrey, for shouldering the responsibility while I was away."

He clasped my arm, "I realised just how heavy is the burden your bear, Sir Thomas. The raids were barbaric."

"Aye, and now I am home with the full backing of the King, we can deal with them but for now we will enjoy a homecoming. We will enjoy the family being gathered together again!"

# Chapter 12
# Across the Border

When William returned, I had a better idea of the problem. The Bishop had been frank with my son. With two days until my men arrived, I was able to put my mind to the problems we faced. I used the night time for my internal debate. Each waking moment was spent with my family or my people. I owed it to them and to myself. The Bishop of Durham had been taken unawares by the attacks. Apparently random I saw a pattern in them. Norham and the border castles had been avoided by the Scots as they had slipped over the border. They had come further south before they had begun their raid and they had targeted places like Sedgefield, Bishopton and other such villages. They had chosen places without defences. Warkworth, Alnwick, Prudhoe and the other castles had been left alone. They had chosen places which were more than ten miles from such a castle. They had come in small groups but the numbers suggested that one mind had been in control. That kind of planning and coordination told me that it was not a random series of attacks. Someone had done this.

"Did the Bishop have any idea who perpetrated the attacks?"

"There were no banners and the Scots took back their dead. The survivors were the lucky women and children. All that they knew were that warriors with Scottish voices had attacked them." William had paused, "And there were knights who suffered. Sir Hugh of Hexham took his men to try to recapture the captives and animals. They were ambushed and their heads placed on spears."

"That is not the work of bandits. That is the work of some lord who seeks to send a message."

"Aye and Sir Robert of Elsdon's wife was abducted. He went north with his men to rescue her. Only the knight and four men

143

survived. He was wounded and is now at Durham with the Bishop. I spoke with him and he begged me to ask you to help."

"What of the Sheriff of Newcastle?"

"The pestilence struck the town and castle. Many died and the Sheriff is ill. It was not his fault, father."

I nodded. This was partly a series of unfortunate accidents and events and, at the same time, evidence of someone taking advantage of England's weakness.

When my knights arrived, my castle was overflowing for they brought their families. We were like one huge family. Many of them had been my squires. My wound and Sir Edward's made them angry. I was touched by their affection. All wanted to know what we would do. I insisted that they enjoy a feast and in the cold light of day we would have our counsel of war. We caught up with one another and we feasted.

The next day it was all business and we sat around my large table. Sir Richard of East Harlsey and the Sheriff of York, Sir Ralph, were with us. My captains, Ridley, Henry Youngblood and David of Wales were also present. Sir William's captain, Johann, who had been left to watch his family, was also present. All would be needed.

"The Scots have hurt Durham and the lands to the north. They think that, now that they have returned across the border, they are safe. They are not!" My men banged the table in approval. "They think that it is winter and we will sit and do nothing. Despite the snows we will encounter when Christmas has passed, we will ride to Kelso and speak with this King Alexander." Once again, they banged the table. I held up the parchment given to me by King Henry. "This is from the King and it means that we act in his name. King Alexander may think that we have a young king who can be easily dismissed. We will show him that he has the backing of the iron warriors of the Tees who have yet to taste defeat at the hands of the Scots." This time the acclamation was so loud that I was forced to sit while they cheered. When they had finished, I rose. "We take mounted men only. We leave our castles with good garrisons. We meet here on St. Stephen's Day!"

I took Sir Edward and Gilles to one side after the others had left. "Are you ready to be dubbed on the Eve of Christmas, Gilles?"

His eyes gave me the answer before he opened his mouth. "Aye lord."

"Then we will make it so. You know that before you may have a manor you need to be married."

He laughed, "One step at a time, lord. I am more than happy to serve as Sir Edward's knight."

I looked over to Edward's son, Henry. His eyes were also wide. "And you, young Henry, are you ready to be a squire?"

"I am, lord."

"And know you that we will be campaigning in winter. That will be a harsh lesson for you."

"I am my father's son, lord and if I cannot campaign in winter then I do not deserve to be a squire, let alone a knight."

"Good. And you, Sir Edward, can you watch our land while we are away?"

"I am become used to the lack of a left arm. I can dress myself and I still exercise my right. I practise with my son and he has yet to defeat me. I am alive and that is good." He nodded to my left arm, "And your wound?"

"It was nothing, although I suspect that it will ache in the damp weather."

"Aye Sir Thomas, that is God's way of telling you that you are alive!"

I spent the rest of the day with my three captains. We would need the best of our men. The mail, weapons and armour we had taken from the French and Poitevin would be put to good use. When we next went to war then we would be far better armed and mailed. I spoke with Alan the Horse Master. The Scots were known as horse killers. He would have the weapon smith make mail hoods for some of the horses. They would protect the neck and chest. I would not be taking Lion. Scotland was not the place for a war horse. The mail hood would be made for Blaze.

Now that Sir Geoffrey had returned to Elton with my daughter and grandson, I was able to spend more time with Henry Samuel and Maud. Winter storms swept in and we hunkered down before huge banked fires. I remembered all the songs and rhymes my aunt had told and sung to me and then to my children. They were silly. They were nonsense and the grandchildren loved them. I learned to do funny voices and to dance around. Maud could not walk but she giggled and laughed as Sam and I danced before the fire. My grandson would hold his hand out for my wife to join us. I was as far away from the battlefield as it was possible. Little Sam took to asking for '*gwandad*', his pet name for me, to take him up to his bed and tell him a story or sing him a song. He would mime for me to lie next to him and I would feign sleep. I would slip away when I heard his regular breathing.

Maud, Isabelle and my wife were all waiting for me two nights before Christmas when I descended. My wife kissed me and Isabelle and Matilda brought me wine, bread and cheese. "What is this? What is it you wish of me?"

My wife laughed, "Nothing. We would not change you for the world. It is just that I have not seen this side of you, husband. When you were younger and the children were growing then you were too weary to put them to bed."

Matilda nodded, "You are the man in their life now, Sir Thomas. You fill my heart with joy for they adore you and that is good."

Isabelle came to sit upon my knee. She sliced off a piece of cheese and ate it, "What we are trying to say, father, is that we do not wish to lose you. This Sir Thomas is a revelation. When you go north to deal with the Scots or when the King summons you to clean up another problem then be less heroic, eh? We like this gentler lord who can cavort like a jester. I wish I had seen him when I was growing."

I smiled and drank some wine, "Perhaps he was always there and it took the death of my eldest to make it come forth. I promise you that he will stay and I will do my best not to die!"

The dubbing ceremony in my chapel was attended by all of my knights. Each of them knew the import of the event. Gilles had passed all of his tests and held his vigil. Father Harold saw that the religious elements were well done and then it was down to me. For some reason this particular ceremony was special. It may have been because he would be replacing Sir Edward or, more likely, it was the first such knighting since my son had died. Soon William would be undergoing it. I was keenly aware that he was paying close attention to all that Gilles did. I saw Isabelle looking particularly thoughtful. I think I knew what she was thinking. At the end of it we retired to my hall. Apart from Sir Geoffrey, the rest of my knights would be spending time with their families. The day after Christmas they would be leaving with me for up to two months away. We broached a firkin of the wine we had bought in Poitou. We ate spiced pies made with minced meat. We spoke of the dead. It was neither maudlin nor morbid. We were just remembering. We did not talk of Alfred's death but we celebrated his life. We spoke of all the other knights and men at arms who had perished. William of Lincoln and Sam Strongarm were remembered. They had no family. If we did not speak of their lives then who would? It was as though by speaking of them we made them alive again. I, for one, felt much warmer. We said farewell. Ralph, the Sheriff of York, would be spending Christmas with Sir William. They had served together. Sir Peter and his wife would spend Christmas with his father in their hall by the Oxbridge.

As the last ones left and with Matilda and her children in bed, and Sir Geoffrey and his family retired, I sat before the roaring fire with my wife and Isabelle. William was with the men at arms. He was a warrior now. He drank with them in their hall. It was good. I saw that Isabelle was sad. "Something ails you daughter?"

My wife shook her head in irritation. "Husband, she is quiet. She is content."

Normally I would have said, 'yes dear' and drunk more wine but speaking of Alfred had made me think about my other children. "Tomorrow I go to punish the Scots. I cannot ride with worries about my daughter. I believe I know what ails Isabelle and I would have her tell me. Who knows, I might be able to solve the problem!"

My wife gave an ironical laugh, "It involves neither your sword nor a funny voice. Isabelle will deal with her problems herself."

Isabelle looked at me. I saw in her eyes that she wished to talk and yet felt awkward. I was a blunt man. "You think that you are too old for marriage and all of the eligible men are married."

"Thomas!"

I waved a hand to silence my wife, "It was brought home to you today when Gilles was knighted and he is but a little older than William." I saw a tear trickle down her cheek. "Come daughter and sit here." I patted my knee. She came and sat upon it, nestling her head on my shoulder. "Your Aunt Ruth lost her husband when she had been barely wed. She lived alone for many years and then found her husband long after she thought she would end her days alone. She and Sir William were happy. Do not give up on happiness. If you wish to travel then I am in a position to help you. I have the King's favour. When spring comes, we can make a progress. There are many young knights who would wish a bride such as you."

She laughed and wiped away the tear, "You would show me off as a prize cow? I think not."

"Not all men are like Sir Jocelyn, you know. There are good knights."

She smiled and kissed me on the forehead, "I know for mother found you, but I have seen little evidence hereabouts."

After she had gone my wife said, "Just let her be. Things will work out. They did for me."

"You were lucky! You found me!"

She shrugged and took my hand, "We found each other and that is the heart of the matter."

Christmas Day was joyous. The food was all that we hoped it would be and some of my men at arms had been out in Hartburn Woods and managed to kill a fine sow. We ate well. The last of the autumn apples were served in a sauce and we had spiced wine with it. It was as perfect a Christmas as I could remember.

Despite the food and drink we consumed I was up before dawn. William was keen to begin for Gilles' knighthood had been the spur he needed. He would no longer be the youngest squire. Henry, Edward's son, had only seen fourteen summers. My wife and I had said farewell the night before but little Sam was upset that his grandfather was leaving. He cried and it broke my heart. When Maud joined in it was almost too much to bear. I turned Blaze and headed up the Durham road. With darkening skies, we would be lucky to reach it in less than four hours. The campaign had begun.

Richard Poore, the Bishop of Durham, was expecting us. My knights would stay with him in his palace. The men at arms and archers would share quarters with the garrison. There would be ten knights in my conroi. The Bishop could field ten times that number and still have many castles garrisoned. In terms of men at arms and archers, however, we had the best and the two hundred men I led were a potent force. There were other knights at the feast held in our honour.

The Bishop had me seated next to him. "Despite all our vigilance the Scots were able to slip over the border so quickly that by the time we had reacted they had fled leaving burned homes, dead men, families lost and animals stolen." He pointed to a young knight who was seated with his squire at the end of the table. The knight looked to be of an age with my dead son, Alfred, but he had the haunted look of a much older man. "That is Robert of Elsdon. The squire is his brother. The two were hunting with their best men at arms when the Scots raided. They slew the servants and abducted his wife. She was with child. When he returned, he hunted them. They found her body in the forests to the south of Kelso. He has been awaiting your arrival more eagerly than any. He wishes to join you."

"He seeks vengeance?"

"Wouldn't you?"

"I would but this must be handled well. I fear that someone plots to make us the aggressor. I will punish those who transgressed but King Henry cannot afford a war." He nodded. "How many of your knights can I take with me?"

"Many are, quite naturally, worried about their families. I have forty who will follow you."

"That will be enough knights. How many men do they lead?"

"A hundred."

I was disappointed and allowed my face to show it. "That is not enough but I suppose it will have to do. I would have a warrant from you. I have one from the King but the support of the Church never goes amiss."

"Of course, and I will send four priests with you. They have a holy banner they can carry. In addition, they are all good healers."

"Now, tell me all you know of the lords who might be behind this."

"King Alexander knows of it. He was away from Roxburgh subjugating Argyll. A clever move for he distanced himself from those he called bandits. King Alexander is married to King Henry's sister, Joan. He has to appear as though he keeps the peace. There is a French lord who returned from France with the King after he and King Louis, the father of the new French King, made their alliance. He was given lands in Lothian. Sir Robert said that when his castle was taken his retainers had fought well and killed some of their enemies. Two were Frenchmen."

"What is this Frenchman's name?"

"Guy de Beaucaire. His cousin is well connected at the French court. He is the Count d'Eu." He must have seen the reaction on my face for he said, "You know him?"

"Aye, let us say I have a clearer picture now of the situation here. This may not be the doing of the young French King. There are nobles in France who seek power. They seek to undermine both King Louis and King Henry. In doing so they will gain both power and land. Where does this Guy de Beaucaire have his lands?"

"You know the King has a castle at Roxburgh, close by the abbey?" I nodded, "A few miles away is the manor of Duns. There is no castle yet but the new Lord of Duns, Guy de Beaucaire, is building one. He wishes to be close to the King."

The servants brought some fowl and we carved them with our knives. I had much to think on. "What I do not understand is how so many attacks occurred at once. They raided from Elsdon which lies close to the Coquet Valley and also Sedgefield which is near to the Skerne. They attacked on a front of more than fifty miles."

"As I said, Sir Thomas, you taught us well and you taught us to be vigilant. They were clever. They crossed the border in small groups and then joined up well inside our borders to form five warbands. We caught some as they returned north but the rest just discarded their captives and animals and crossed back to Scotland. I do not think we killed above twenty or thirty men. The Constable at Norham knew nothing about the attacks. His men patrol the border for ten miles on both sides of his castle."

I discarded the bones from the bird I had eaten. I wiped my hands on the cloth the Bishop's servants had provided and I drank some wine.

The Bishop waited and then said, "You have a plan?"

"The captives and animals could be anywhere. We can try to get them back but it will be hard. I want none of your people under any illusions about that. The King has given me free rein. I intend to punish this Frenchman but first I must speak with the

Scottish King. I would have you come with me to Roxburgh. I believe that King Alexander is a pious man?"

"He is."

"Sir Robert's wife was found on the road to Kelso and Roxburgh. She was a lady and with child. That is how we shame him into allowing us to find her killers. You can return to Durham when we have spoken with the King and I will go to Duns and confront this Frenchman."

"It is winter, my lord."

I could tell that Richard Poore did not relish travelling through inhospitable lands in winter. "Your Grace, they will not be expecting us to face them down. King Alexander may know about the raids but he might just think they stole sheep and cattle. I doubt that he knows of slavery, murder and worse. The longer we leave it the less truthful it becomes. We go now. We show outrage, as we should, and to do that we need someone like yourself who is a respected churchman. I have fought the Scots too many times to have many friends there. Although I speak the truth, they may suspect my motives. I need you!"

He smiled, "Of course. I shall try to prove to you that I am a better Bishop than some of my predecessors."

I saw Robert of Elsdon stand, "Your Grace I need to speak to that knight. He is key to our success." I reached him as he and his squire left the hall. "Sir Robert, may I speak with you?"

"Of course. Richard go and prepare our beds." He hurried off. "You are Sir Thomas of Stockton, the Earl of Cleveland, I believe."

"I am and I am sorry for your loss."

I saw the sadness in his eyes. It was as if he bore the pain of the world. "Eleanor was my world. She was bearing our first child. I would have crossed the border and killed every Scotsman I could find had not my brother persuaded me that we needed more men than the handful I had." He stared hard at me. "Tell me that we will punish them!"

"We will. Know this, I travelled deep into France to avenge the death of my son. I understand vengeance but I need you cold. You will ride at my side but you will neither speak, nor act without I say it is good."

"It will be hard but I will do as you say for I know you to be a man who speaks the truth."

"Get some rest tonight. Tomorrow we ride for Scotland and I would have close conference with you on the journey north." He nodded. "And how is your wound?"

He rubbed his leg, "It is nothing. I am healed. Others suffered far more."

His words told me that he was a warrior. I returned to the hall. Unlike many of the other knights there present my knights had barely touched their wine. They looked at me as I returned. I walked over to Sir Ralph, the Sheriff of York. "We ride early tomorrow. The Bishop comes with us and the journey will not be swift. I believe I know who is at the heart of this."

# Chapter 13
# The Road to Roxburgh

It was over ninety miles to Roxburgh. Despite my misgivings the Bishop was able to ride well and we were not unduly slowed. We first headed to Otterburn. Despite Elsdon having been ravaged the tower at Otterburn had deterred an attack. The tower was close to Roxburgh. We could spend the night there before crossing the border. Speaking to Robert of Elsdon I learned that his castle had not had enough men and was in a state of disrepair. It was one of his many regrets. We were heading for Sir Robert's land. I avoided asking him why his castle was so ill defended and needed repairs. They had not attacked Otterburn but had chosen Elsdon. I had my suspicions. They must have been watching and known he was away. The raiders had planned and plotted. I would need to use my mind to defeat them for they were clever.

I questioned him about his pursuit of those who had abducted his wife. I learned that he had gone north with just his squire and eight men. He had two good scouts. They were both local men whose families had lived in the borders for generations. Oswald and Cedric, as their names suggested, had Saxon blood in them. They had found the trail. That in itself had not been easy. Other warbands had met up and joined together but the two men were able to follow Lady Elsdon's prints. They had found her body. The Scots were still close by and in the fight to recover her body only the knight, his squire and the two scouts had survived. The two scouts became as important as their lord. Their skills might help us to find those who had done this deed. They were at the rear of the column with the baggage of the knight. I would need to speak with them.

"Will you return to Elsdon?"

"No, my lord. I inherited the manor through a distant relative. I was desperate to have a home so that I could marry. My family had lands close to Oxford. As the third son I had little to inherit. When my father died in the baron's war, I lost everything as did my brothers. Eleanor was my childhood sweetheart. We hoped to make a home at Elsdon but if I returned there then it would be like a mausoleum to me. Every wall hanging and pot would remind me of her. When she is avenged, I will take the cross. Perhaps God might help me to atone for whatever sin I committed."

"You committed no sin, Sir Robert. You just lived in the most dangerous part of England. I have fought the Welsh and the Scots. Believe me the Scots are deadlier. Do not make a hasty decision about crusade. I have been to the Holy Land as has my grandfather. It is not the answer." We stopped for water and I called over Padraig and Richard Red Leg. "With the baggage train are Sir Robert's two scouts, Cedric and Oswald. Get to know them. They will be of great use to us. They know the land well."

"Aye lord."

I had studied the maps at Durham with the Bishop. He had a great number and they had given me a clear picture of the land through which we travelled. As we neared Otterburn I knew that we were just a few miles from the knight's home. I saw Sir Robert's gaze drifting to the east. His home lay there. Otterburn had a tower and had resisted the attacks but the farms which were adjacent were burned out ruins. The Scots had almost emptied the land of the English. We were just fifteen miles from the Scottish border. The last populous place we had passed had been the New Castle! The valleys north of the Tyne had been ravaged and razed by the Scots. I had seen such raids before but never on this scale. My father had told me of such raids in the time of the Warlord. Just as I would tell Henry Samuel of the deeds of the men who followed me so my grandfather had filled my father's head with such tales. Sir Hugh Manningham of Hexham had died not far from where we rested. Sir Ralph, Aunt's Ruth's husband, had been just a few miles south when he had been slain. This was a land of blood. The devastation of the valleys north of the Tyne made me wonder. This was not a raid for cattle. This was an attempt to rid the border of the English. Now I understood why the raids had covered such a larger area. Someone wished the English to pull back from the border. When I spoke with the Scottish King I would discover if it was him.

The men camped and made hovels. The tower was small but accommodated the Bishop, myself and some of the senior barons. I would have stayed with my men but the lord, Edward, insisted that I use his tower. Before I entered Padraig brought the two scouts to see me. They were both hardy men from the north country. The inclement weather did not bother them. Both wore seal skin coats. The seals who lived near the Holy Island were a bounty for the folk who lived close by. The two men had the weathered faces of men who spent more time outdoors than beneath a roof. They had short swords but it was the deadly looking knives which drew attention. They were the kind of knife which could skin an animal quickly and efficiently. In the right hands they could gut a man just as easily.

"Sir Robert says that you two found Lady Elsdon."

When Cedric spoke, it was with the thick accent of the north country. Anyone who lived south of York would struggle to understand it. "Aye lord, a pity we did not see the ambush or we would have had the bastards who did that to the poor woman." He shook his head, "She was a bonny lass."

I nodded, "I am sworn to help your lord to avenge those you lost." I saw a thin smile appear on both of their lips. To those who lived on the border vengeance was a savage affair. "I want you to do something for me. We will be speaking with the King of Scotland tomorrow. North of Roxburgh there is a wood by the river. When we cross the river, you will leave us and secrete yourself in the woods. I suspect a rider wearing livery will pass northwards. Follow him home and then report back to your lord." I was guessing but if the Bishop was correct and there was a Frenchman at Duns then he would be warned of our arrival.

"You know the land, lord, and you seem to know what will happen before it does. Are you a wizard?"

Like all north countrymen Oswald was superstitious. The old ways were never far from the surface. I smiled, "Apart from having seen the maps I have fought the Scots before. I know this land and as for predicting the future, I will confide in you, I

155

believe I know who ordered the attack on your home. He lives at Duns. When you return with the proof, I can confront the King."

"Our word is proof? We are villeins, lord. We are nothing and have no voice."

"Aye but you do. When the King's father signed the charter, he gave rights to those who work the land just as much as those who profit from the land. You need to trust me that justice will be done."

"We do, my lord."

I returned with them to the camp and spoke with Sir Robert. He was their lord and he deserved to know what was in my mind. I saw relief on his face when he saw that I was not just coming to speak with King Alexander. There would be a result from the meeting. William had been with me the whole time. He was like my shadow. Part of it was fear that an assassin might try to strike me down. It was not unheard of and it was partly to help him learn how to be me. The death of Alfred meant he would be the next Lord of Stockton. My title was not hereditary. I had had to fight for it but William knew that he would be lord of the land around the Tees and he wanted to know what to do.

One of the knights who had been granted accommodation was Sir James of Wessington. I needed to speak with him. His father, William, had been lord of Hartburn before I had returned to become Earl of Cleveland. He had exchanged Hartburn for Wessington. I needed to know why. I did not want bad blood with a knight I would be leading into battle.

He was seated close to me and I leaned over. "We have not met. I am Thomas of Stockton. I believe your father once had the manor of Hartburn. That is now the manor of William of La Lude."

He smiled, "And you would know if there was a reason why my father chose Wessington over Hartburn?"

"Bearing in mind the reason why we are here is because of Scottish raids and your home is closer to the Scots than was Hartburn, you can understand my concern. I do not wish resentment amongst the men I lead."

"Then fear not. It was simply a matter of money. Wessington is a much larger manor. There is more land and it is flatter and requires less work. It is better for farming. My father was a clever man and we have prospered. And I confess that we liked not how we were given the land. My father liked the Warlord and did not like the way his family was treated by King John. As for the Scots? We are close enough to Durham to take shelter within its walls. I am here because I know that the Earl of Cleveland will punish these Scots and we will not have to endure such attacks for some time. By then I may have built a castle."

"Good. I am pleased I spoke. I like clear air between my knights."

"And I have sharpened weapons which I hope to whet on the blood of the barbarians who murdered Lady Elsdon." He shook his head. "She was a fine lady and a cousin of my wife. I have a personal interest in this."

After I had prayed that night, and lay down on the cot the Lord of Otterburn had provided, I thought about the tenuous ties we all had. There was a link between Sir James and myself. The granddaughters of the same lord had tied him to Sir Robert. There was hope for Isabelle. She would find a husband and he would be a man worthy of her and not one like Sir Jocelyn.

We rode towards the Tweed with banners flying and our best raiments beneath heavy oiled cloaks. Sleety rain was at our backs and it made the fourteen-mile journey distinctly unpleasant. We reached Roxburgh bridge before noon. The weather had spurred us on. I looked at the bridge and the ground with military eyes. If things did not go the way I planned then I would have to fight and it might be here at Roxburgh. The Bishop sent two of his priests as heralds to warn both the prior and the King of our arrival. It was another reason I had insisted upon the Bishop's presence. King Alexander would have just his personal guards with him. The site of such a large number of knights might preface a war I did not want. The Abbey of Kelso was not far away. Roxburgh Castle was built on a high piece of ground in a loop of the Tweed. A royal borough lay below it. I would not have wished to assault it. The only avenue up which an army could attack was similar to Warkworth and channelled between the natural moat that was a river. We were met at the town gates by two Scottish lords. They wore no helmets and had no shields but their faces were serious. They addressed the Bishop but the looks they gave me told me that they had recognised me.

"Your Grace, your priests told us that you wished conference with the King and he has agreed to that but he has spied your army and he is concerned that you do not wish him well."

Richard Poore smiled, "In these parlous times it does not do to travel the borderlands with a tiny escort. It is just the Earl of Cleveland, myself and four or five knights who need to be admitted. The rest, with your permission, can camp here."

The knight who had spoken shook his head, "Have them return to the other side of the river, Your Grace. They can camp in England." He smiled, "If your purpose is peaceful then that should not be a problem."

We had discussed the various responses they might make and the Bishop nodded, "And it is peaceful. That will be acceptable." He turned to me, "Earl?"

I shouted, "Sir William, take charge of the men. Camp over the bridge in England. It seems the Scots fear us. We will be safe for I have seen nothing which might detain us." It was a deliberate barb.

One of the lords who had come to greet us snapped, "We fear no Englishman." I saw that he had red and yellow diagonal stripes on his surcoat and that there was a black hawk on his chest.

I turned back and said slowly and quietly, "King William the Lion discovered that it is wise to fear those of my blood. My great grandfather led the knights who slew his bodyguard and captured him. That led to more than twenty years of peace. I would not put ideas into my head, my lord. I am the great grandson of the Warlord and his blood courses through my veins."

He stared at me, "I am the mormaer of Fife, Duncan of Dunfermline. I will remember your words Englishman. My grandsire died in that treacherous attack through fog."

The Bishop said, reasonably, "My lords, we are here for peace. Sheathe your words for they can hurt just as much as blades."

We rode through the gates. The Sheriff of York and Sir Robert were the only two knights who accompanied me. We had our squires and the Bishop had his priests and the Dean. My men outside were surety for our safety. Servants and grooms waited to take our horses. When we entered the hall more servants took our wet cloaks.

The King and Queen were waiting for us in the feasting hall where a fire was banked up. The King looked serious but I saw that the Queen was smiling broadly. She was young. King Henry, her brother, was three years her elder. She had been a pawn used by her father. Originally, she had been intended as a bride for the King of France. That had not happened and she had been used to join England to Scotland. Poor Queen Joan was ill equipped to control her husband. He was twelve years her senior and she was barely a woman.

"You are welcome, Bishop, but as you have brought the wolf of the north with you then you will understand our scepticism that this is a peaceful mission."

King Alexander's words sounded stronger than they were. The look in his eyes showed me that he was fearful of our presence. Had he ordered the raid? I was not offended. I did not take the appellation as an insult. I kept a straight face. I knew that Sir Ralph and Sir Robert would do the same.

The Bishop smiled, "The Earl of Cleveland has been sent by the King and only the enemies of England need fear him."

I bowed and took out the locket the King had given me. I slowly approached the Queen, "The King, Your Majesty, sent this to you with his warm regards and felicitations." I handed the young Queen the locket. She opened it and saw that King Henry had had her portrait and his painted in miniature. I had examined it in my castle. It was a fine piece of work. It showed a sensitive side to the King I did not know he had.

She was young enough and innocent enough to show her natural feelings. Her face lit up, "My dear brother! How is he, Earl?"

"He is doing well. He has just recaptured the lands of Poitou and, even now, seeks to retake Normandy. Your father's lands will soon be whole again. He has learned to be a good King despite treachery all around him." As I spoke, I looked at the faces of the lords who faced me.

I saw a worried look pass over the face of the King and his ministers who stood close by. Queen Joan showed no such fear and she beamed, "And that is how it should be. I look forward to speaking with you at the feast."

The King said, "Perhaps you should leave us now, my dear, for we have matters of state to discuss."

Disappointment was etched all over Queen Joan's face but she curtsied to the Bishop and left with her ladies. "I will see you tonight, Sir Thomas. You shall sit at my right hand." From the look she was given by the King I suspected this was the first sign he had had that his wife would stand up to him.

The King said, "I pray you sit."

We had discussed, the night before, how we would proceed. The Bishop would speak. I would listen and we would choose our moment. We had evidence and, although it was flimsy in nature, used at the right time could be devastating.

The King was flanked at the table by his steward, chamberlain, thePrior of the abbey and the two lords who had met us. He looked at them before he spoke. "What is your grievance, Bishop Poore?"

"I think you know already, King Alexander." He glanced at the prior who could not meet his gaze. "However, I will explain. Scottish raiders came over the border more than a month since. They ravaged the lands of the Palatinate as far south as Sedgefield and as far north as Elsdon." He paused.

The King spread his hands apologetically, "I am sorry, Bishop but there are brigands and bandits on both sides of the border. Short of building a wall it is hard to see what we could do."

The Bishop smiled a sad smile, "The Romans built such a wall. Perhaps it was not a bad idea. However, these were not brigands nor were they bandits, King Alexander. They were led by men wearing spurs."

For the first time the King looked a little nervous. "Did you identify their livery?"

"No, King Alexander, their purpose was sinister and they disguised themselves."

The King and his lords looked relieved but I saw the priest finger his cross. The King answered, "Then they could have been anyone." He sounded reasonable but I knew, in that moment, that the King knew who had orchestrated this attack.

"They could, King Alexander, but one of my lords followed those who had abducted his pregnant wife. They found her body."

"I am sorry that this lord lost his wife and it is deplorable that a woman with child should have been abducted but I say again, what could I have done?"

It was my turn to speak and I did so with authority. I looked not only at the King but the two lords who flanked him, "Her body was found but ten miles from where we now sit. Either those who perpetrated the deed came from here or just a little further north. We crossed the Tweed today and this is the only crossing for many miles. The killers crossed this bridge. They passed through or close by Roxburgh. You may have been indoors or busy but the guards on the walls would have seen them. If they did not tell you of the crossing then they are guilty. They are murderers by association!"

That brought a reaction. The Earl of Fife waved over a servant and whispered in his ear. The man hurried out. The King looked from the Prior of Kelso to the Earl of Fife and back. He was shocked by the news. That did not mean he did not know of the deed merely that he did not know it pointed to him.

The Earl of Fife said, "I am sorry, Your Grace, but that cannot be true. None crossed the river with captives."

I leaned forward, "Interesting, mormaer, the Bishop never said that they had captives with them."

Blustering he replied, "I assumed as one died then the rest would have been brought across the river." He waved a hand before him, "This is an English plot to ensnare us. I do not believe that a lady was abducted. No Scotsman would do that."

"My lord you and I know that Scotsmen have done that and done so many times." I smiled, "And a Frenchman might."

Once again, our knowledge had surprised them. The Earl of Fife ploughed blindly on. I could see that the King was discomfited by the news he was hearing. Perhaps the gory details had been kept from him. I was reminded of the young French King. He too had been manipulated. "There is no proof. There is no charge to answer."

I put my hand on the back of Sir Robert and when he turned, I nodded. He spoke. His voice was cold and like ice. Beneath the veil of courtesy was the threat of violence. "That lady was my wife. It was I who found her. When we tried to carry her back, we were attacked by Scottish warriors. I recognised their voices and

161

they wore your livery, lord. My word is my proof or would you question me also? If you do then my sword is ready to put it to God's judgement."

The Earl was visibly shaken. I added, "And I will second Sir Robert."

Silence fell and the air was stiff with tension. King Alexander showed his nobility, "I am sorry for your loss, Sir Robert. This should not have happened and no-one," he glared at the Earl of Fife, "doubts your word. Make no mistake. When we discover who are the guilty parties then we will punish them."

Silence fell again. The Bishop looked at me and nodded. I put my hands together, "King Alexander that is not good enough. I will not impugn the honour of a King but I believe that there are men in this room who know the identity of the man who led this raid. We have enough priests and prelates in this chamber to have a Bible brought forth and for men to swear an oath. However, it is not enough that you say you will punish the men who did this deed. The deed took place on English soil. I have brought men with me to bring back whoever is guilty. They will be tried and executed in England." The Earl of Fife made to open his mouth. "King Henry has given me authority to act as I see fit in this matter. I have brought a small number of knights, men at arms and archers." I emphasised the last word. Our archers had wreaked a terrible toll on the Scots in battles past. "This is a force merely to apprehend the guilty. If we are denied justice then I will bring the full might of England to punish Scotland. If that happens then the Treaty of Falaise will seem as nothing compared with the reparations we shall demand. Do you really want a war with your wife's brother, King Alexander?"

Even the Earl of Fife slumped back in his seat. The Treaty of Falaise had made the King of Scotland pay huge sums to England and he had been forced to bend the knee to English kings. The King looked at his advisers. We had given them information which needed to be discussed and digested. "Sir Thomas you have brought us disturbing news. I need to speak with my advisers and discover the truth, or otherwise, of these events. I must also discuss the legal aspects of the case. I pray you retire to your rooms and prepare for our feast. We will speak again on the morrow. For the rest let us be friends and enjoy the festival of Christmas and all that it entails."

The Bishop rose, "That is good, King Alexander, my priests and I will pray to God for guidance and I am sure that Sir Thomas, the Sheriff of York and Sir Robert will wish to cleanse themselves."

Once we were in the hallway we stopped. I waved the four servants, who were to take us to our chambers, away to the side so that we could talk. The Bishop nodded to me, "That upset them. What think you, Earl?"

"I think that while the King might know of the chevauchée he does not know of the captives, the deaths and of your wife, Sir Robert. The Earl of Fife is a different matter. His lands are north of the Forth and I think he knows what went on. It was he sent the servant out of the room. If Cedric and Oswald are as good as I think they are then we will have news by the time we have feasted with the King. If the messenger goes to Duns then we see the whole web. Scotland, Fife and the Count d'Eu. By tomorrow we will be in an even stronger position."

"And if the King maintains his stance that this is a Scottish matter?"

I raised my voice a little so that the servants could hear me, "Then I will do as I told the King. I will bring an army and reduce Roxburgh, Kelso, Jedburgh and Berwick to piles of stones and this land will become England."

The Bishop nodded, "You are a hard man, Earl, and I am glad that you are on our side."

Once in our chamber William helped me to change. My arm had healed but it was still difficult to raise my arm. It was getting easier. By spring I would be back to normal. "How will it help if they have sent a rider to Duns?"

"I do not think that the King knew what the Earl of Fife did. The King can only plead innocence so long as he thinks we do not know the identity of the Lord of Duns. That was why I spoke of French knights. Tonight, watch for treachery. Serve me nothing but that which the King or the Earl of Fife consumes." Our squires would act as servants at the feast. "Tell the other squires too. I do not think the Bishop will be at risk. When the food is finished then say you have to take a message to the camp. It will

163

worry them. I want you to wait until the two scouts have returned and bring me their news."

We were summoned to the feast. I saw that Queen Joan was seated next to the King and that a place had been reserved next to her, for me. The Earl of Fife was with the other Scottish lords well away from us. The Prior of Kelso Abbey was next to the Bishop who was next to the King. We three English knights were outnumbered by many Scottish lords and I saw the animosity in their eyes. I could endure it.

The Queen looked radiant. She was younger than William. I felt sorry for her. She had been married off and sent far from the world in which she had grown up. She put her hand on mine, "Thank you for coming, Sir Thomas." She smiled, "When I was growing up, I heard your name often." She giggled, "My father did not like you." She became serious again, "But I know that you did what you did for England. Did you see my mother?"

We chatted away while various courses were brought. Being seated next to the Queen I was able to take the food which she was offered first and knew it was safe. I told her all that I could about her mother and her brother. She glanced over to Sir Robert. Once again, he had the cold and serious look which had been his countenance since I had first met him. "One of the servants said that Sir Robert's wife was with child. She was abducted and died."

"She was abducted and killed."

"Killed...?"

"Do not ask more, lady. It is not for your ears. You are a lady and should not hear of the privations of such men. I am here to bring the perpetrators to justice."

"The Lord of Duns..." although she said it quietly, I knew that it was involuntary. She put her hand to her mouth, "Do not tell the King I pray you, I..."

I shook my head, "You have told me nothing I did not know already. Fear not, my lady, you will not be betrayed by me."

The feast went well once we had put the abduction behind us and the Queen became gay and joyful. It was an act for her husband. I saw, in her eyes, sadness. The King and Queen retired first. It was the signal for us all to retire. "Thank you, Earl, for entertaining my wife. She has not looked this radiant for some time. You have brightened the darkness of her winter."

As we headed to our chamber William appeared. "They are back and the messenger rode to Duns. They waited until they had seen the town roused. Riders left the town. The Lord of Duns is prepared for us."

"Good. They have no castle and I would rather all of his men were gathered together. When he is punished then all will be punished. I have no desire to travel the length of Scotland seeking enemies."

When we had prepared for bed William took the goose down filled mattress and placed it behind the door. "What do you do, my son?"

"Tonight I will be your chamberlain. When I went to the camp Padraig said to do so. He said the Scots were cutthroats but a body behind a door is hard to shift! It is one night. I am content."

We woke and the night had been without incident. We broke our fast with the other Scottish lords but the King and Queen kept apart. I spoke quietly to the Bishop, Sir Ralph and Sir Robert and told them what I had learned. I sent William with a message to the camp. When the King arrived, he was alone. The Queen was not with him. He sat, not at the table with us, but on his throne. He also wore his crown. The previous day had been informal. Now he was using the authority of his crown. We were winning.

"Bishop we have spoken with our advisers. We will deal with those who committed these crimes ourselves. They are Scottish and will be subject to Scottish law."

"I am afraid, King Alexander, that is not good enough. Sir Thomas?" The Bishop held his arm out.

I stood, "The man who organised the attacks and led them was the Lord of Duns, Sir Guy de Beaucaire." If I had made lightning appear from my sword, I could not have had a greater effect. "We suspected so before we came. He is a Frenchman. Frenchmen were amongst those who raided England. Last night the Earl of Fife sent a rider to Duns to warn the Frenchman." I looked at the Earl. "My men followed your messenger. They saw Duns preparing for war. He is the guilty party and I will take my men now and apprehend him. I hope to have your permission, King Alexander, for I do not wish to make war. However, I should warn you that my men have broken camp and they are already on the road to Duns. You I trust but not the Earl of Fife."

Duncan of Dunfermline stood, "You insult me!"

"Then ask for satisfaction and you and I will put our honour to God's test. I know who will win. Do you?"

It was when he sat that I knew we had won. The King looked at his advisers. It was as though he had been abandoned. He had a choice. He could refuse to allow us to go to Duns and, effectively, declare war on England, or he could accept our act with good grace. He nodded, "You have my permission to arrest Sir Guy. We suspected his involvement but had no proof. When he is taken then this is over?" The King's words showed his complicity in the whole raid. He was not an innocent. King Henry would have a Scottish war.

I nodded to the Bishop who spoke, "It is, King Alexander, but we would urge you to control your border knights. We will ensure that no rogue knights cross the border. If you do the same then there will be peace."

The Bishop had done well. His calm voice had been heavy with the threat of war. King Alexander would not condone any more raids but I had made another enemy in the Earl of Fife.

# Chapter 14
# The Battle of Duns

We parted with the Bishop and his escort of five knights and men at arms at the Tweed. "God speed, Earl! I pray you have success." I nodded. "I will leave you two priests. The captives may need their aid. I will await you at Durham. I have no doubt that you will be successful for you have thought all things out well. By the time you arrive there will be beds and shelter for those who have been so basely abused."

We hurried up the road. I could already see the tail end of my column. We galloped through them to cheers and shouts. The day was cold and overcast but the rain of the last two days had gone. That had been my only worry for I had feared my archers might be impaired. They would be the key. At the front of the column rode Sir William and my household knights. Cedric and Oswald were with them. We did not rein in but spoke as we rode. "Well?"

Cedric spoke, "We recognised two of the men who we fought in the woods, lord. These are the same. They have a hall with a ditch but no keep. The foundations for the castles are laid but they offer no defence. The new castle is on a hill above the houses. They do not have a river."

"You did well and you shall be rewarded."

"Nay, lord, our reward will be when you take the heads of these murdering bastards."

I waved forward David of Wales, "David, take our archers and go with Cedric and Oswald. Find somewhere that we may attack them. Cedric says there is a wood to the north of the new castle they are building. Send me word."

"Aye lord." The one hundred archers and two scouts disappeared in the twinkling of an eye. It showed how poor was the visibility.

Sir William and Sir Ralph flanked me. The Sheriff said, "Well lord, what is the plan?"

"If they were going to flee then they would have done so. They intend to fight. They have been sent word of our numbers and think they outnumber us. That means they will improvise a defence. They will block roads and build barricades. They might hope we will not come but they will prepare. They have had one night and a morning to do so. We dismount and fight on foot. There is naught to be gained from a mounted attack. We will rely on our archers keeping their heads down as we advance."

Cedric had told me that the hall was being built a little out of the settlement on a patch of higher ground. They would use the slope and assume that our horsemen would be slowed down. If David of Wales could infiltrate the woods then an attack from there might surprise them. We passed a tiny hamlet. It was deserted. We later heard it was called Gavinton. It was a mile and a half from Duns. We could see the hill through the murk. We dismounted and left the servants with the horses. We would need the squires. I ordered a dozen of the Bishop's men at arms to stay with the horses. I was unsure of their reliability. Our squires and my men were more certain.

We prepared to attack on foot. We removed our cloaks. We took spears.

Dick One Arrow rode in, "My lord, we are in the woods to the north and west of the hill. We were not seen and all of the defences face this road. They are using the unused timbers of the building as defences. David of Wales awaits your command."

I shook my head, "He will be in the best position to time his arrows. Let him loose when the time is opportune. We will draw the enemy to us."

"Aye, lord."

I divided our forces into two. Sir James of Wessington led the men of Durham. I had them skirt the south of the village and sweep up toward the hall. I led my men cross country, over muddy fields to the hillside. "Sir James, I will sound the horn when we are about to attack but attack whenever you feel that the time is ripe."

"I will, my lord."

"Spare the women and children. Keep a sharp eye for captives. We come not only to punish but to rescue captives."

"Aye, Sir Thomas."

I had my shield on my back and my helmet hung from my sword as we began to move towards the hill. I could see little. When I saw movement, I knew that it had to be men who moved as we neared their defences. We were in one long line. I relied on the superior skills of my men. We had better armour and were better trained. No matter how many men faced us we would give a good account of ourselves. The ground was cloying and we did not move as quickly as we might have liked. In one way that favoured us. Our enemies were able to move their men around to face the threat. They would move men away from the village to meet us. Sir James would have fewer men to face. They thought that they were in control but a hundred archers led by two scouts were already moving towards their flank.

We were just two hundred paces from them when their boys and archers stepped from behind their defences. They were using the timber they planned on using for the castle's palisade as a barricade. It came up to their chests. Holding up my sword to steady my men, I turned to William. "As soon as they launch their first arrow or stone then sound the horn and signal Sir James to attack."

I donned my helmet and pulled my shield around. I pointed my sword forward. I was flanked by the Sheriff of York and William of Hartburn. The archers sent their arrows towards us. They were using neither bodkin tipped nor war arrows. They were hunting arrows. If we had had men without mail or horses then there was a chance that they might have hurt us. As it was, they were just an annoyance. I held my shield up. A hunting arrow could strike and tear flesh. Two arrows hit my shield but failed to penetrate the cover and dropped to the ground. David of Wales would have been disgusted. Their bows were not powerful. If the wind had not been from the north east then the missiles would not even have reached us. William sounded the horn and I heard a cheer from my right as James of Wessington led the Bishop's men to attack the village. We ploughed on steadily up the muddy and increasingly slippery slope. The defenders would be heartened by our laborious approach. David of Wales would judge his moment to launch his arrows. I knew that whenever he did so would be the perfect time. Then the stones began to hit our shields and our helmets. They were deadlier than the arrows for if they hit a helmet, they could cause damage. I risked peering over the top and saw that they had a line of warriors ready behind the barrier. The slingers and the archers were arrayed before the barriers. The stone that came towards me was so fast and the light so bad that I barely had time to bring up my shield. The stone clattered off the shield. It had been a powerful throw. The archers and stone throwers were now less than thirty paces from us. The sound of stones on shields sounded like hailstones. I was lucky and all of the stones and arrows hit my shield.

I raised my sword and shouted, "Charge!" William waved the standard and I opened my legs to run.

The effect of our charge on the ones with bows and slings was instantaneous. Throwing from a distance was one thing but they would not face the wrath of a mailed warrior who had had to endure their missiles and was seeking revenge. They ran. David of Wales had judged his arrows to perfection. Even with my helmet and coif I heard the whoosh of arrows as David of Wales sent his bodkin tipped missiles and war arrows towards the defenders. I had been right. It had been the perfect time. As the archers and slingers tried to clamber over the barricade, they and the men defending it were hit by one hundred arrows. The attention of the defenders was drawn to the wood to their right. I reached the barricade and found two dead archers and a dead spearman. I was able to clamber over the timbers unmolested. I saw that the men on the barricade had been without armour. Most looked to be brigands or bandits. Ahead of me, however, I saw, in the shell of the new keep, the knights and men at arms of the Lord of Duns. The light was poor but I saw helmets and mail. I recognised the two headed eagle he bore on his chest and the single fleur de lys. His men at arms bore the same sign. The other knights all had a single fleur de lys on their shields too. They were French. I had time to gauge their ability to defend for Sir William and Sir Ralph, along with their squires, had cleared the rest of the barricade. The slingers and archers who had survived had fled and were streaming north and east. To my left David of

Wales led my archers from their place of concealment. They were targeting the mailed men. We had time to form up.

"Shield wall on me!"

Geoffrey FitzUrse and my other knights ran towards me. All had surcoats spattered and smeared with mud. As my men at arms joined me, I looked to my right and saw that the men of Durham were driving back the defenders from the village. There was a low stone wall which was the foundation layer of the keep. The enemy were behind it. Had we not had archers then that might have been a serious obstacle. Our archers could use plunging arrows and that would hurt the enemy. We began to march towards them. The newly knighted Sir Gilles was in the front rank. This would be a severe test for him. The French knights we faced knew their business. Their shields were locked and spears prickled along the edge of the wall. David of Wales kept pace with us. His arrows kept the heads of the enemy down. It also irritated the Scots. They did not like to endure an arrow storm. Before us was a mass of men. Whatever one might think of the Scots they had courage. They ran at us.

A Scottish knight, recognisable by his spurs, shouted something in Gaelic and he and a half dozen of his clansmen ran from behind the wall and charged us. I did not risk my sword against his broader sword. My edge would be dulled. Instead I took the blow on my shield. I let him swing his sword a second time. I was aware that, to my right, William was holding my standard with his left hand while fighting a warrior with a target shield and short curved sword. Sir Gilles was standing and defending his right side. I would have to deal with the knight before I could go to the aid of my son. This was war! This time, as the knight's sword hit my shield, he was concentrating on hurting me. He was trying to use his broader sword and strength to batter me into submission. I lunged down toward his legs. They were protected by chausse but unlike the Scotsman's blade my sword had a tip. As I punched, I tore through one of the mail links and into his thigh. I twisted as I pulled. My blade brought some links with it and, tugging his leg on the slippery slope, unbalanced him. He used his left hand for balance and I swung my sword in a sideways sweep. I hit him in the side. My sword had an edge and it was sharp. My sword was made of the finest metal and it ripped through his mail, gambeson and into his side. I sawed the blade backwards and he fell. I whirled to help William. I was not needed. Even as I turned, I saw him lunge with the standard as though it was a spear. As the Scot raised his shield, William hacked across his neck and the man fell gurgling in his own blood. I watched as Sir Gilles, closely followed by his squire, Henry, run to the aid of Sir Peter who had three Scots trying to hack him and his squire to pieces. This was a baptism of fire for the young knight and squire.

Suddenly the five enemy knights, who bore French devices, jumped up and ran. I wondered where they were going. The half-finished walls of the keep's base meant that there was dead ground ahead of us. We hurried forward to finish off the others. The five knights would be caught for David of Wales was advancing from our left and I saw the survivors from the village running away from James of Wessington and the knights of Durham. As the other defenders realised what was happening and tried to flee, I saw that the five knights had mounted horses. Their heads appeared and they tried to escape north and west. David of Wales and his archers would not reach them in time. Guy de Beaucaire was going to escape! He was less than one hundred paces from us and I saw him urge his horse on. There was, from my left, what sounded like a flock of birds taking to the sky. I looked and saw that David of Wales and his archers had sent a hundred arrows at the fleeing men at arms and knights. The mail and the armour of the five knights gave them some protection but none to their horses. David and his men had all sent their arrows, war arrows this time, at the five horsemen and their mounts. We would catch those on foot. The arrows could not miss and horses and riders were all struck repeatedly. The arrows sprouted from surcoats, mail and shields but none of the knights was hurt. All five horses died. One gamely carried on for twenty paces before falling. Their riders were thrown from their backs.

The Scots who had been fleeing now realised the futility of flight and turned to face us like men. If they turned their backs then David of Wales' arrows would kill them as easily as they had the horses. They were not knights and had neither mail nor breastplate. They ran towards us. One had a war hammer which he swung above his head as he ran down the slope towards me. A war hammer is a terrifying weapon but it is hard to control. Once he was committed to the swing, I merely dropped to my right knee and swung across his thigh with my sword. I severed his leg and he fell forwards screaming. The weight of his hammer made him tumble down the slippery slope. I reached the wall and climbed up. Guy de Beaucaire, I guessed it was him from his livery, had extracted himself from beneath his horse and led the four knights who had survived towards us. The Scotsmen who remained alive had nothing to lose and were wild enough to sell their lives dearly. I still had my knights with me and, leaving Ridley the Giant and my men at arms to deal with the other raiders, we moved through the shell of the keep towards the knights. Three of their squires had survived and joined their lords.

"Watch out for breastplates beneath the mail. These are French knights!"

They nodded. William, Peter and Fótr had met them before but they were new to Sir Ralph and Sir Gilles. I headed to the knight I assumed was Guy de Beaucaire. I had seen the double headed eagle in France. He was not as tall as me but he was broader. The ground was slippery and that would be a disadvantage to me. I placed my feet further apart as he swung his sword at my chest. I blocked it easily with my shield but he had fast hands and swung again. I used the flat of my sword to fend it off. He was trying to finish me quickly. He must have known who I was for my livery was well known. I was no longer a young man and perhaps he thought I might tire. I had the slight advantage of higher ground. Even as he pulled his arm back, I swung. I made the move appear as though I was going to go for his chest. I was not for I suspected he had a breastplate. He barely raised his shield. At the last moment I flicked up my arm and hit him on the side of the helmet. It unbalanced him and he reeled.

As he struggled to regain his balance, I saw that the rest of my men were winning. The French were relying on their breastplates but my men attacked their more vulnerable parts: arms and legs.

"Yield or you will die! Your men are dead or fled!"

"I will not yield to you and all is not lost until I am dead. Lay on!" He lunged at my chest with his sword. His sword, like mine, had a tapered point and tip. His hands were so quick that my shield barely stopped the strike. My left arm was still not totally healed. I had strength but not as much mobility as I once had. The tip penetrated two of my links and burst them. It was a well-made hauberk but I could not afford for this to continue too long. I brought my sword over from behind me. The movement told him that I would strike his head again. He brought his shield up to block the blow but, instead, I punched his sword arm with my shield. He reeled. I pulled my left hand back and hit him again with my shield. I might not be able to raise and lower the shield quickly but I could punch with it. When I pulled my sword arm behind me to swing again, I had him confused. I struck the side of his helmet again with the blade and this time he fell. I dropped onto his chest with my left knee. I felt the breastplate there. I rammed the edge of my shield across his left arm, breaking it. I heard him scream in pain. "Now you will yield for you have no sword arm. I can break every bone in your body if I have to but you will be my prisoner!"

His head nodded, "I yield!"

I stood and looked around me. I took off my helmet and shouted, "Your master has surrendered. Yield!"

The men who had raided, ravaged and raped were in no mood to surrender and be hanged. They fought on. David of Wales and his archers ended their resistance with deadly arrows. There was neither honour nor reason in wasting men at arms. Two other French knights and four Scottish knights had surrendered. I turned to Ridley the Giant, "Have these knights bound and assign a man to watch each one."

Guy de Beaucaire, now that he had taken off his helmet, I could see that he was about the same age as Alfred would have been, protested, "My lord we surrendered! You cannot bind us. We should be treated with dignity!"

"You are to be taken to Durham where you will be tried for your crimes."

One of the Scottish knights shouted, "King Alexander will hear of this! It will mean war!"

"Before we came here, we spoke with your king or did not your messenger from the Earl of Fife tell you that?" My strike had been a blind one but it struck home. His reaction told me that they were the men of the Earl of Fife. "We stay in the village this night and leave on the morrow. Find the captives."

Sir James of Wessington had already located the eighty captives. They were women and children. Some of the women's faces told of the pain they had endured. They were barefoot and blue with the cold. As my men found them cloaks and furs, mainly from the dead bandits, fires were lit and food put on to be cooked. I saw Sir Robert speaking with the handful of people from his manor who had survived. He was closer to peace now but so long as the knights lived there would be a need for revenge. We had but fifteen prisoners to be taken back for trial. The rest were dead or had managed to escape. The bodies of the dead had been stripped. We found stolen items on them. They would be taken back to Durham. The Bishop would see that they were returned to their rightful owners. We ate horsemeat. The five knight's horses were butchered and we all ate well. Our losses had been relatively light. The dead were buried by the two priests in the cemetery of Duns church. Their souls would be in heaven for the priests had shrived them before we fought.

With the prisoners secured I spoke with the captives. As in all such raids there were leaders amongst those who had been captured. Some of those who had been taken might be women but they had steel for backbones. Seara, wife of Egbert of Embleton, was one such matriarch. She had seen forty summers and the children who had survived were less than ten summers old. The others had died. The boys, along with their father defending their farm, east of Sedgefield, and the elder girls during the march north. Some of the orphans of dead mothers had attached themselves to her and they nestled close to her. I could tell that she was the leader.

"I am Sir Thomas of Stockton, Seara wife of Egbert, I would hear your tale."

She nodded. I saw that she did not enjoy telling the story but she was a strong woman. Many of my men at arms and archers had married such women. They were as much a part of my land as the castles and the warriors. They held families together while men made war. "I am Widow Seara now and that is sad for my husband was a good man. We had eight children. The Good Lord had blessed us, we thought, for I only lost two before the savages came." She made the sign of the cross and touched the cross about her neck. "They did not kill all. they left me four. I should be grateful. Some of these other bairns lost mothers, fathers, brothers and grandsires." She shook her head and I thought she was going to break down. She coughed and shook herself. "Get a hold of yourself, Seara, tears help no one." She looked at me with steel in her eyes, "We will remember the dead when they are buried. They will be buried will they not, lord? You will not allow the foxes to feast on their flesh!"

"I swear that all will be done to give the dead that which they deserve and," I pointed to the prisoners, "your testimony will see that justice is served to their killers."

"We are women, lord. We cannot testify."

"The Bishop of Durham will hear your words. They will be given under oath. Your testimony will be heard!"

"Good." She began stroking the hair of a four-year-old who was falling asleep, nestled next to her bosom. "The first we knew was when the dogs barked. We thought it was wolves. They are rare in the valley but they do come in the depths of winter. When my husband went forth, he was killed as were my sons. We tried to defend ourselves but there were too many." She pointed to the Scottish lord who had objected to his treatment. "He was there. They left us with four men and they abused my elder girls. Poor bairns, they died on the march north and that is a mercy for they endured that which should not be endured." She bit her lip and, seeing that the girl was asleep covered her. "The next day the butcher brought the survivors from Sedgefield and we were forced north. We were all tied together and tethered behind horses. Many died on the roads and their bodies were hurled in ditches. As we went north more joined us. There were many animals. We crossed the Tyne and the numbers doubled. It was though the north had been emptied of women and children. When we reached the Tweed, we were met by a lord. He had many more men there."

"What was his livery?" She frowned. I pointed to my own surcoat.

She nodded, "It was yellow and red stripes. There was a bird upon it."

I turned to Sir Ralph, "The Earl of Fife! Go on."

"There we were split up. The cattle and sheep were driven north and we were brought here."

"That explains why we found so few animals. I will need to have words with the Earl of Fife."

Seara said, "What will happen to us, lord? It was hard enough farming our land with my husband and my sons. With no animals and none of my children older than eight how can I eke out a living?"

I stood and addressed all of those who were gathered in the barn we were using, "Any who do not wish to return to their own homes can have a home with me. I know the Scots travelled far to attack you but Stockton Castle is a rock." I turned and glared at the prisoners. "These savages would not dare to attack my castle. It is as safe as the King's home in London. You will all have a home in my valley."

For some reason my words made the steel of Seara melt and she began to weep. She grasped my hand and kissed it. "Thank you, lord. I could not lose any more bairns. It would kill me."

I strode over to the captured knights. "None of you have any honour. On the journey to Durham you will feel what these people felt. You will be tried fairly but I have no doubt that you will be found guilty and executed."

One of the French knights said, "This was a chevauchée! We did nothing wrong. I never touched a woman or a child! I only killed men!"

"You killed men who were not mailed. You killed men who had wood axes to defend their homes. You may not have harmed a woman or a child but the men you led did. You were their leaders and you bear the responsibility!" I shook my head, "I have met your King, Louis, and I know that he would not condone such actions. He would have you executed too. Make your peace with our priests, my lords, for you will die and I will see that it is well done!"

We headed, back to Roxburgh the next day. We would spend the next night at Otterburn but I intended to go, with five knights and confront the King and the Earl of Fife. We had carts and wagons for the captives. We took all the animals that we could find and we set fire to the building of Duns. Those who had lived there had fled. The blackened buildings would be a reminder of the folly of attacking England. I had the prisoners tethered and they were each pulled behind the horse of one of my men at arms.

They would have a long march to think on their sins. As we neared the bridge, I took four of my knights, squires and the priest who had heard Seara's story to the castle at Roxburgh. We were seen from afar and greeted at the gate by men at arms.

"I would speak with the King."

"He is expecting you, lord."

There were fewer lords present this time when we entered his hall and the Queen was seated at the side of the King. "We saw smoke in the sky, my lord. Is it done?"

"It is, King Alexander, and we have rescued many captives. The Queen is present and I will not go into details for their suffering was great and she is too delicate a lady to have to endure such tales. Suffice it to say that we bring back many orphans and there are young women who will fear the touch of men. They will wake in the night screaming with the nightmares which haunt them." The Queen's hand went to her mouth.

"Are you sure you do not exaggerate, Sir Thomas, to enlist the support of my wife."

I clenched my fists. He was trying to make me out to be a liar. I spoke quietly, "Brother Paul."

The priest stepped forward, "King Alexander, the Earl speaks true. The Scots and French did not behave as men. They behaved as animals. I was ashamed to be a man. The Earl neither lies nor exaggerates!"

There was little respect in the priest's voice and the King was taken aback. "I am sorry, Earl, I did not mean to impugn your honour. And you have those responsible?"

"We have most but not the man who sent them." I paused, for effect. "The Earl of Fife was the one who ordered this raid. He was not captured and I need him to stand trial too. Is he here in the castle?"

"I cannot believe that of the Earl but he is returned to his home. He will be far to the north. He left soon after you did. You have proof of his guilt?"

"We have proof. He met with the raiders on the other side of the Tweed and took the animals from them. I daresay they are already grazing in Fife."

The King said nothing and we just stared. I had wanted knights and a priest as witnesses to the King's conduct. He said, very quietly, "Sir Thomas, the Earl of Fife is a powerful man. It does not do to make accusations. He has lands in France as well as England."

The King was telling me that the Earl would remain unpunished. I nodded, "That comes as no surprise. His estates in England will now be forfeit." I turned to look at the other lords who were watching us. "I am guessing that there will some lackey of the Earl's who will take that message to him." I saw one knight redden and squirm. "I have captives to house and prisoners to execute so the Earl is safe for a while. Know this, King Alexander, I will travel to Fife and I will apprehend the Earl. It is only a matter of time." I glared at the knight with the reddened face, "Tell him that I come for him and this will be settled once and for all. If any try to stop me, any, then I will destroy them."

King Alexander nodded. "I would not have you as my enemy, Earl. You know not when to stop."

"But I do know, King Alexander. I stop when justice is done and the innocent avenged. We will now take our leave of you."

As I turned the Queen said, "Sir Thomas!"

I turned, "Yes, Queen Joan?"

She flashed an angry look at her husband and took a red ruby ring from her finger. "We are innocent in all of this but I feel guilty that my brother's subjects were so ill-treated. This ring was given to me as a wedding present. I would have you sell it and use the proceeds for the people who were abused."

"My Queen, I cannot take this ring. It is valuable."

She shook her head, "It has no value to me. It was given to me by the Earl of Fife. I cannot bear to look at it again for each time I did the red would remind me of the English blood shed by a foresworn and venal man."

I took it from her, "In that case I promise that I will put it to good use." Queen Joan was a good woman and Scotland had, in her, a good queen.

# Chapter 15
# English Justice and English Peace

The Bishop was as good as his word and the captives had new clothes and beds waiting for them when we arrived in Durham. The closer we had come to the Palatinate the more the captives had realised that they were in dire straits. They pleaded for their lives and, in doing so, implicated even more people. We listened to their pleas but promised nothing. The Count d'Eu was key to the plans. His sister had married the Earl of Fife. The Count had acquired estates in Normandy and the Vexin. They had been given to the Earl of Fife. One of the French knights suggested that the Earl had aspirations to be King of Scotland. None of this would change their fate. The further south we had progressed the more stories of the privations of the captives had been revealed. The priests listened to the revelations and made notes on wax tablets. Their testimony would be heard.

The Bishop convened a jury. It took five days to do so. The Sheriff of Northumbria and the Sheriff of York as well as myself and the Bishop of the New Castle formed that jury with Sir Peter and Sir James representing ordinary peers. The testimony of the captives was given by the two priests who had accompanied us. The only argument the knights had was that they were following the orders of the Earl of Fife. His fate was sealed in absentia. A written record was kept of the trial. The punishment was death. The only question was the form it took. Hanging, drawing and quartering was an option but the Bishop chose the less dramatic death. They were beheaded in the cloisters before the cathedral. Their heads were displayed on pikes on the city walls. A warning was sent across the border and across the sea. There was justice in England. The heads of the dead brought some relief to the captives and Sir Robert and his brother. The dead had been avenged.

Some of the captives chose to stay with the Bishop. Winter gripped the land and if they had gone home, they would have starved to death. Most, especially those from the south of Durham, chose to come with me. When the trial had begun, I had sent Sir Fótr and Sir William back with the majority of my men to warn my wife and the town of the influx of refugees. I had visited the Jews of Durham. In those days they were still able to ply their trade. They purchased the ring from me and I divided the money between all of the captives. It was just a few pennies for each of them but was welcome. For most it was more money than they had ever seen in their lives. They would all have something to begin their new lives in the Tees Valley.

Robert of Elsdon sought an audience with the Bishop. He asked for me to be there. He had come south only to see the trial of those who had been responsible for the death of his wife. He wished to go on crusade and he would give up Elsdon. I saw the sadness on the face of Richard Poore. He felt that he had let down his knight but he would not stand in his way. He gave him permission and another lord would be appointed to the troubled manor. Sir Robert came with me. He would stay with me in Stockton until the weather was clement for such a long sea voyage.

We had been away for a month and the winter snows had set in. We were lucky that the Scottish raiders had had so many furs. Our new people were warmer than they might otherwise have been. When we reached Stockton, it was after noon. The Sheriff and Sir Peter stayed just one night for they were anxious to get home. I was sad for I knew there would be fewer meetings with my old comrades. Their departure was offset by the presence of Sir Robert and his brother. This was where I missed my aunt for she had a way with such damaged people. My wife was busy with the captives. She understood their plight and so it was left to William and his sister, Isabelle, to entertain and brighten the lives of the two brothers who had lost everything. For Isabelle her own sadness was temporarily forgotten.

I had been away so long that I was closeted with Leofric for the first hour. A huge manor such as mine took a great deal of organisation. I had much to do. None of it was dramatic and most was mundane but a lord of the manor had to do these tasks. "Lord, will you be here long? I only ask as we need to hold an assize. There are many outstanding cases. None are serious save to those who bring the cases."

I nodded, "I should be here for a few months. The King is not due to begin his attack on Normandy until the spring. He has yet to send for me and I am reluctant to leave my family."

He nodded as he understood. Leofric had a wife, children and now, grandchildren. He was far luckier than I was as he got to see them all the time. He had watched them grow. I had seen mine but in fits and starts. In the month I had been away Maud, Sam and Alf had all changed. Henry Samuel was now speaking groups of words as was Alfred. I would not call them sentences and I did not understand them all but both of them were changing. Henry Samuel would soon need a tutor. He had to learn many languages. He would be a lord and there were skills he needed. Alfred and Maud would have the same teacher. I went through the list of tasks which Leofric had written for me.

"When you have time, speak with Father Harold. We need a teacher for the children. At first it will be just Henry Samuel but the others are not far behind and I am sure that Sir Geoffrey and Rebekah will want more children. We have funds aplenty." We had brought treasure back from Duns. Little of it belonged to the captives but we gave them half and shared the rest out between our men. Coin was never an issue.

The jobs which were urgent done, I went to the hall in which my wife had accommodated the captives. I saw that Seara had helped to organize them. I was also surprised to see Padraig there. His wife had died many years ago. When we had been in France, he had not shown any signs of wanting another woman and yet here he was, the only man, save me, in a room full of women. I said nothing to him for I saw that he was embarrassed. Instead I went to my wife. "I am sorry that I gave you this task."

She squeezed my arm, "You are a goose! Men!" She shook her head. "You are a kind man. I know that in the heat of battle you are not but you are thoughtful in matters domestic. This was the Christian thing to do and it was the right thing. This hall was largely empty. Most of the archers and men at arms are now married and have homes beyond the walls. The ones who had beds here were more than happy to go to the warrior hall. This is good." She smiled, "Besides I can see that many of those who are single will soon be married. These women all have children. They are mothers." She nodded towards Padraig. "I believe your man at arms has his eye set on one."

I looked at the women who were organising the beds and tables. The prettiest of the women was Mary. She was a redhead and, despite her ordeal, was always laughing. She had two children under the age of five and I had no doubt she would soon find a man. "Mary?"

My wife laughed, "You do not know your own men! He is sweet on Seara and she returns that affection."

"But she is older than all the rest!"

"And not as old as me!" She playfully smacked my behind. "That is what they both need, comfort and someone that will not be flighty. It is good for them both. Padraig lost the love of his life when his wife died. Seara will not be the love of his life but they will be happy!" I saw Padraig helping Seara to put sheets on the mattresses. "Come, let us leave them. They do not need us to stare at them!"

I helped her to put on her cloak and we hurried across the inner ward to the main hall. "Is there food enough for them?"

She nodded, "When Sir Fotr brought the message I had Edward bring up some of the emergency supplies. Tam the Hawker says there are herds of deer yet to be culled. We can replenish our stocks. And I have had Alice the sow slaughtered. I thought to wait for the end of the month but this is as good a time as any. We will eat well and the bones, offal, head and feet will keep them fed for a week."

We entered my hall and Tancred took our cloaks. I heard laughter coming from the hall. We edged along the corridor so that we could peer in without being seen. My son and daughter were with Sir Robert and his brother. They were playing the game where you had to balance a stick on your head after having been turned around a number of times. It was one of the exercises we did with squires. It helped them when they became knights and had to fight enemies who were all around them. My daughter was doing it and managing to do so better than most squires might have done. That was not the surprise. It was the smile on Sir Robert's face. My son and daughter had done the impossible. They had dragged the knight from his pit of despair.

I went to my chamber and I prepared for the feast. My wife joined me after she had ensured that the food had been prepared according to her instructions. We had guests and my wife always went that little bit further for those that we did not know well. She smiled as I took off my tunic. When I took off my undergarments, she frowned. I realised that this was the first time she had seen me semi-naked since I had returned from France. She put her hand on the wound to my left arm. "You did not tell me you had another wound!"

I shrugged and, taking her hand, kissed it, "It does not bother me and, in truth, I had forgotten it. Now you should."

"Thomas, you are no longer a young man. There are others who can take on the mantle of defender of the King. The Earl Marshal's son, Richard, he is much younger and has all the skills which would be needed."

I nodded, "I know and yet his father chose me and not his sons."

"Perhaps his sons were not ready then. It may be that you are needed to make the transition."

"That might be true but I cannot change who I am." I put my arm around her and pulled her to my lap. "Let me enjoy my time at home. I am enjoying my grandchildren. They do not seem terrified of my scar and for that I am grateful. My land is now at peace and we have coin enough to indulge ourselves. Let affairs of state wait! The King and his Justiciar are in Normandy. Hopefully they will retake Normandy without recourse to me."

She kissed me, "I hope so."

I was less embarrassed about the scar on my face. Time had passed and my grandchildren seemed not to notice it. I was still their grandfather or, as Henry Samuel now called me, '*grandda*'. His earlier '*gwandad*' had gone. He was growing. He had learned the word from Mary, his nurse. She was a local girl and they called their fathers dad or da and their grandfathers, granddad or grandda. She had used that term since he had been born and he now thought it was my name. I still had their love without measure. I combed and oiled my hair and beard and led my beautiful wife down to the feasting hall. We were the first to arrive although William soon joined us. I saw that he had also combed and oiled his hair and beard. He had adopted a beard in the French style. He had seen many knights in Poitou with such facial adornments. I did not like it but I accepted that many young knights sported one.

He grinned when he saw me. "After all this time it is good to know that I will be sleeping in my own bed for some time to come and I need not worry about the food. Life is good, father."

"It is and you did well. If you wish me to dub you...."

He shook his head, "I have spoken to Richard, Sir Robert's squire. I know how lucky I am. I have the opportunity to become more skilled and a better knight. I am content." He lowered his voice and looked over his shoulder, "They have both had a hard time, father. Their own father died in the baron's war. Their family lost everything for King John was vindictive."

"And that is no surprise but they have the chance to start anew. If they do not wish to go to the Holy Land, I have need of another household knight." I squeezed my wife's hand, "We have yet to replace Alfred as a knight. We can never replace him as a son but..."

My wife squeezed my hand back, "Thoughtful, husband, as ever."

We heard laughter. It sounded like the tinkling of a mountain stream. It was Matilda and Isabelle. As they entered the hall they both looked radiant. I had not seen Matilda look so since before my son had been murdered. "You two are happy!"

Isabelle came and linked my arm, "I have my father and brother back. Why should I not be happy? The war in Normandy is a lifetime away and we can be gay and enjoy a feast. Christmas had a shadow hanging over it. Let us make this feast a second Christmas. My father has brought back gifts worthy of the Magi!"

Matilda nodded, "Aye, lord. My son is happy for his grandfather is back and he and his sister are both asleep. The wet nurse feeds Maud and I can enjoy some wine this night. Let us, as my sister says, make it a celebration. From what Isabelle says you saved those women and children from a life of slavery. We will celebrate Sir Thomas, the true knight!"

I laughed, "I do not know about that but I agree with the celebration." I waved over Leofric, "Tell the steward to broach one of the barrels from Royan. Let us enjoy a good wine this night and impress our guests!"

By the standards of my feasts this was a small one but it was one which warmed my heart more than most. There were four people who each bore a stone of sadness in their hearts. Sir Robert and his squire were a little quiet at first but Matilda and Isabelle had decided to throw off the shackles of sadness. Sir Ralph and Sir Peter sat with my wife and just enjoyed the evening. They were anticipating the homecoming that they would have. Both had wives and children. I knew how much they missed them and we had been away for a month. That night there was laughter around the table. The instigator of the humour was my son, William. My men at arms had taken to my son and, when on campaign, he often rode with them. Their rough humour had rubbed off on him. He was a good mimic and he had the hall laughing with his impression of one of the fussier priests who had accompanied the Bishop. Sir Robert came out of his shell and, laughing, said, "You have him Master William. Why, it is almost as though he is in the room!"

Isabelle laughed, "Oh I pray that the Bishop brings him to visit." She laughed and then shook her head, "No, I do not for I would not be able to constrain my laughter as soon as I saw him!"

William then told some jokes. They became racier and racier. He had almost crossed the line, for his mother was about to speak, when he was saved by the arrival of the pig. The cook had done everything perfectly. It had been roasted and the skin scored and salted. It would be so tender that carving would almost be unnecessary. As host it was my task to carve the first piece and then the others would cut first for their ladies and then for themselves. I cut some of the crackling and placed it on my wife's platter. I then cut some for myself. I sliced some thinner slivers of meat for Margaret and then thicker ones for myself. We still had apples in the store and cook had made spiced apple sauce. My wife put generous spoonfuls on my platter for she knew I was fond of it. Sir Robert and his brother put crackling, meat and sauce on Matilda's platter while my son served his sister. When all was served the laughter at William's jokes was replaced by the sound of well-cooked pig skin being crunched. The servants brought in side dishes of beans and winter greens. Platters of venison carved in the kitchen were brought in along with a compote of the last of the plums. This was food served to my taste. I was pleased that my guests all seemed to enjoy it. The wine flowed. Matilda and Isabelle drank it watered but my wife enjoyed strong wine. When the meat had been finished the fresh bread and cheese were brought in along with the pudding. My cook made a wonderful pudding made of honeyed fruit, minced meat and spices served with cream. Even I enjoyed it.

After the meal Sir Peter said to William, "You are soon to be a knight. Go fetch your crowd and we will judge if you are ready."

Alfred would have baulked at the attention but William was more confident. He happily left to fetch his musical instrument. Sir Robert turned to me, "Thank you for this merry gathering, lord. It has lifted our spirits. You are lucky to have such a fine family. I envy you."

My wife leaned forward and said, "And yet, Sir Robert, we too have had to endure losses. Our son was recently murdered and my husband's aunt, who was the head of this family, also died. We know of your pain. This is our way to relieve it. It does not disrespect the dead, rather it honours them by celebrating life. God gives us but a short time on this earth for we spend eternity in heaven and it would be an insult to him if we did not make the most of it."

"You are right, lady, but I fear the hole in my heart can never be filled."

Richard shook his head, "You do not have to fill it. It seems to me, brother, that your heart is big enough to have the hole there as a reminder of what you lost but fill the rest of it with joy. I have not lost as much as you although, I confess, I still weep at night over the loss but I am determined now to be a knight. I will seek my fortune. Sir Thomas here began with less than us. He was alone in the Holy Land and yet look what he has now. He is a confidante of the King and kings and princes walk in fear of offending him. If Sir Thomas can change his life then the least we can do is try!"

Sir Robert nodded and sat back in his chair. For the rest of the evening he was more thoughtful. It was as though someone had placed the idea in his brother's head for the message to be given to Sir Robert. I believed that it was the spirit of my aunt. Almost her whole life had been spent in the castle. She was part of its fabric.

William returned and walked confidently forward with the crowd under his arm. He then made a feigned stumble. It was a trick which Sam Strongarm had taught him. It made Matilda, Isabelle and Richard roar with laughter. William looked accusing at the floor as though it had tripped him. He struck a note. It was off key and he nodded and smiled as though he had meant it. He began to run through some vocal exercises all of which were off key. There was even more laughter. He then said, "I have been practising for the day when I shall gain my spurs and I have, as I am supposed to, composed a song. I will give it an airing."

He adopted a serious pose and then, striking the crowd perfectly, began to sing.

*Hubert de Burgh is a fine fat man*
*He can count his numbers better than a miser can*
*He roars and struts when the enemy cheer*
*But when they are close he flees in fear*
*You know where he is for he cannot hide well*
*With the doxies and...*

The laughter was great, especially from those who knew the Justiciar but I saw his mother frown when he sang the word doxies. I think he always intended to stop there for he ceased playing and said, "Of course this is a work in progress. I will have it refined when I sing it before the ceremony. Here is a more appropriate song."

He then sang, beautifully and in perfect tune, the story of Saint George, the dragon and the princess. The version he used came from Sir Peter's mother, Marguerite. She had learned the song as a child in Sweden. In that tale the princess who is rescued represents Sweden while the dragon, an invading army. Marguerite had translated it. I saw Peter smiling for he had been brought up on the story. William had embellished the song and changed some of Marguerite's words. It was still allegorical but the princess now seemed more like Isabelle than a blond Swede. I saw her blush a little when she realised what her brother had done. At the end of the song she and Matilda wept and my wife, while applauding, leaned over and said, "Our son has talent. Did you know he was such a fine singer?"

I nodded, "He often sings and makes up songs while he is cleaning my mail. I suppose I am used to it. I take it for granted but you are right. He has many knightly skills."

She kissed my cheek and whispered in my ear, "Do not be in a hurry to knight him, husband. I would have my child for as long as possible."

None wished to retire but I was aware that Sir Ralph and Sir Peter were keen to return home and so my wife and I left the room. It allowed Sir Ralph and Sir Peter to follow. The others were still laughing as we entered our chamber. The sound echoed around my castle walls and filled me with joy.

I was awake early to bid farewell to my knights. Sir Ralph and Sir Peter, along with their men, would share the road as far as East Harlsey. They would enjoy food there with Sir Richard before they went their separate ways. It would be late in the evening before Sir Ralph reached his home. He would have to change his horses twice to do so.

After they had left, I walked my castle walls. I had heard Sam and Maud playing with their nurse but I decided not to intrude. Matilda had had a late night and she would wish to dress her children. I would have all day with them. I was at the gate which overlooked St John's well when I saw Padraig and Seara emerge from the hall. He held her hand. My wife was right. This was a tryst. I was pleased. When I had been in France Padraig had told me how much he missed his dead wife. We had been on the road to Pontoise and he had said, "It is the comfort, my lord, of being comfortable in the arms of someone with soft skin who does not smell of blood. It is just the feeling that there is someone who would weep if you did not come back from a battle." He had shrugged, "I daresay my fellows would miss me but within a month or more I would just be a name. When you have a wife then you live in her heart forever and that, somehow, keeps you alive. That is my belief anyway."

As I watched the two of them, I knew that my wife was right and this was good. Padraig would be a good father to Seara's children. It also meant that Seara would stay in my town and I liked that thought too. She had been the reason so many of the captives had survived the privations of the raiders. She deserved to be treated well. Padraig was paid well as a sergeant at arms and, like all of my men, could have any plot of land in my manor which he chose. It was a sensible arrangement for it meant my land was protected by a ring of warriors and their families. It was one reason why the raiders had not dared to attack my lands.

When I entered my hall I could hear, from the feasting hall, the sound of voices. One was Isabelle and the other was Sir Robert. Some thought prevented me from entering and, instead, I went to the chamber of Matilda and her children. I could hear Matilda's voice as I approached and so I knocked on the door.

"Come!"

When I entered Henry Samuel shouted, "Grandda!" His nurse had been dressing him and he hurled himself from the bed into my arms. It was a prodigious leap and I saw the looks of horror on his mother and nurse's faces. He landed safely in my arms. His tiny fingers wrapped around my neck, he hugged me.

"What if I had dropped you?"

He laughed, "You are grandda! You would not drop me!"

I held him away from me and smiled, "That was two whole sentences!"

Matilda smiled, "He has been practising. He has missed you, lord."

"So, my young cockerel, what shall we do this day? The air outside the castle is too cold to ride. We will have to find amusement in my hall and inner ward."

He looked at me seriously and I could see him struggling to choose the word he wanted to, "Hoops!"

I smiled. I knew the game he meant. It was the game squires used to practise their hand skills. They each had a stick and a hoop. The game was to throw the hoop in the air with one stick and the other would catch it with his stick. It helped to develop sword skills and reactions. I thought he was a little young but I had played it with Alfred and William when they were but a little older. I knew how to adapt it. "Let us go then, my little warrior!"

I spent the morning with Henry Samuel. I wished Alfred was there too. It would be good for them to practise together. When they were older and knights, they would ride to war together. Bonds made in childhood were strong. Richard and William joined us in the inner ward. They practised too but they were squires and they used the wooden swords which were heavier and more awkward than swords. It built strength and made it easier to use metal swords. Henry Samuel stopped playing with his grandda to watch, enviously, his uncle and the new squire as they fought with swords.

I was about to end the practise when Sir Robert and Isabelle, wrapped for the cold, appeared. Isabelle said, cheerily, "I thought to show Sir Robert the manors of Hartburn, Elton and Norton. It is a good day to ride."

I shook my head, "It is a cold day and I chose not to ride because of the cold!"

She laughed and it was good to hear, "That is because, father, you are old! We are young and the cold does not bother us. We will be back before dark!"

They went to the stables and within a short time emerged on two good palfreys. My daughter was a good rider but this was winter and we had had raiders. Who knew how many bandits had remained in the valley? I waved over Mordaf. He and the other archers were practising at the butts. "Take your brother and trail my daughter and Sir Robert. Be discreet but keep them safe!"

"Aye lord."

When I returned inside, I felt better. I was fond of Isabelle. A man should not have favourites but she was my youngest.

Henry Samuel still had afternoon naps and I was seated before my fire talking with William and Richard when the two reappeared after their ride. Isabelle was glowing. It was not just the warmth of the hall after the cold of the day it was something from within her. Her eyes sparkled. "See father, we came to no harm! All those we met were pleased to see us and were most kind. They all asked after your health!"

"Good. Did you like my land, Sir Robert?"

"Aye Sir Thomas; Elsdon is wild and a farmer has to fight the land. Here I see that the battle was fought long ago and the land is tamed. Even in the depths of winter I can see that it is fertile. I wonder that the savages did not raid here."

William laughed, "They have learned to avoid annoying my father. Our knights keep a close watch on our borders. We know when a new hunting bird appears and any strangers are greeted and either welcomed or despatched. We do not take chances in this land."

"Aye, I can see now that we took too much for granted. Looking back, I see how foolish we were but it was the only manor I was offered and I needed to provide for my wife…"

His voice tailed off. Isabelle put her hand on his arm, "Sir Robert, do not berate yourself. You blame yourself when it is the Scots and the French who are to blame. My father keeps this land safe." The love in her eyes as she looked at me made me melt inside. She deserved happiness.

Over the next weeks we settled into a routine. When the weather was good, I rode with William and young Sam, on my saddle before me, to Elton. There the two young cousins played with each other and I spoke with Rebekah. I saw little of her now and the loss of my son had made me aware that I ought not to waste opportunities to speak. Isabelle, Sir Robert and Richard would also ride. They rode further afield. Tam the Hawker went with them sometimes and they hunted with Isabelle's marlyon, Prince. It made Sir Robert envious. He asked me if I knew where he could obtain a sacre falcon. I told him to ask Tam. My hawker knew birds better than any. He was always asking why I did not have an eagle as was my right as an earl. As I told him, I had too many calls on my time to go hawking.

By the end of February, I could see a change in both my daughter and the troubled knight. He smiled more and that, in turn, made Richard happier. William and Richard had grown close. That was good. William led a lonely life as my squire. The other squires were older than he was and were rarely around. The greatest change was in in my daughter, Isabelle. She became a younger version of Aunt Ruth. She always had time for her nephews and her niece. She was patience personified. She and my wife fell out less. She was always ready to help Matilda. God had sent Sir Robert to us for a purpose. He was here to make my daughter happy.

We also had a wedding. Padraig and Seara decided to get married and the banns were read in the first week of March. Spring weddings were always believed to be lucky! Padraig had asked for one of our deserted farms. Lonesome House, which had lain empty since the time of my grandfather. It lay just a mile or so from the Oxbridge and half a mile from the farm of High Hartburn. It was not a large farm but there was water and it lay on the track which led from the Oxbridge to Redmarshal and Bishopton. It suited them both for while it had little arable land it would support sheep and goats. Seara had the idea of growing barley and brewing ale. The nearest ale wife was in Stockton. None brewed in Hartburn and they both thought that there might be company from those archers and men at arms who had homes between Stockton and Elton. I gave them one hundred pennies as a wedding gift in addition to the leasehold to the farm.

They married at the end of March. It was at the celebrations, which were held in my feasting hall, that Sir Robert approached me and seated himself in the chair vacated by Ridley the Giant. "My lord, this is a good day."

I had had enough wine to feel sleepy already and I nodded, absentmindedly, "Aye. Padraig is a good man and he and Seara deserve happiness." I patted his arm. "And you have much to do with it. Had you not searched for your wife we might never have discovered where the captives were to be found. Your loss was their gain."

He smiled, "The pain grows less each day lord and that is in no small part due to you and your family."

I waved a hand, "My family has a history of welcoming those who need a home. I am pleased that you are happy here. You have given up on the idea of crusade?"

"Aye lord. I spoke with some of your men who had been on crusade. They were disillusioned. I think I wished to become a crusader so that I could die a glorious death and be with my wife. I realise now that it was selfish. My brother would have been with me and I could not consign him to an early death."

"Good. I had already advised you not to go. I thought you needed time to think when you were less pained."

I sipped some more of the wine. We had just one barrel left from that which we had bought in Royan. If the King sent for me to help him retake Normandy then I would buy some more. As I stared into the wine, I reflected that the King had not sent any message to me. I wondered if he was waiting until he had recaptured Normandy and then he could impress me with his achievements.

"My lord?"

I turned. Sir Robert was looking at me, "Yes, Sir Robert?"

"I asked a question but you seemed distracted. Perhaps I should speak with you on the morrow." He began to rise.

"I am sorry. I was thinking of the King. No, ask your question now. I will give you my full attention."

He nodded and, as he sat, I saw him take a deep breath, "I would marry your daughter, Isabelle, if you will allow it."

I was stunned. I had not expected this and yet it was now obvious to me that the couple had been moving closer for some time. The wedding would merely have accelerated the process. I looked down the table and saw that my wife, daughters and Matilda were all staring at me. Of course, they would have known. I was aware that the room had grown quiet. Sir Robert's eyes pleaded with me. Had I given him an answer? His eyes said not. I smiled, "I am sorry, Sir Robert," his face fell, "I was not expecting the question. If the lady agrees," I smiled again, "and I have no doubt that she will, then of course you have my permission."

His eyes showed his joy, "I have little to offer, lord. I am a landless knight."

I laughed, "I know the feeling. King John took my lands and I was a sword for hire. Fear not about land. When you are ready for a manor, I will find one for you." I had one in mind but first I would need to speak with the Bishop.

I gave him my hand and he kissed the back of it, "Thank you, lord!" As he stood the whole room erupted. They had all known about it. I was the only one who was in the dark! My wife came to sit next to me as Isabelle kissed Sir Robert. My wife said, "You had everyone worried." She pushed the wine away, "You have had more than enough!"

# Chapter 16
# Rebellion!

The couple were married in May. The preparations for the wedding drove all thoughts of King Henry and Hubert de Burgh from my mind. It was not until a week after the wedding that I had the opportunity to think about King Henry and the campaign in Normandy. My wife, when I mentioned it to her, was philosophical about it. "The King may not need you. Do not take offence at that. There are other lords."

"And yet Hubert de Burgh is not a good adviser. Perhaps you are right."

It was four days later that a ship sailed into my port. I recognised the standard. It was the banner of the Bishop of Winchester. What was Peter des Roches doing in Stockton? I had heard he was back in England but I thought he was still out of favour with the King. I wondered if he was seeking my support. If so, he was in for a disappointment. I did not do politics.

I quickly sent a messenger to my wife to prepare rooms and I hurried with Leofric and William to the quay. We had plenty of time for ships always turned around in the river. The Bishop, wearing mail and accompanied by knights, disembarked. He had been in the Holy Land and his skin still showed the sign of the sun. I did not like Hubert de Burgh and I liked Peter des Roches even less. However, he had been appointed by William Marshal and I felt honour bound to greet him.

I bowed, "Your Grace, what brings you to my manor?"

The former regent never wasted words and he said, simply, "You are needed by the King, Sir Thomas. Hubert de Burgh has all but ruined King Henry's chances of taking Normandy. I would have you come with me on the next tide and we shall go directly to London. The King, himself, has sent me." I was stunned. I had enjoyed so many months of peace that I think I believed it would continue. I was wrong. The Bishop said, "I will explain while we walk to your castle."

"Of course." I turned to Leofric. "Tell her ladyship that the Bishop does not stay and neither do I. We will eat and then leave."

"Yes lord. I will speak with Master William too."

"Good man." I turned to the Bishop. "Lost Normandy?"

"Hubert de Burgh persuaded him to wait too long. I was in London else I might have advised him better as would you. The rebel lords in Normandy were quashed by an alliance of the Count d'Eu and the Count de Pontoise. King Louis himself led some of the armies. King Louis is now seen as the saviour of Normandy. You should not have left the King's side." That was an unholy alliance. Had I driven the two of them together?

We had reached the outer ward. "I was sent by the King to deal with Scotland."

"Aye and now it becomes clear that the attacks were initiated to draw you thither."

"I thought that you were in the Holy land."

"I returned last year. The barons of Poitou sought my help. Hubert de Burgh had punished the Poitevin lords who rebelled by taking their lands in England."

I shook my head, "He is a fool! He knows coin and that is all! But what can I do?"

"I seek to impeach the Justiciar. He has squandered royal money and lands, and was responsible for a series of riots against foreign clerics. The man is a fool."

"The King is back in England?"

"He arrived in March. That is why we need you. Hugh de Lusignan told me that it was you who recaptured Poitou for the King despite the incompetence of de Burgh. Once he is impeached and imprisoned then we can right the wrongs. There are lords in the west who do not pay taxes and conspire with our enemies. The King's attention was distracted. The King sees you as someone he can trust." He shrugged, "He is still suspicious of me. Perhaps I cannot blame him but you are seen as spotless. You have done nothing to earn his disapproval."

"Lords in the west?"

"It saddens me to tell you this, Sir Thomas, but Richard Marshal, the new Earl of Pembroke, leads them and he has had many meetings with Irish lords and Prince Llewellyn. He did not fight the Welsh as he was ordered. He came to an agreement and sent de Clare back to the King. He is not the man his father, the Earl Marshal, was. The Earl's elder brother, William, died recently. William was a more reasonable man than his hot-headed younger brother. His younger brother Gilbert is more reasonable and would make a better earl. Richard speaks rebellion."

My wife smiled when she greeted the Bishop. "I understand you will be taking my husband from me, Your Grace. I hope there is good reason for this."

"England needs him and King Henry needs him more. The Kingdom balances on a knife edge. Unless your husband can help me to restore order then we may have another civil war and this time the French have a leader in whom they can put their faith."

From what he had said he was not exaggerating. I waved over Richard Red Leg. "I need five more single men at arms to accompany me along with yourself. I want them armed and mailed."

"Aye lord. I will pick them and pick them well."

I waved over William, "Pack for me. We go armed and mailed."

"We go to fight?"

"We go so that we are ready for anything!"

By this time the hall was full of my family and those who lived within the walls. Sir Robert said, "Do you wish me to accompany you, my lord?"

I shook my head, "Stay here. With me gone then you can watch my land. I will send word of my return." My head was spinning. This was a case of no news being bad news. The King had not sent to me nor let me know of the disastrous events in Normandy. I had failed. The Earl Marshal had asked me to watch over the King and to guide him. I had obeyed the King and in doing so let him down. As my bags were packed my wife came into the bed chamber.

"My husband, this is unfair. From what I can gather this has naught to do with you. The King has made bad decisions and you must mend the broken pieces."

197

"The Earl Marshal set me on this course and I cannot abandon the ship because the going is a little rough. I do not go to fight. I go to advise and to offer counsel. All will be well. I am not taking my men. The King does not need warriors. He needs counsel. I will do that."

I was touched by the affection of all of my family. Matilda was quite tearful when she came to say goodbye. Maud was complaining else she might have stayed longer. Isabelle had eyes heavy with tears, "Father, you are a great man. You are too great to waste your life on the dreams of others. You deserve to enjoy your grandchildren and children." She kissed me on the cheek and whispered, "Soon I hope to add to your grandchildren. I want my children to know the man I regard as the greatest in the land. Be safe father, for me, my husband, your family, your unborn grandchildren and the people of this valley. Without you we are nothing."

I was touched and found it hard to make the words form without unmanning myself. "I will return and know that I will be here to watch my grandchildren grow. My father was denied the joy. I will not be!"

I felt drained of emotion by the time I reached the ship. My wife hugged me so hard that I thought I would be crushed by her love. William had carried my war gear aboard and I was the last to step on to the deck before the gangplank was raised and we followed the current, through darkest night, towards the sea. I stood by the tiller and watched the lights of my castle disappear. The bends in the river soon made all dark. I turned and saw Peter des Roches watching me.

"I am sorry, Your Grace, but this was a hard parting."

"Do not apologise, Earl. I envy you. I am a man of God and can never have a family like yours. When I leave no one sheds a tear and yet here, in Stockton, there were tears enough to fill a sea. How you are loved." He shook his head, "I am sorry to drag you hence but I genuinely believe that you are the only hope for King Henry and for England."

I never truly understood the motives of Hubert de Burgh and Peter des Roches. I think that both of them wished the best for England but there was such animosity between them that they spent more time trying to undermine the other. I never manage to unravel the rivalry. We sailed south to London. I did not even get to see my land as we sailed down the river. It was night and we passed through shadows. Once we hit the open sea and left the estuary of the Tees then I began to feel the motion and I retired to the tiny cabin I shared with William. I spoke with William as we headed south. He was a man now and we could talk. I was able to formulate my thoughts and ideas through speech with him. He now filled Alfred's boots.

The King was at Westminster when we arrived. I learned, on the voyage south, that the King had been in contact with the Bishop of Winchester and it was he who had suggested summoning me. Suggested is too gentle a word. I was ordered to London. The King was growing. He had attained his majority and was flexing his muscles. It was mid-morning when we tied up at the quay which was adjacent to the palace. I recognised many of the young knights who were waiting in the Great Hall. They were the de Clare and Bigod boys. Humphrey de Bohun gave me a warm greeting. Now grown to be men they were the protectors of the King. For some reason I felt relieved. I was here as an adviser and not as a sword to protect the King. When the King realised that we had arrived we were summoned to his presence.

I said, "William, watch the door!

"Aye, Earl!"

As we walked into the chamber where two clerks were copying out decrees the King waved one piece of parchment before him, "You were right Bishop! He has been taking estates from loyal lords who had land in Poitou and giving it to his own supporters. Richard Marshal, especially, has benefitted. This is intolerable! I would have you ride to Oxford. He is in Merton College Chapel. Fetch him hence! You are a Bishop and you can do that which a battle of knights could not!" The Bishop nodded, "Put him in the Tower until we can hold a trial!"

"Yes, Your Majesty. It is good to see you roused."

He waved an irritable hand and the Bishop left. The King then said to the clerks, "Take your scratchings and leave us. I would speak with the Earl in private!" The door closed, he waved me to a seat, "You should never have left me! De Burgh made me dally and dance around the French and Normans. We have lost Normandy and I fear the rest will soon follow!"

"King Henry, had I not returned to England then there would be many women and children enslaved yet in Scottish halls."

"I sympathise but they are few in number. I have lost Normandy! Brittany is close to capitulating and here at home I have enemies emerging like wood lice to gnaw at my power and my lands! I need you!"

I sighed, "I am here, Your Majesty. What would you have of me?"

"The same as you did in Poitou. There you retook my land from the rebels."

"Are there rebels?"

He frowned, "There are people who oppose the Bishop of Winchester and question my authority."

On the voyage south, I had learned that the Bishop had been retaking the estates back from the supporters of Hubert de Burgh. He, in turn, gave them to Lusignan lords who had supported him. "The Bishop takes manors from the Justiciar's supporters and gives them to his friends."

"They are my friends too, Earl. The Poitevin lords supported me after you had gone. They kept the French and the rebels from the border. They are loyal. You will not know that Richard Marshal attacked some of the men sent by the Bishop of Winchester. When I summoned him to Gloucester to answer charges, he refused citing treachery as the reason he would not attend! He accuses me of treachery! I would have the Earl of Pembroke come, now, to London and to seek my forgiveness in person. This is rebellion, pure and simple."

Part of me wondered if their loyalty had been bought. The Bishop of Winchester had returned from the Holy Land through Gascony. I could smell a conspiracy and yet I was powerless to do anything about it. "King Henry, you are now able to rule alone. Why do you need these advisers? Why do you need me?"

"You are right, I do not need these advisers and one of them, de Burgh, will soon pay the price for his corruption. I am not a fool, Sir Thomas, I know that Peter des Roches does much of what he does because he hates de Burgh." He smiled. "I wonder if that was why the Earl Marshal chose them to be my regents. He thought they would cancel each other out. It has not worked out that way. I will use the Bishop of Winchester and then he will be gone too." The King had learned to be ruthless. He poured us each a goblet of wine. "Your health." I toasted him back. "You, however, are different. When you left, I fell under the spell of de Burgh. He had a honeyed tongue. De Bohun warned me but I did not listen. You had told me to be bold but the Justiciar advised caution. We did not advance. Men deserted and the French reduced the castles of the rebels. Had you been with me then Normandy would be mine. I need you to stay with me until England is under my rule once more."

"And then I can return to my home?"

He looked hurt but he nodded, "If that is where you wish to be rather than at the side of your lord, then aye."

"Let me be blunt, King Henry, I think that this is a harder task than retaking Poitou. There, enemies were easier to see. From what you say the Earl Marshal's son, Richard, is a potential enemy. Who else lies in that camp? I would not expect the son of the Earl Marshal to side against the King."

"That is what I have been told, Earl."

"The truth and what you are told are often realms apart. You will have a trial of the Justiciar to organize and, I imagine, the city of London to control. Give me a month to speak with the Earl of Pembroke. He will speak the truth to me, of that I am certain." He nodded. "I would advise against any more confiscations of estates. The Justiciar was wrong but, it seems to me, that the Bishop is behaving in the same manner. It is you who rule and you should take back the reins of power. That means being merciful and just, as well as swift and authoritative."

He sighed, "I know. I allow you to speak to me like this Earl when others would suffer my wrath."

"A good king knows when to offer the hand of peace and when to use the iron fist. I believe you are such a King."

"Then ride to Richard Marshal. I will wait to show which hand I will use until your return. You have my word! But I will raise men ready to crush any rebellion. The Bishop already has his men mobilised and moving towards Gloucester. I will not be inactive again!"

I spoke with the King to discover who might be enemies and who might be friends. I took some of the parchment, ink and a quill. When I left with William to join my men I had much to do.

I had a warrant for horses. I spoke quickly to William for the one thing we did not have was time. My conversation with the King had told me that the country, in the south at least, was like a pot simmering. It could boil over at any moment. I gathered my men. "Roger of Hauxley, I am sorry but I need you to ride to my home. I need Ridley the Giant and twenty men at arms along with David of Wales and twenty archers."

He nodded as though a two-hundred-mile ride was the most reasonable of requests. "And I bring them back here, lord?"

I shook my head. I did not know Westminster Palace well. There was a room for the royal pages close by. I went in and said, "I require this room for a short time. Find food and ale for me and my men!"

"Yes, Earl."

When we were alone I said, "Roger, you will bring the men to Chester." I sat and began to scribble. "This is for the Countess of Chester. She is a trustworthy lady and rules Chester for her brother. I go to speak with Richard Marshal and then either I will come to Chester to fetch you or send another to bring you." The men who had fought for the King in Poitou had been from Cheshire but Ranulf de Blondeville was a sick man. It was the Countess, his sister, who was now the power in that county.

"Aye lord."

I finished writing. I read it and, folding the parchment, dropped wax upon it. I used my ring to seal it.

"Give this only to the Countess of Chester. Keep this safe. If enemies try to take it then destroy it."

"I will lord."

We left at noon. I used the King's authority to take the best palfreys that were to be had. The King had given me a warrant. It was not for Richard Marshal. It was to use on the journey west. We rode hard. I wanted to be in Pembroke within four days. The flames of rebellion were yet to be fanned. Hubert de Burgh was an ally of Richard Marshal and I needed to douse those flames before he heard of the Justiciar's incarceration. I was largely silent as I rode. I had much to ponder. Roger would reach the Tees at roughly the same time as I reached the Marches. Sir Ralph would give him a fresh horse and he might reach there sooner. It would take a further three or four days for my men to reach

Chester. The men of Chester and my men were a back up plan in case I failed. During our stops I spoke with my men. I was honest with them and told them what the King had told me. They needed to know all of the problems that we faced. They now understood why I had sent for my men. They were there in case my words were not sufficient. If we had to then I would use force to enforce the King's will.

We reached Chepstow Castle as the sun was setting behind it. We crossed the Severn by ferry. I was able to see the work which had been done by the Earl Marshal to the mighty castle formerly called Striguil. It stood on the River Wye and with the Severn close by would take a huge siege to reduce it. It was a formidable fortress. Richard Marshal's father, the Earl Marshal, had a good eye for defence. I counted on my reputation gaining me access to the castle. I was recognised by the sergeant at arms who was at the gate and we were admitted. Leaving my men to see to the weary horses William and I hurried to the Great Hall to speak with the Earl.

I confess that I was taken in by the smile. It had been some years since I had seen Richard Marshal. When first I had met him, he had been little more than a squire. His brother I had known better. I had fought alongside his brother and he had shown himself to be his father's son. If I was to judge Richard Marshal by the King's words then he was nothing like his father. I would, however, reserve judgement. The King's views were second hand. They were reported to him by the enemies of the Earl of Pembroke.

"Sir Thomas, this is an unexpected pleasure. I thought you were still watching the northern marches."

"I was, my lord, but King Henry sent me here to deal with a delicate matter."

"Delicate matter? I pray you sit."

I joined him before the fire. "Aye, Earl, it seems that you were summoned to Gloucester to clear up a misunderstanding and you did not appear."

The smile left his face, "I am Lord Marshal of England! I do not appear before mere Sheriffs to answer false accusations."

I could see this was going to be difficult. The title of Lord Marshal was inherited through the Earl Marshal. Richard's predecessor had not wielded the title like a war axe. So far as I could tell Richard Marshal had done nothing to merit the title. I smiled. This was going to be harder than I thought, "Then it is all the more important that you meet with the King at Westminster and clarify the situation."

He shook his head, "Me, travel to London and make obeisance before that boy? He would not have his crown but for my father."

Diplomacy had failed, "My lord, the King demands your presence in London. To refuse would be treasonous."

The smile reappeared, "So he has finally come from behind the skirts of his ministers!" He waved a hand. I should have known something was afoot but I trusted that the Earl would follow the conventions of hospitality. I was wrong. "I will tell you what, Sir Thomas. You shall be my guest until the King comes to me! I summon him to my presence!"

I jumped to my feet, "My lord, I protest."

Suddenly my arms were piniored by the two men at arms who had been behind me and William was similarly guarded, "You have a choice, Sir Thomas, you may keep your sword if you swear not to escape. Do that and your stay will be a pleasant one. Refuse and you will be locked away."

"I cannot swear for I would be breaking my oath to the King. I stay here under protest."

"Then take their weapons." He pointed a finger at me, "Prince Llewellyn knows my worth. With Welshmen at my back I will teach this boy king a lesson! Gilbert, fetch their men." His younger brother, looking decidedly unhappy, hurried off. "The King has neither wife nor heir. He is in a most dangerous position, Earl. He cannot bargain with me. We hold the whip hand. The lords of Poitou are far away and there is much bad feeling in the land. The King and des Roches have alienated many of the barons. When Hubert de Burgh has raised the army then we shall see who rules this land."

"He will find that hard to do, Sir Richard, for he is in the Tower!"

His face darkened. He had not realised that he was alone. Now my speedy ride had actually helped us. We had outstripped news from the east. "Then perhaps I will exchange one prisoner for another. We will see if the King holds you in high regard or not.

If he does not want you then your life will be forfeit!" My men were brought in. I saw that there were two men for each one of my men. They still had their swords. "You are the men at arms of the Earl of Cleveland?"

Richard Red Leg nodded, "Aye, lord."

"As you see I have his sword and that of his squire. He will be my guest. He refuses to give his word not to escape. You have a choice. You can join him in my dungeon or you can take my coin and become my sergeants." He smiled, "I will pay more than the Earl."

Richard Red Leg was quick thinking. He had been with me for a long time. I saw a smile crease his face and he rubbed his chin. "We have been with Sir Thomas for a long time but we are swords for hire. I know not about you lads," He turned to face them and neither the Earl nor myself could see his face, "but I would rather sleep in a bed and have coin in my purse." He turned back to me, "I am sorry, Sir Thomas, I will not raise my sword against you for I swore an oath but we are far from home and the nearest help to you is in Stockton. If there were any friends closer then I might join you. I am your man, Lord Earl."

One by one my men all agreed to follow the Earl of Pembroke. I said nothing but William could barely contain himself, "Treacherous traitors! Apologies of men! When this is over, I will slay you all!"

Richard laughed, "You are a feisty cockerel, lord. Well, if you survive, we will not hide from you."

The Earl of Pembroke laughed, "Gilbert, take them away then send a rider to the King and tell him I hold his emissary! He exchanges Hubert de Burgh for the Earl or I execute Sir Thomas."

My son tried to throw off the arm of one of the men at arms. It was futile. The two men were strong. I said nothing. All the way down my son cursed and struggled. I went meekly. We passed through the kitchens and descended to the cellars used to store food. One was obviously used as some sort of dungeon. The cell into which we were placed was not as bad as I had expected. There were two cots, a large straw filled mattress and a blanket. There was a pail for our waste. I heard the sergeants at arms speaking as they locked the door, "I had expected more from the Earl."

"He is old. It happens to all men."

"It did not happen to the Earl Marshal."

"Aye but he was made of sterner stuff. If he is the best that protects the King then the throne will soon be lost."

William snapped, "I am disappointed; I thought better of our men!"

I put my finger to my lips until the sound of the men's voices had receded. My son frowned. Smiling I said, "Our men are still loyal to us. They were playing a part. There was nothing to be gained from being prisoners with us."

"But they joined the Earl!"

"Did you not hear the words of Richard Red Leg, *'we are far from home and the nearest help to you is in Stockton. If there were any friends closer then I might join you.'* We know that forty-one of our men are riding towards Chester. That was a message from Richard. They are still loyal. But your outburst was good for it reinforced the Earl's view that they were traitors. Now let us rest. We have travelled far and we know not when we might be freed. Fear not, my son, and trust our men. Richard is clever and will find a way to effect our escape."

I lay down on the cot and was soon asleep. I was woken by William when the bread, cheese and water arrived. I smiled at the guard, "Is it the cook's night off?"

He had the good grace to smile, "You are lucky to have the cheese my lord. Sir Gilbert provided that. The Earl wanted you on bread and water."

There was no outside light in the cell. They had provided but a tallow candle which smoked. "What hour of the day is it?"

"It is the tenth hour of the day. The feast is well under way. You are a great catch, my lord. The Earl is so pleased that he has broached a barrel of good ale. The garrison send you their compliments!"

I gave a mock bow. "I try to be of service."

The sergeant at arms nodded to William, "You could take lessons from your father. He knows when he is beaten and makes the best of it."

When he had gone, I divided the bread and cheese and began to eat. William sat there, sullenly. "Eat. The candle will soon burn out and we will be in the dark. We will need our strength before this night is out."

He began to eat as the candle started to splutter and spit. "You think we will escape this night?"

"If they feast and drink strong ale then this will be our men's best chance. They can feign drunkenness. The problem will be in securing horses and getting out through the gate. The main gate will be guarded but there is a smaller gate at the west. It would mean we would have to pass the warrior hall."

"We are not out of the cell yet!"

"Trust our men, William. We have trained them well, have we not?"

"Aye, father, but we have given them a mighty task."

"Do not despair."

Some time later the candle sputtered out and died leaving a smoky smell to the air. I closed my eyes but it was not to sleep. I wanted to listen. The darkness accentuated the silence and I began to hear footsteps above us. We were below the kitchens. There must have been storage cellars close by for we occasionally heard servants as they came to fetch what I assumed was more ale. Eventually all passage ceased and we were left with silence except that it was not true silence. There were mice and there were rats. Doors were no barrier to the rodents. There was the sound of air moving along the corridor and I could hear William breathing. He was anxious. I said nothing for I needed to listen.

The first I knew that my men were there was when I heard the key turn in the lock. It showed the skill of my warriors. A dim light filled the cell as the door opened. Richard Red Leg put his finger to his lips. I nodded. We stepped into the corridor and Ralph of Appleby and Edward Long Leg handed us our swords and daggers. The three men knew their way better than we and so we followed them. We went up the steps and passed through the kitchens. There was the dim glow from the fire and I could smell the bread which was proving. We went through tiny corridors until we emerged into the cool night air. We waited. I could sense William's impatience but I trusted my men. They had a plan. I heard the sound of creaking leather and the snort of a horse as my other men led our horses towards us. I took the reins of mine. I pointed to the west and Richard Red Leg nodded. He handed the reins of his horse to John and Ralph gave his to Edward. They disappeared in the dark and Edward Long Leg led us towards the gate. We were lucky that this ward had not been cobbled. It was bare earth and the hooves of the horses did not clatter. To me the noise they made sounded like thunder but I was listening for it. A sentry on the walls, watching outside, would not make anything of it, or so I hoped.

We passed the warrior hall. I heard laughter from within. There were men awake. The laughter was punctuated with incoherent words. They were drunk. We walked in the shadow of its walls and I saw a sentry leaning out over the battlements looking at the River Wye. If he looked around then all would be lost. Ralph appeared and took the reins of his horse. We kept walking and I heard the gate give a slight creak as Richard Red Leg opened it. I saw the bodies of the two guards lying next to the wall. Their throats had been cut. We led our horses through the gates. I thought we had escaped detection when a sentry on the wall above us who had obviously been in the garderobe stepped out and saw the horses.

"Sound the alarm! The prisoners are escaping!"

I threw myself onto the back of the horse and we galloped through the gate and headed along the banks of the Wye. We had escaped the castle and the Earl's clutches. Could we now escape the inevitable pursuit?

# Chapter 17
# The Road to Shrewsbury

I shouted, "Follow the road along the river! Head north!" I remembered that the road headed north. The river looped a number of times. The first bridge across the Wye was north of Tintern. I wanted to be further north before we crossed the river. We would head to Ross on Wye and cross there. We would be pursued and I wanted to be as far north as I could be before they caught us. The road was a good one and that helped us. We had our swords and daggers. We had our coifs and arming caps but our helmets and shields had been taken. If it came to a fight our enemies would be better armed. I could not read the numbers on the mile posts for it was too dark but I counted them as we passed them. When I had counted fifteen and we had skirted the castle at Monmouth I shouted for Richard to slow.

"We need to water and rest the horses."

"Aye lord."

We found a small hamlet with a water trough. We stopped. No one came out of their homes. I daresay our pursuers would ask questions of every villager along each route out of Chepstow. As the horses drank, I said, "Thank you, Richard. How did you manage it?"

"We pretended that we could not handle the ale. Edward Long Leg even managed to make himself spew up some ale and we retired. They jeered us!" He turned to my son, "Sorry about the cockerel comment, Master William."

"I am sorry that I reacted as I did. My father trusted you and I should have too."

Richard Red Leg nodded, "We sneaked to the stable and found our horses. We saddled them and hid them closer to the west gate. Then we searched for you. We saw that there was just one guard at the end of the corridor close to the kitchen. I pretended to be drunk and came close to him. I offered him ale and he drank some. I promised him more and said I would fetch it. I found an ale skin and when they stopped serving food and the last of the barrels had been fetched from the cellar I returned. While he drank Ralph hit him on the back of the head with a bag filled with sand. We tied him and hid him in a store cupboard then I sent the lads for the horses. Their lordships had retired early and only the hardened drinkers were left. They had a drinking contest. Finally, we took the keys from the gaoler and rescued you. Easy really, my lord."

"It was your skill which made it look easy."

"And what now, father?"

"We cannot trust anyone between here and Chester. Shrewsbury is the only stronghold about which I am confident and the Welsh may well threaten that one. We have more than two hundred miles to travel. They did not take our purses and so we can buy food."

Ralph of Appleby knew horses, "We cannot keep pushing these horses, lord. We will need to rest them and for longer than this."

I nodded, "North of Ross on Wye there are the Malvern Hills. It has forests and there are no castles. We can hide there for a few hours. I chose not to cross the Wye further south to throw off our pursuers."

William said, "Perhaps they will not chase us for too long."

"They will, my son. Richard Marshal sent word to the King that he had captured me. The Earl is an arrogant man. He is neither his brother nor his father and he will not wish to be made to look a fool. He will follow us and he will use all of his allies in the Marches. We have escaped but it may only be temporary."

We reached Ross on Wye just as dawn was breaking. We were still in the Welsh Marches. While it was a small place and without a castle, the wooden bridge would signal to those who lived there that horsemen had crossed. It could not be helped and we galloped across just as the sun peered over the eastern hills. Doors opened and we were seen. We would be reported. We headed north on the road. Our horses were labouring. Six miles from the bridge we left the road and headed up a greenway into the wooded hills. A soon as the trees gave us cover, we dismounted and walked. We twisted and turned as the greenway, which served some of the farms, climbed the hills. Richard found us a dell with grazing for the horses and a small stream which bubbled down the slope towards the Wye.

"We each watch for an hour. We will all need sleep. When we have all done one watch then we move."

"But the Earl!"

"If they have followed us hard then their horses will need a rest. They can obtain fresh mounts in Monmouth but each time they stop will delay them. More people will use the roads and our trail will become colder. I am hoping that they think we went to Gloucester. That would be the logical place for us to go. The Sheriff is the King's man. I will take the middle watch. Richard, you take the first and Ralph, the last."

I covered myself in my cloak and slept. Edward woke me. He curled up in his cloak and I went to check on the horses and to make water. The horses looked better for the water and the grazing. Grain would have helped them even more but we had none. There were water skins on the horses. I drank from one and then went to the stream to fill it. I chose the part which bubbled. That was always the healthiest part. I used my fingers and my thumb to estimate the position of the sun and then I walked back to the greenway. I sat on a rock and listened. The only sounds were in the distance. There were birds in the trees and their noise was comforting. It meant we were hidden. I had time to think. The King had been right but I saw now that his two ministers, between them, had created the crisis. The Earl of Pembroke had benefitted from Hubert de Burgh and suffered when Peter des Roches had taken over. The King was better off without any ministers. From what I had learned when I had travelled south with the Bishop of Winchester, he was not a man to sit idly by. He had been a warrior priest in the Holy Land. When the demand came to exchange de Burgh for me, he would bring an army and he would fight the Earl. I had not seen Richard Marshal fight or lead men. He was an unknown quantity. His father and elder brother had been good generals whom men would follow. The army he would lead was a good one. They had been trained by the best. I was unsure if the Bishop could defeat them. My men would be within a day of Chester. With my own men behind me I

211

would be happy to face any enemy. I checked the sun. An hour had passed. I woke William.

"You know how to estimate the progress of the sun?"

"Padraig taught me!"

"Good."

I went back to my cloak and tried to sleep. It did not come but I rested. I heard William change the guard and then I heard Ralph as he was woken. I rose and joined him. "Ralph, when we ride today, I want you half a mile behind us. If we are followed you will hear them and can warn us."

"Perhaps your son is right, lord. They may give up."

"They may but I am sure that there will be men who follow us if only to find out where we go!"

We needed food but we could tighten our belts for a couple of days. We would need at least one and perhaps two more long rests to be close enough to Chester to be safe. Richard led us along the greenway and back to the road. We were cautious as we joined the road. We listened for traffic along it but there was none. God favoured us or perhaps we were due a little luck. We made many miles before we took our next long stop. It was coming on to dark and we had taken a long detour to avoid Ludlow and its castle. We had stopped in a village just after Ludlow and bought some bread and cheese. The bread was rough oat bread but it was better than nothing. We knew that the villagers would report us to any who asked and so we took the east road at the next crossroads. It was only when we dropped into dead ground that we resumed our northern path. Once again, the horses were weary. We were pushing them too hard and we were all mailed. We found a greenway which led to some hills in Shropshire for we were now in that county. Here we risked the Welsh as well as Richard Marshal's men. The son of the Earl Marshal was dining with the devil for he had allied himself to the Welsh. I had fought the Welsh and knew that they were a daunting foe. They would retake, if they could, all of the lands of Shropshire, Powys and Gloucestershire. He had become blind to the danger.

"We sleep and then head back to the road. We can make good time at night travelling the road. We just need to avoid Wrecsam and we should reach the plain of Cheshire safely."

We made a fireless camp and ate the rough bread and runny cheese. I was starving. We took the saddles from the horses and let the weary animals graze. We took it in turns to sleep for the four hours we rested. When we led our horses back to the road, I felt the stiffness from so long in the saddle and so many nights sleeping rough. I was unused to it. We mounted on the road and Ralph was almost three-quarters of a mile behind us. We struck trouble just two hours into the ride. Richard Red Leg's horse picked up a stone and we had to stop. We could not afford a lame horse. We were lucky in that there was neither house nor farm close by. A small stand of elder trees and blackberry bushes afforded us some shelter and Richard set to cleaning the hoof.

He had almost finished when I heard the sound of hoof beats. I drew my sword as did the others. It was Ralph. "Lord there are the men of Chepstow behind me. They saw me and come at the gallop. There are twelve of them!"

I acted quickly knowing I could rely on my men, "Richard take half the men over there in the bushes. The rest with me. Listen for my command. We hit them and we hit them hard." I had with me Ralph, William and Edward Long Legs. I heard the hooves as the horsemen galloped up the road. Dusk was not far off and they were chasing hard. I waited until the leading horsemen had passed me and then I spurred the horse, "Charge!"

They wore mail and helmets but their swords were sheathed and the shields hung from their cantles. They did not have any weapons ready and first blood went to us. My sword hit the side of the helmet of one man at arms and he fell to the ground. I wheeled my horse to go for the leader. William came with me. I saw that it was Gilbert Marshal. He had managed to draw his sword and rode at me. William rode at his squire. Behind me I heard the clash of steel as my men engaged the Chepstow men at arms. Gilbert was the youngest of his brothers. He had the look of his father. I dropped my reins and stood in my stirrups. I brought the blade down and Gilbert Marshal had to block it with his own sword. My elevated position added power to the strike and his sword was driven down to strike his saddle. My original plan had been to disrupt them and flee but as William unhorsed Marshal's squire I realised that we could win. I punched at the helmet of Gilbert Marshal with my sword. I connected with the nasal and saw his head reel. I swung my sword again and he tried to block it. The punch to his head had disorientated him and his block was weak. When I lunged, he tried to parry and his sword was knocked from his hand.

In a flash my sword's tip was at his throat. "Yield Sir Gilbert. I would not have your death on my hands!"

He nodded, "I yield!"

With his squire unhorsed and four men lying on the ground the others had little choice. They sheathed their weapons. I turned and saw that my men had all emerged unscathed. Gilbert's squire rose somewhat unsteadily. He held his left arm. "William, see to the squire. Richard Red Legs take the spare horses. We have use for them." I sheathed my sword.

Taking off his helmet Gilbert Marshal asked, "What now, lord?"

I smiled, "You go back to your brother and you tell him that he should reconsider his position. Your father lost lands to King John and he did not rebel. He used the law to take back what was his. If Peter des Roches has circumvented or abused the law then the courts can remedy the situation. Men do not need to die." I pointed west, "An alliance with the Welsh is the worst act of treason I can imagine for it opens England's back door to the wolves."

I saw that Gilbert agreed with me. "You will let us go?"

"You surrendered your sword and I believe that you are a gentleman. I did not surrender my sword to your brother. My escape was one with honour. Besides, I assume that the others who search for us are further south and east." He nodded. "By the morrow we will be safe." I made a stab in the dark. "And I am guessing that the Bishop of Winchester has your brother's full attention now."

"Aye. His men are gathered at Gloucester. War is come to the Marches."

"Then return with my message to your brother. It is one thing to fight the Bishop but if you fight the King then there will be but one end for you, the executioner's block. Then you would lose all of your lands. Think on that." I turned to William, "How is he?"

"I believe the arm is broken but it is a clean break. I have put on a splint using his dagger but he needs a healer." He helped the squire to his horse.

I nodded, "God speed, Sir Gilbert. We part in peace. The next time we meet it had better be as friends for I have given you your life once. I do not do so twice."

They clattered down the road with the bodies of the dead draped over the saddles of the men who had escaped injury. The horses we had were little better than ours but we had four horses we could use to give our mounts relief. We mounted and walked slowly up the road. With the pursuit ended we did not ride all night. An hour into darkness we found a farm. My purse bought us hot food and the use of a barn. We and our horses needed the rest. From the farmer I learned that the village of Condover lay ahead and that was just south of Shrewsbury.

As we ate I changed my plans. The pursuit had ended. John Fitzalan was the lord of Oswestry and High Sheriff of Shropshire. I had known him in the past for, like me, he and his family had suffered at the hands of King John. If he had been an ally of Richard Marshal then men would have been sent south to search for us. I took a chance. I still had the warrant from the King in my saddlebags. The Earl of Pembroke had been so keen to get my body that he had failed to search my goods.

The next morning we rode into the walled town and headed for Sir John's hall. We must have looked a sorry sight. We had not changed our clothes from many days. They were besmeared and bespattered with blood, mud and dung. My livery, however, was still visible and it afforded William and I entry to the hall.

"Sir Thomas, this is unexpected," he smiled, "and yet not so. Welsh forces are gathering in the west and I hear that the Earl of Pembroke has risen in rebellion. Are you the harbinger of doom?"

"I was sent by the King to bring the Lord Marshal to London for judgement. I failed. Aye, I suppose you are right. The border is in great danger." I took out the parchment from the King. "This gives me the King's authority. We need to raise the levy."

He nodded, "You need no paper to do that but Prince Llewellyn has many times more men than we do. He is marching from his mountain stronghold to join with the Earl."

"Then we must stop him."

"I do not have enough men, Sir Thomas. Yet if I hide behind my walls the Welsh will ravage my land."

"Just raise the levy. I will fetch the men of Chester. We use you as the bait. You have to trust me."

He nodded, "There are many of King Henry's advisers I would not trust further than I could throw them but I know you and I know that you seek only the best for England. We will raise the levy. Will you refresh yourselves?"

"I fear we have little time. Some food and a change of horses and then we will need to ride. We can make Chester before dark and then try to be back here in a few days."

"I will have my border knights harass the Welsh and draw them hither. I will send a messenger to Gloucester. I believe that is where the Bishop of Winchester gathers his forces."

With fresh horses and food inside us we rode hard to Chester. There was no standard flying over the keep and I began to worry. Was the castle manned? Had they been summoned to Gloucester? If so it was a disaster for us. We could not stop the Welsh with just the men of Shropshire. We rode through the gates and I was relieved to see Ridley the Giant and my men practising. I had been worried they might still be on the road. Leaving Richard Red Leg to speak to him I went with William into the hall. I saw Countess Maude, the wife of David of Scotland, sister to the Earl and her son John, Earl of Huntingdon.

I dropped to a knee, "My lady, where is your brother?"

She shook her head, "He is in Wallingford and has gone there to die. There is no Earl of Chester." She held up the letter I had sent. "I received your letter and I have raised the levy but there is no Earl of Chester. My brother is childless. I hope that King Henry will confirm my son, John, as Earl."

She was asking me to intercede with the King. I nodded, "I will do all that I can to ensure that he is confirmed but we have little time, Countess. Prince Llewellyn's Welsh army advances on Shrewsbury. The High Sheriff cannot hold them alone. We must march on the morrow." I looked at her son. "I will lead the army."

The Earl of Huntingdon was just a few years older than William. Had his father not died then he might be King of Scotland yet he looked happy to follow me. He smiled, "I will happily learn from you, Earl. We will be ready to ride at dawn."

"I take it that the knights of Cheshire who went to Poitou with the King have not returned?"

The Countess shook her head. We have my brother's household knights and the knights who live to the west of us."

"Then with the levy that will have to do!"

My men had brought with them not only spare horses but also fresh surcoats. That was my wife's doing. "Sir Robert asked to come but your wife said he should stay in the valley." Ridley the Giant looked to me for approval.

"She did right. We will need helmets. William go to the armoury and find them. Send Mordaf and Gruffyd to me. This is their land and this is where they will come into their own." My two Welsh scouts were more than happy to find the enemy. The men of Gwynedd were no friends of theirs. I sent them off with orders to meet at Shrewsbury.

The Earl of Huntingdon sought me out as I was speaking with my two captains, "My lord, do you have a plan?"

"Not exactly for until I know the size of the enemy force, I can do nothing. However, I know that we can use the River Severn and the town of Shrewsbury as allies. How many men will Cheshire and Lancashire provide?"

"There are perhaps forty knights from Lancashire. There would be more but they will not arrive in time. We have eighty knights of Chester and west Cheshire."

"And you still leave a healthy garrison?"

"Aye lord. I would not leave my mother undefended."

"And the rest?"

"There are two hundred sergeants and one hundred and twenty Cheshire archers. We have four hundred in the levy."

"The levy is an unpredictable element. Have them armed with bows and slings. They can guard our flanks. The Sheriff of Shropshire has another one hundred and twenty knights as well as two hundred sergeants and a hundred archers. His levy will guard the walls of Shrewsbury." I saw a worried look on the Earl's young face. "You think we do not have enough to face the Welsh?"

"In my experience they could bring two thousand men."

"We do not need to defeat them. We just need to stop them. That is the whole purpose of our battle. If they join with Richard

Marshal and the rebels then England is lost. If we can stop the Welsh then that gives King Henry the opportunity to rally his men and defeat the rebels here in the west."

He said, quietly, "This will be my first battle."

"And at the end you will remember little. A battle is not one large event. It is a whole series of small encounters. The will of the stronger determines the outcome. You must show yourself to your men. Lead by example. I have seen too many battles lost because lords fled."

"You stood at Arsuf."

I shook my head, "I would have run for that was my first battle but my father stood and, when he fell, I guarded his body. It was my father's courage which won Arsuf not me."

We had but forty miles to travel and, leaving before dawn, with well-rested animals it meant we were at Shrewsbury by noon. The Sheriff was pleased to see us. "We have had reports from my knights sent to harass the Welsh that they have taken Oswestry. The survivors fled here. It seems you are right, Earl. Normally when they capture somewhere, they celebrate for a long time. They are approaching us and will be camped here by dark."

"Do you have numbers?"

"Unreliable ones. Those who fled talk of hordes. It justifies their flight. I believe there could be thousands."

"We will have a better idea by the time they arrive for my scouts are following them. They do not exaggerate and we will have a more accurate estimate of the force we face."

Although we had arrived by noon the levy and the baggage did not reach the town until the middle of the afternoon. We set them to work building a Roman style camp with a ditch and stakes. In my experience the levy was more reliable if horsemen could not ride them down. We seeded the ditch and the ground before it with caltrops. I did not think we would be fighting there but I wanted a safe refuge for the men of Cheshire and Shropshire. We planned on using the loop in the Severn for our battle. With the town and wall behind one loop we would entice the Welsh towards us. I went across the river with the Sheriff, the Earl of Huntingdon and my captains.

"When darkness falls, we will bring our men across the river. There is a convenient loop here. I want a ditch from one bank of the river to the other and stakes embedding before it. We put the levy, our men at arms, squires and our archers behind the ditches in the morning. We shield them with our knights."

Sir John shook his head, "I know we do not have true numbers yet but two hundred and fifty knights would be ground up by the Welsh!"

I smiled, "We are bait. We charge and we fall back. We retire into the fortress we have made. Our stakes and ditch will stop them; our men at arms and archers will slaughter them. All we need to do is to break their spirit. If I were the Welsh Prince, I would avoid battle. I would march to Chepstow and join my allies. I am the bait. I have bloodied his nose more than enough, he will not want me behind his line of march. He will seek vengeance and if I offer him two hundred and fifty knights then he might nibble the bait."

The Sheriff said, "A good plan, my lord. I will set the men to lopping trees now."

We saw the Welsh scouts appear even as we rode back across the river. Behind them we saw the long line of banners and men. They were briefly silhouetted by the setting sun and then, as the sun disappeared behind the mountains, all became dark. We then saw the flickering fires of their camps ripple to the west. My two scouts returned soon after dark. Already the ditch had been started and the stakes were ferried across the river.

"Well?"

"The Welsh have brought three hundred and more knights. We counted their banners and there were at least that number. We counted more mailed men with spurs." I nodded. There would be unattached lords who had yet to have their own banner. They would be seeking fortune from the battlefield. English knights always fetched a good ransom. "They have less than two hundred men at arms and three hundred archers. Their strength is their levy. There are almost a thousand of them. There could be as few as eight hundred or as many as fourteen hundred. They were hard to count. They are armed with spears, bows and slings." I knew what he meant. The Welsh excelled at archery.

"What sort of arrows did you see?"

"We saw that most had their arrows in their belts. They would have had more in the wagons but the arrows they had about them were war arrows."

"Not bodkins?"

"No, lord. It is easy to tell them apart."

"You have done well. Go and rest." I joined the Sheriff and the other leaders of the conroi in the hall. I told them what we had learned.

Once again the Earl of Huntingdon, the least experienced of the knights, looked the most worried. "They outnumber us two to one."

The Sheriff shook his head, "Do not worry about the levy. We outnumber their men at arms. We have almost as many knights and it is just their archers who pose a problem."

"And we minimise the risk by putting in our front rank those with the best mail. The Welsh use war arrows. They can hurt horses and, if they find flesh, will incapacitate but they will not hurt men in mail. My plan still works. I want everyone in position before dawn. When the Welsh see dawn behind us, I want them to see a thin wall of knights. There will be fifty of us in each rank. I will make them think that we intend to take their Prince. There will be just one squire with us, my son William. When he makes three blasts on the horn then we turn as though we flee. We ride back without any order. There will be four safe paths through the stakes. They will be marked with red flags. All the rest will be covered with caltrops."

One knight, Sir Harold of Evesham, asked, "Will not the Welsh follow that path?"

"I will have four volunteers who will remove the flags when the last man is through. The last man will be me. We ride to the rear, dismount and then join the men at arms at the stakes. Do not worry Sir Harold, I have used this device before and it works."

The Earl of Huntingdon said, "And if they do not take the bait?"

"Then we have won for they will stay where they are and not go to the aid of the Earl of Pembroke. They dare not leave for we are a large battle and we would be able to fall upon them. They either attack us or they have lost."

The Earl said, "And you gamble that we are better?"

Ridley and David of Wales, the two captains of the men at arms and archers, were with us. Ridley said, "With respect, lord, we are English. It is not a gamble for we are better! Better blood courses through our veins!"

Even though he was common born his words had a dramatic effect. Men stamped and banged the tables with the hilts of their daggers. They were the right words and even the Earl of Huntingdon nodded and smiled.

# Chapter 18
# The Last Battle

I had one of the French breastplates we had taken from the men we had fought in France. I wore it that day for the first time. I did not find it comfortable. I was not sure that it would be adopted by knights. It gave protection but it seemed to constrain me. I commented so to William as he strapped it on. He nodded, "We could ask the blacksmith to cut it down close to your arm. It is the front of your body which needs protecting and not under the arms."

We slipped the mail over the top followed by the arming cap and coif and then the surcoat. I felt overdressed. The breastplate added to the weight I was carrying. William handed me the helmet. It did not have a face mask. The one my men had found in the armoury had been an open-faced bascinet. It had hooks, however, to allow me to use a ventail. I also had a courser from the stables at Chester. It was jet black and called Crow. It had been the Earls' second horse. It did not seem a noble name but the horse appeared to know its business. I mounted him and rode him around the stable yard while I awaited the rest of the knights. He appeared to respond well to my touch. The Earl told me that he had been his uncle's favourite horse. I would discover the truth of that when I rode to war.

The men at arms and archers had already crossed when I led the two hundred and fifty knights across the Severn. The men at arms were still seeding the ground with caltrops as we formed our lines. The red flags were being placed while we wheeled our horses around. The borrowed shield was still hanging over my leg and my helmet from my cantle. It would be some time before we fought. I saw the fires of the Welsh still burning. From what Mordaf had told me the Welsh had had a hard day's march. I did not think they would be rising early. The Sheriff's servants brought us ale and some fresh bread as we saw the first of the sun's rays illuminating the Welsh. Their horns told us that they had seen our serried ranks.

"You have the horn ready, William?"

"Aye father."

"Then when we charge stay as close to me as you can. I intend to make them believe they can catch us."

I saw the enemy moving around their camp. Neighing horses and the sound of horns and shouts filled the air. I had fought Llewellyn before. I had beaten him then. Had he learned from his defeats? My banner fluttered over William's head. The breeze, coming from the north, make it clear who led our army and where he was to be found. The Welsh would be doing as Mordaf had done and counting banners. They would see just two hundred and fifty of us. They might wonder where the rest of our army was waiting but as we had the levy behind the walls of Shrewsbury, I hoped that we had fooled them. They could not know that I had brought the men of Cheshire with me. We just had to hold our nerve until they attacked. Normally I would have dismounted to save our horses but I needed to remain mounted to hide our true numbers from them.

It took until mid-morning before the Welsh were arrayed. They had their archers on the two flanks and their knights, and, I assumed, their men at arms in the centre. The writhing, wriggling mass of men behind suggested the levy. I counted on making them charge too. It had worked for King William at Hastings and it might work for us. Their Prince was not amongst the knights. That made sense. He would be saving himself for later battles. The liveries of the knights I could see five hundred paces from us showed that they were the Prince's men. They would be eager for glory before the eyes of their Prince. One would have been given Oswestry as a reward. The others would hope that they could have Shrewsbury.

A horn sounded and the whole line moved forward. They were going to allow their archers to attack us first. I shouted, "Earl John, your men will attack the archers to my left. Sheriff, yours will attack the ones to the right." My two leaders each commanded fifty knights each. I would still have a hundred and fifty knights with which to attack their knights. When they were three hundred paces from us the Welsh knights halted and the archers moved eighty paces closer. I saw them string their bows.

"At the walk, forward. Earl, Sheriff, now is your time!"

As we walked closer the last two ranks of fifty split off. The slow pace would not alarm the Welsh. Our fifty wide line was too narrow to use in battle. A one hundred and fifty wide line was more efficient. My men and I had worked with archers so often that we knew their routines as though they were second nature. I watched them ram arrows into the soft ground before them. After donning my helmet and pulling up my shield I said, "William, sound charge!"

As he sounded the horn, I spurred Crow. The courser leapt forward. My men on the flanks began to gallop toward the archers. I heard a shout from the Welsh lines and their arrows filled the skies. We were cantering. The Earl and the Sheriff were galloping. We confused their archers. They had released but not as one and not at the same target. Some went for the quicker moving horsemen on the flanks but more than half came at us. I was obviously a prime target for I saw a flock of arrows coming for me. Holding up my shield three arrows thudded into it. One clanged off my helmet. One struck in my cantle and two hit my mail. They penetrated the links but were held by the breastplate. A cheer went up from the Welsh as they saw me, apparently, stuck like a hedgehog. I did not lower my spear, I watched as some of the knights on the flanks were hit. All carried on. A Welsh horn sounded and their knights began to move towards us. Our charge had made them counter charge us. Their archers would not be as effective.

The Welsh knights were charging my one hundred and fifty knights in the centre. Even though they had taken casualties my flank attacks were closing with the archers. There were no stakes before the archers. When my horsemen were less than fifty paces from them, they broke. It was too late for the vengeful knights speared the backs of the unarmoured men as they ran.

We had to concentrate on the Welsh knights who attacked us. They would soon outflank us. Of course, our flank knights could turn and attack them but I did not count on that. I would stick to my plan. This time I had neither my household knights nor my men at arms flanking me. I was relying on knights I did not know. This would be harder than normal. I saw that the lances and spears of the Welsh knights were aimed at me. I chose the leading knight as my target. The Welsh dragon told me that he was one of Llewellyn's household knights. He had a full-face helmet and he wielded a lance. I pulled my shield a little tighter and lowered my shield. This would be a test of the Earl of Chester's courser. I spurred him and he leapt forward. It was not much of a move but at the speed at which we approached each other it was enough to make the longer lance of the Welshman waver a little. My spear did not waver. I rammed it towards his middle. His lance crashed off the side of my helmet. It made my ears ring. The combined speed drove the head of my spear deep into the knight's middle. As he tumbled from his saddle his body tore the spear from my grasp.

Even as I dragged my sword from my sheath a second knight saw his opportunity and he rammed his spear at my chest. I could not bring my shield up in time. The spear head shattered as it struck my breastplate. It hurt but it did not penetrate and the shocked knight had but a heart beat to wonder why his strike had failed before my sword struck the side of his helmet and he tumbled to the ground.

"William, sound fall back!"

We had done more than enough. We had broken their front two ranks. Their archers had fled. To stay longer would invite disaster. The horn sounded and my men began to disengage. Two knights rode at me. I blocked the lance of one with my shield as the other hit the side of my helmet. I reeled and I would have perished had not William galloped at the second knight and rammed my standard into his face. I began to turn my horse. I hacked at the sword arm of the second knight who blocked it. To my horror a third knight galloped directly at William. My son had no shield and his sword was sheathed. The lance came at him. He did the only thing he could. He wheeled his horse around. The lance head missed William but was driven deep into his horse's flank. Mortally wounded the horse managed but a few steps before its heart gave out and it fell. William was thrown from its back. I rode at the knight who had lanced the horse, He was pulling back his arm to spear my son when my sword, with all the power I possessed, hacked through his mail and his spine. We had created a gap around us but the rest of my knights were obeying my orders and fleeing back to our lines. The Welsh knights sensed victory and were charging towards me. I saw my son stagger to his feet. I galloped at the Welsh and rode Crow directly at one who rode a poorer courser. The horse flinched and as it did so I slashed across the knight's leg. Blood spurted and as he fell, he pulled the horse to the ground. It created a space for the other knights had to avoid the obstacle.

I turned and rode towards William. I kicked my left leg from my stirrup and, pulling down my ventail, shouted, "Climb up!"

I barely slowed but William managed to throw his foot into the stirrup and, still holding the standard in his left hand, used his right to pull himself on to Crow's rump. As we galloped towards safety, I saw that we were the last ones left alive on our side of the battle. The others had withdrawn close to the river. Ridley and Padraig along with Richard Red Leg and Ralph of Appleby stood waiting by the red flags. My men would not trust any other for my life was at risk. I heard hooves behind me as the Welsh tried to get me. I did not look around. Crow was a great horse. He carried two mailed men but, even so, another twenty paces would have seen him falter. David of Wales' archers sent arrows above us but I still heard and felt the hooves of horses as they followed us. Richard, Ralph and Padraig tore their flags away as I headed towards Ridley the Giant. I saw him pick up his two-handed war axe as we galloped into the safe channel. It was then that I risked looking behind. I saw two knights. One suddenly fell from his saddle as six arrows struck him. Ridley the Giant's axe hacked across the neck of the second knight's horse. He was thrown from its back and was speared by a sharpened stake.

I reined in by the other horses. The knights were rushing to join the men at arms. William slid from Crow's back and I followed him. "Are you hurt?"

"Winded and I think I cracked a rib or two." He smiled. "I will live. "Thank you for saving me!"

"You saved me first. Stay here and watch Crow. He was the real hero!"

I hurried to the men at arms. The knights and men at arms allowed me through. I reached there just as the Welsh knights, with the rest of their army in hot pursuit, arrived at the stakes and caltrops. The effect was dramatic. Horses reared as the deadly many pointed spikes dug into hooves. They threw their riders. The arrows from our archers and the arrows and stones from the levy began to smash into knights, men at arms and the Welsh levy. Men fell, horses reared and warriors died.

"Lock shields. Men at arms of England, your Earl stands with you. None shall pass! Let the Welsh bleed their treacherous lives away!"

The whole army, small though it was, cheered. Part of it was that my son and I had come so close to death and yet been saved. I knew that it was luck but they saw it as some sort of miracle and a sign that God was on our side. The Welsh had courage. Those who found, by accident more than by skill, the four paths through our maze faced men at arms who had been waiting for the chance to hew Welsh horses and knights. The horses and men at arms who came down the other channels had to endure the pain of caltrops and arrows and stones sent at point blank range. They died. Their best weapon had fled. The archers, routed by the Earl of Huntingdon and the Sheriff of Shropshire, were running back to Wales. They were broken. I suppose the Prince could have rallied them but he led his reserve for he thought he still outnumbered us. I was between Ridley the Giant and Padraig. I felt invulnerable.

A horn sounded and the Welsh, little by little, drew back. The Welsh Prince was reorganizing his men. It gave me the opportunity to look around me. We had three rows of men at arms and, behind them, the survivors of the attack of the knights. That was a further two ranks. Behind those came the archers and, on the flanks, were huge numbers of the levy. This would be bloody if they succeeded but we were preventing reinforcements reaching the Earl of Pembroke. We were thwarting his rebellion.

The Welsh dismounted. With knights at their fore and the Welsh Prince in the second rank they advanced on a wide front. This was when I feared for those on the flanks. They were the levy. They were our greatest numbers but they were our weakness. I braced myself for their attack. The Welsh had to step over the bodies of their dead, both human and equine. Protected by shields and mail our archers reaped a smaller harvest but they thinned out our foes. Many who would reach us had arrows in shields and mail and they would impair their ability to fight. Less than two thirds of those who tried to make their way through the stakes actually reached us. My men at arms, the archers and slingers accounted for one in three of them. After they had slipped and slid on mud and gore, they were weary beyond words. Where I stood was the strongest part of our defence. Ridley had kept his axe and he swung it like a Viking of old. Padraig had a long sword and knew how to use it. I had been fighting in battles such as this for more than forty years. The first who tried to break us were eager young knights. Fitter than the older ones, they had rushed to get at us.

The young knight with the green dragon swung his sword from on high. Had it connected then I would have been laid unconscious. I saw the blow coming and it did not hit me. I stepped away and it hit the mud. I lunged with the tip of my sword and, catching an eye hole in his helmet, drove his head around. Unsighted he did not see my shield as it smashed into the side of his head. I stabbed down as he lay at my feet and skewered his right elbow. He would never raise a sword again. Ridley and Padraig were in no mood to be so generous. Their sword and axe took heads, limbs and lives. As the Welsh fell the pile of bodies before us grew. It became a barrier.

Suddenly a Welsh horn sounded. A few knights and men at arms continued to fight on but most fell back. We had lost men but the Welsh had lost more. I turned, "Knights, mount your horses. Let us make them think we are ready for more."

The Earl of Huntingdon said, "Sir Thomas, we have fought to a standstill. We can do no more."

"We can because I say we can. William, fetch Crow!" William was already leading Crow towards me. I mounted although I felt weary beyond words. The Sheriff and his knights joined me. I saw Sir John shake his head and call for his squire to bring his horse. By the time we had mounted and formed a line the Welsh had regrouped. I saw a debate going on. When the Welsh herald came towards us, I knew that the battle was over.

"Sir John, Sheriff, come with me. I believe we are going to hear terms!"

We met in the middle of the body littered field. The Prince was there with the Bishop of St. Asaph and his leading lords. The Prince had fought for there was blood on his surcoat. He shook his head when he saw me, "Will you not stay in your valley? Why must you constantly come to plague us?"

"Because I serve King Henry of England!" I saw his shoulders sag. "You came here with terms but here are mine. You withdraw and return Oswestry to the Sheriff of Shropshire. There will be no rebellion in England. Now that I have dealt with this irritation, I take this army and we go to scourge the Earl of Pembroke. I am anxious to do so for I have grandchildren I wish to see and this takes me away from them."

"We still outnumber you!"

"Your archers have been decimated and the survivors have fled. We hold twenty knights for ransom. If you wish to continue then let us do so, now! I am ready! Are you?"

He shook his head, "It is over! Let us collect our hurt and our dead."

"Aye you may do so but if you are still here at the same time tomorrow then I will draw my sword in anger once more."

We waited three days to ensure that they had, indeed, gone and then I led the men of Cheshire to Gloucester to meet with the King. We arrived two days after we left Shrewsbury just as the King arrived. The Bishop of Winchester had managed to hold the Earl of Pembroke at the Severn. The King was pleased to see me. "You have defeated the Welsh?"

"I have but we have still to deal with Richard Marshal."

The Bishop's forces had lost heavily. I could see that the King was less than enamoured of Peter des Roches. The three of us sat in the Sheriff's hall and had a counsel of war. "Bishop, I fear that it is your polices which have driven my lords to rebellion."

"My Liege I protest!"

"Protest all you like. I have been speaking with Edmund Rich, the Archbishop of Canterbury. He advises me to be lenient with these rebels for they have just cause for their grievances. What say you Earl?"

"I agree with the Archbishop. When a baron loses land and there is no justification then it can change a good man into a rebel."

"Then when time allows and we can meet with the Lord Marshal in a meeting free from anger we will do so."

We spent a week in Gloucester planning our strategy. In the end it was unnecessary. Gilbert Marshal rode with his herald to say that his brother had left, with his men, to Ireland. He had the intention of making Ireland his kingdom. We could not have had better news. The King showed his new-found maturity. He confirmed the Earl of Huntingdon as Earl of Chester and appointed Gilbert Marshal as Lord of the Welsh Marches. It was a master stroke. With his brother away the far more reasonable youngest brother was happy to support the King, especially when the King promised to look into the wrongs done by Peter des Roches.

My men and I were able to leave for Stockton within a month. I had the Welsh ransoms and the King gave me four more manors in Yorkshire. They meant nothing to me. I was going home but I now had a King in whom I could trust. King Henry had come of age.

# Epilogue

By the time we finally reached our home it was November and winter gripped the land. Events meant that we could not come back as soon as we might have liked. Richard Marshal was wounded in Ireland. The King dismissed Peter des Roches deciding that he would rule without advisers. That included me. I advised him on that. With the Bishop of Winchester out of the way the path to peace was clear. The Archbishop of Canterbury sent his representatives to Ireland to broker the return of the Earl. He agreed but God decided to punish him. He died of his wounds and Gilbert Marshal became Earl of Pembroke. The King tried to persuade me to take the title of Earl Marshal. I declined. I was not my great grandfather and I had seen what the title had done to others. I would return to my home and my life as a border knight.

When I reached Stockton, I had another grandchild, Elizabeth, and Isabelle was with child. As I was greeted by three toddlers desperate to see their grandfather, my world was complete. I needed neither King nor Bishop. I had my family and I had my people. I was content. I did not need to be the Warlord. I needed to be Sir Thomas, Earl of Cleveland and knight of King Henry. I needed to be the head of a family which was now recovering from hurts beyond words. They needed me to be with them and I would be. King Henry had come of age and he could rule alone.

# The End

# Glossary

Chevauchée- a raid by mounted men

Courts baron-dealt with the tenants' rights and duties, changes of occupancy, and disputes between tenants.

Crowd- crwth or rote. A Celtic musical instrument similar to a lyre

Fusil - A lozenge shape on a shield

Garth- a garth was a farm. Not to be confused with the name Garth

Groat- English coin worth four silver pennies

Hovel- a makeshift shelter used my warriors on campaign- similar to a '*bivvy*' tent

Marlyon- Merlin

Mêlée- a medieval fight between knights

Pursuivant – the rank below a herald

Reeve- An official who ran a manor for a lord

Rote- An English version of a lyre (also called a crowd or crwth)

Vair- a heraldic term

Wessington- Washington (Durham)

Wulfestun- Wolviston (Durham)

# Historical Notes

This series of books follows the fortunes of the family of the Earl of Cleveland begun in the Anarchy series of novels. As with that series the characters in this book are, largely, fictional, but the events are all historically accurate.

William of Herrteburne did exchange the manor of Herrteburne for Wessington in the late 12$^{th}$ century. One of his descendants was George Washington who became President of the U.S.A.

King Henry did manage to subdue Poitou easily but he failed to retake Normandy. King Louis was a pious king and he was canonized. He went on crusade twice. The first time, in Egypt, he was captured and France was bankrupted by the ransom. The second, in North Africa, saw his death. He died of dysentery and was 56.

## Book of St. Albans

This fifteenth century book lists the hierarchy of hawks.
Emperor: Peregrine falcon and merlin
King: Gyr falcon and the tercel of the gyr falcon
Prince: Falcon gentle and the tercel gentle
Duke: Falcon of the loch
Earl: Eagle
Baron: Bustard
Knight: Sacre and the sacret
Esquire: Lanere and the laneret
Lady: Marlyon
Young man: Hobby
Yeoman: Goshawk
Poor man: Tercel
Priest: Sparrowhawk
Holy water clerk: Musket
Knave or servant: Kestrel

## Books used in the research:

- The Crusades-David Nicholle
- Norman Stone Castles- Gravett

- English Castles 1200-1300 -Gravett
- The Normans- David Nicolle
- Norman Knight AD 950-1204- Christopher Gravett
- The Norman Conquest of the North- William A Kappelle
- The Knight in History- Francis Gies
- The Norman Achievement- Richard F Cassady
- Knights- Constance Brittain Bouchard
- Knight Templar 1120-1312 -Helen Nicholson
- Feudal England: Historical Studies on the Eleventh and Twelfth Centuries- J. H. Round
- English Medieval Knight 1200-1300
- The Scandinavian Baltic Crusades 1100-1500
- The Scottish and Welsh Wars 1250-1400- Rothero
- Chronicles of the age of chivalry ed Hallam
- Lewes and Evesham- 1264-65- Richard Brooks
- Ordnance Survey Kelso and Coldstream Landranger map #74
- The Tower of London-Lapper and Parnell

*Griff Hosker*
*December 2018*

# Other books
# by
# Griff Hosker

If you enjoyed reading this book, then why not read another one by the author?
For more information on all of the books then please visit the author's web site http:www.griffhosker.com where there is a link to contact him.

## Ancient History

## The Sword of Cartimandua Series
(Germania and Britannia 50 A.D. – 130 A.D.)

Ulpius Felix- Roman Warrior (prequel)
Book 1 The Sword of Cartimandua
Book 2 The Horse Warriors
Book 3 Invasion Caledonia
Book 4 Roman Retreat
Book 5 Revolt of the Red Witch
Book 6 Druid's Gold
Book 7 Trajan's Hunters
Book 8 The Last Frontier
Book 9 Hero of Rome
Book 10 Roman Hawk
Book 11 Roman Treachery
Book 12 Roman Wall
Book 13 Roman Courage

## The Aelfraed Series
(Britain and Byzantium 1050 - 1085 A.D.)

Book 1 Housecarl
Book 2 Outlaw
Book 3 Varangian

## The Wolf Warrior series
(Britain in the late 6th Century)

Book 1 Saxon Dawn
Book 2 Saxon Revenge
Book 3 Saxon England
Book 4 Saxon Blood
Book 5 Saxon Slayer
Book 6 Saxon Slaughter
Book 7 Saxon Bane
Book 8 Saxon Fall: Rise of the Warlord
Book 9 Saxon Throne
Book 10 Saxon Sword

## The Dragon Heart Series
Book 1 Viking Slave

Book 2 Viking Warrior
Book 3 Viking Jarl
Book 4 Viking Kingdom
Book 5 Viking Wolf
Book 6 Viking War
Book 7 Viking Sword
Book 8 Viking Wrath
Book 9 Viking Raid
Book 10 Viking Legend
Book 11 Viking Vengeance
Book 12 Viking Dragon
Book 13 Viking Treasure
Book 14 Viking Enemy
Book 15 Viking Witch
Bool 16 Viking Blood
Book 17 Viking Weregeld
Book 18 Viking Storm
Book 19 Viking Warband
Book 20 Viking Shadow
Book 21 Viking Legacy

## New World Series
## 870-1050

Blood on the Blade

## The Norman Genesis Series
Hrolf the Viking
Horseman
The Battle for a Home
Revenge of the Franks
The Land of the Northmen
Ragnvald Hrolfsson
Brothers in Blood
Lord of Rouen
Drekar in the Seine
Duke of Normandy

# The Anarchy Series England
## 1120-1180

English Knight
Knight of the Empress
Northern Knight
Baron of the North
Earl
King Henry's Champion
The King is Dead
Warlord of the North
Enemy at the Gate
Fallen Crown
Warlord's War
Kingmaker
Henry II
Crusader
The Welsh Marches
Irish War
Poisonous Plots
The Princes' Revolt
Earl Marshal

## Border Knight
### 1190-1300

Sword for Hire
Return of the Knight
Baron's War
Magna Carta
Welsh War
Henry III

## Struggle for a Crown England
### 1367-1485

Blood on the Crown
To Murder A King

# Modern History
## The Napoleonic Horseman Series
Book 1 Chasseur a Cheval
Book 2 Napoleon's Guard
Book 3 British Light Dragoon
Book 4 Soldier Spy
Book 5 1808: The Road to Corunna
Waterloo

## The Lucky Jack American Civil War series
Rebel Raiders
Confederate Rangers
The Road to Gettysburg

## The British Ace Series
1914
1915 Fokker Scourge
1916 Angels over the Somme
1917 Eagles Fall
1918 We will remember them
From Arctic Snow to Desert Sand
Wings over Persia

## Combined Operations series
### 1940-1945
Commando
Raider
Behind Enemy Lines
Dieppe
Toehold in Europe
Sword Beach
Breakout
The Battle for Antwerp
King Tiger
Beyond the Rhine
Korea

## Other Books

Carnage at Cannes (a thriller)
Great Granny's Ghost (Aimed at 9-14-year-old young people)
Adventure at 63-Backpacking to Istanbul